A Dueler's Fate

Tanner Lee

Table of Contents

Map of Athren

To my wife and son:

You are my rays of light.
Thank you for blessing my life with your
love.

To my family:

We've never had it easy,
but every struggle brought us closer
and I wouldn't trade it for anything.

8 | P a g e

Chapter One:

Niklas

My brother is a pompous prick. Every time we duel, he always takes it too seriously, as if he were the champion of Athren.

The clanking of the swords is like an orchestra to my ears. Each stroke in the symphony is perfectly placed and serves its purpose.

My older brother, Nate, and I battle each other to a hypothetical death on the rocky dirt road leading to our family farm. He always starts high above his head with his sword, attempting to strike down in a single power swing. I have practiced with him enough to know precisely what counters are needed to stand a chance. Nate is good at helping me practice proper balance; one of his powerful swings could fling me onto my buttocks. That's why I focus most of my attention on my legs, creating a sturdy base. Dad always says a firm foundation will help you weather any storm.

I can tell Nate wants to follow in our eldest brother, Niklas's, footsteps and join the Loyalist guild. He has always aspired to contribute to the enactment of laws and achieve personal fame by becoming a champion. I, too, wouldn't mind becoming a household name as a dueler.

Nate swiftly strikes from side to side with such force that I stagger backwards. As I try to gain my proper footing again, he sweeps my leg out from under me, causing me to land on my bony ass. He places the tip of his dull sword on my chest.

He scoffs, "Amis, I know you're five years younger than me, but you're still old enough to join a guild. Don't be so predictable!"

I chuckle with a quick jab of words. "Nate the almighty, you are as fierce and impenetrable as a nun." I bow, mocking him.

We turn quickly when we hear a horse galloping up on our farm. "It's Niklas!" I yell for all to hear. The sight of my eldest brother coming home brings life to my depressed soul. Niklas has been gone for months; I've missed him dearly.

Niklas slows his horse as he nears us on the road. "Amis, are you just going to let him knock you on your keister?" He teases from on top of his horse.

"Think you can do better?" Nate sneers, egging Niklas off his horse with an open palm.

Niklas squints hard in Nate's direction. "Without a doubt, now stop overcompensating and act your age."

"Nate, he's a dueling champion! He hasn't lost in a duel." I say to Nate with concern.

Nate proceeds to throw my practice sword through the air at Niklas. Before I can blink, the two are aggressively trading blows, brandishing their swords in a tense exchange.

Niklas is a renowned dueling champion; Nate doesn't stand a chance. Niklas is taller, longer, and more agile. Nate's power and muscular build are the only things going his way.

Niklas' sword whips through the air with precision and skill. He is calm, controlled, and strikes with ease. Nate parries at will, attempting to stop the onslaught. Niklas's elegance with the blade is unlike anything I've ever seen. No wonder duelers have never come close to beating him.

Niklas pauses and smiles at me mid assault, like he's trying to tell me something. Out of nowhere, Nate forces Niklas' sword into the earth, disarming him. Nate raises his sword to his neck.

Nothing like letting your egotistical brother win, I think to myself, grinning.

"Brother, you have bested me; now show some mercy." Niklas smirks ear to ear.

Nate's pride engulfs his face as he lifts his chin and pounds his chest. "I beat the champion of Athren!"

"First time? Get off your high horse, or I'll cut you at the knees to take you down a notch." Niklas pauses with seriousness now in his eyes.

With lightning-quick succession, Niklas raises his feet off the ground, kicking Nate square in the chest. Springing himself backwards into the rocky dirt road. The painful result of Niklas's kick is worth it, as the enormous frame of Nate's topples to the ground with a 'thud.'

Nate groans in agony, like his diaphragm is barren of air. Niklas again bounces back on his feet, motioning me to attack. We double team the arrogant blonde shit, Nate, wrestling him on the earth. I grabbed his arms, pinning them behind his back in a double arm-bar, exposing his torso. Nate kicks and screams in agony as Niklas batters Nate's useless abs with his fists.

Blissful joy washes over mine and Niklas' faces as Nate yields, saying, "Alright, you dirty wankers! I yield; I yield!"

"Finally! Don't be such a cocky dirtbag." Niklas says, as we laugh in unison.

"Now, on a serious note, brothers, are you ready to join the Loyalist or Federalist dueling guilds?" Niklas asks.

"I'm not even considering the Federalist! Why would I risk fighting you? We want to join you in the Loyalist guild?" Nate questions.

Niklas purses his lips. "Nate, you might be better off in the Federalist."

"Why would you say that? I don't want to fight you to the death. We know who will win." Nate sneers, pointing at himself.

"Nate, if you were on fire, I wouldn't piss on you to put it out. Don't think I'd let you win in a real duel. Now, where's Dad? I really need to talk to him."

Nate, feeling accosted, points to the east pasture with the wisp of his hand, saying, "Over there, why?"

Niklas, with his tall, lanky build, says, "Nothing that concerns you… yet."

Waiting for Niklas to be out of earshot, I say, "That was weird." I exhaled, opening my brown eyes with concern.

A few minutes later, I spotted Dad and Niklas off in the distance, walking across one of our fields by a lone apple tree, not yet in bloom. Dad stands next to Niklas, looking rugged and worn, from his physical life as a farmer. Comparing the two, Niklas traded the persistent farming life for one of a violent dueler. Both are terrible and painful in their own way.

They are having an intense discussion of some sort. When they finish conversing, Niklas walks with an exaggerated pace, eager to head back to Lyon.

As he mounts his horse to leave, I shake my head towards him, "So you don't even care for ma's cooking anymore. Is your Loyalists' food better than ours?"

Niklas grabs the reins, looking flustered. "There's no time for dinner; I'm late for a date with a girl in town. Don't let Nate push you around, you are my favorite brother!"

I give a half smile and nod, waving him off.

The evening passes in its typical fashion and night has come in typical fashion.

I wake to loud knocks echoing throughout our small two-bedroom farm home. Bloody hell, what is the hour? I think to myself as the dogs' bark relentlessly. Deep darkness still permeates throughout the house.

"Who is it?!" My father yells, hatchet in hand.

Peering through the glass, I make eye contact with one of the conscripted Athren officers. He looks young and very antsy, holding a lantern shakily. I threw my gray wool coat over myself and yelled, "There are two scumbag officers here."

An audible rustle sounds as my father scurries to the door. I noticed the hatchet was now in his back waistline.

"What can I help you with?" My father says while answering the door.

Expecting them to ask for more crops for the battalion inconveniently, the senior officer with grey whiskers responds, "You are to report to Lyon courtyard, midday tomorrow. The sovereign officers will be waiting for you and your family." Both officers then turn and walk off the porch.

My father yells with aggression, "What happened?!"

The young officer hesitates for a moment, looking conflicted, the senior officer nudges him and they continue walking.

Dad immediately turns to the darkness in the house and firmly orders, "Kids, get over here!"

Mother immediately lights a candle. My sister Sofia, of course, drags her happy, nonchalant ass out of bed. I swear, no fire or flood would quicken her pace. And she could get away with murder if she wanted. She is devious and very unpredictable. I tend to keep my distance, given her morbid condition.

Mom begins to eye us over, ensuring we are all present, have no lacerations, and no signs of injury. To her surprise, my two brothers and my sister are all normal. Whatever our norm is.

"What did they want?" Rupert, the third born, says intriguingly.

"They are probably ready to finally take you in as one of their pets," I say sarcastically.

Dad then gives a perplexed look, saying, "They want us to report to the courtyard tomorrow at midday, as a family."

"If anyone wants to fess up for something, now is the time," my Mom says, giving my father a long stare.

Everyone else seems to glare at me. I shook my head, "Mariam and I did not get caught skinny dipping in the canal again. She's in the capital, remember!"

Nate chuckles but can't keep it in, saying, "You know you guys swam through a bunch of shit, right? There's a clean giant lake just a few miles away!"

Dad shakes his head and says, "You'll need to get an early start on your daily jobs. There's no excuse. Your mother and I will meet you in town. Rupert, make sure you feed the chickens before you go in town to your judicial duties."

Rupert then exhales, "There aren't any duels scheduled tomorrow, so there's nothing I'll need to oversee and judge… Dad, you don't think Niklas got caught trying to find a new way to get high, do you?"

I look at him sideways, saying, "No, he's in a dueling guild! He can't smoke joints there!"

Mom sighs in annoyance, saying, "Go to bed. You'll need the rest for an early day."

The morning starts abruptly and painfully as Rupert shakes me awake, saying, "Stop fantasizing about Mariam; she left you alone in Lyon with us, remember."

I blink rapidly and punch him square on the right side of his ribs. He may be two years older, but I'm not scared to dish out some punishment. I roll my 6'2" dark frame off the mat I call my bed.

I grab a quick slice of stale bread and some water. I try to inhale the brisk air of the long day ahead as the cold March breeze smacks my face. Our farm, located just outside Lyon, is spacious and beautiful. The trees have not yet regained their color, and the Oquirrh Mountains to our east are still capped with snow. I'd like to know what type of practices Niklas would experience up there. I lack the conviction to fight in the Loyalist guild. Every law made based on who wins or loses in a duel? Not to mention the possible death in every duel.

At least in Lyon and the Province of Murcia, we only fight to the death on matters of utmost importance, not like the capital of Athren, Harpstedt. Thinking of Harpstedt, I wonder what the political scene is like for Mariam. Is she finding it hard to be a Loyalist there? I couldn't care less for either group, the Federalist and Loyalist can all go to hell for all I care.

We work efficiently, ensuring we do our best to prepare the fields for the new life of spring. Nate and I find ourselves in the cornfield, going over the rows of dirt that will soon be lush and green. We ensure the rows are clear, ready for irrigation.

"Amis, stop daydreaming. It's time you pulled your weight." Nate grumbles.

I put my head down with a grin and work the plow across the cornfield. Nathan is a little shorter than I with a stockier build and bigger biceps, and he is not afraid to keep me in line. It's about time he took Niklas' advice and got out of my hair by joining a guild.

We finish our chores as the warm sun begins to warm the fields. With dirty, riddled clothes, I finish my duties in the nick of time.

My sister Sofia, Nate, and I walked into town, filthy and disheveled. After the two-mile stroll, we reach Lyon and notice a large crowd of people congregating in the courtyard.

"That's strange, isn't it?" I turn to my siblings.

"Yeah, it is," Nate agrees.

"Maybe there is a duel today, and a big one?" Sofia happily quirks, as if she is excited to see some blood.

We finally find Mom and Dad at the entrance of the courtyard. The two- and three-story buildings tower over the courtyard, where all decisions and judgments are dueled over. The atmosphere feels like an entertainment venue. Sometimes I forget how detailed the architecture is.

The provincial buildings' stone architecture is immaculate. They say that the former King who built it sealed his enemies alive within the walls.

Queasiness rises in my stomach, and my nerves tighten when I can see the Loyalists and Federalists in their black robes between the tall pillars of the provincial building. My Dad approaches the officers as directed; they stand in the central part of the yard. Usually, there is a ring in the center of the yard for duels, but currently, there are no ropes for a ring; instead, in the center, there is a stone block.

"Why were we ordered here?" My Dad quickly fires off at the senior officer.

"You'll see, you will need to be compliant. If you are not, there will be consequences," an officer retorts.

The officers position us in the front and center of the large crowd in the courtyard, for all to see. Well, except for Rupert, he is watching from his judicial position on a balcony above. There may be a duel for him to watch over.

Why are we in this position, for what? Where is Niklas?

Excitement grows overwhelmingly in front of the Murcia provincial building. The murmurs grow to a rumble, working their way towards us.

Then, my heart skips a beat. As a person, I know better than anyone else who rises, step by step, onto the platform, where the stone block lies.

"It's Niklas!" I burst out in shock.

My sweet Mom screams in absolute horror and uncertainty. No mother should have to watch their child die.

She whispers in torment, "He's shackled, they are going to kill him. Henry, do something!"

Dad remains still, frozen.

An execution is why we are here. Bloodshed is the reason for the crowd. We must stop this.

Why am I going to witness the execution of my eldest brother?

Let them scowl, let them mock. Many have died where my brother now kneels. His head is on the stained block, painted red from those before. This courtyard is death.

My mother continues whimpering loudly for all to hear. The noise will forever echo in my soul.

My father, Henry, abruptly turns to her, saying, "He is forever yours. Do not give these swine the satisfaction of your emotion."

His head is held high. My father is a quiet, observant, and tall man, standing firm amidst all the robust mockery and public shaming.

A rust-ridden soldier wearing dented and dirty armor steps up, standing in front of my kneeling brother. A hush settles over the impatient crowd. The round, relatively short man with his chin out holds parchment in front of his eyes and begins to read:

In the name of Tyren, it is hereby ordered and decreed that the Loyalists and Federalists of the City of Lyon, Murcia Province, and Country of Athren, on March 20th, find Niklas Hastings guilty of murder. Sentencing him to death by execution for the murder of Heather Brookshard. Mr. Hastings will face the same axe he used to kill Ms. Brookshard wrongfully.

The crowd erupts, shouting vile vulgarity. An individual from a balcony above can be heard screaming, "Curse his soul and his family."

Nathan lowers his head in agony, knowing that Niklas, the eldest, is undoubtedly going to die. My younger sister Sofia, on my left, has a sense of power in her stance as if the execution and outcry of the crowd have no hold on her. Rupert, high above, is nothing more than petrified with a straight face.

I watch as vegetables (surely from my father's fields) splatter, pummeling the kneeling Niklas. Nothing in the foundations of my childhood could prepare me for this. Could he have killed Heather? The girl from the most prominent family in Lyon. Wasn't he the champion for the Loyalist guild?

Now seeing my poor mother hide her face within her hands, what a terrible sight.

Pure rage boils in my Dad, and he unleashes a fury of anger I have never seen. "Mr. Flemming, you put a stop to this! That's my son; he is guilty of no such crime."

He rushes towards the stage. The guards try to stop him, but to my surprise, they are outmatched. Dad's strength and will outdo their own. I've never seen him in this manner; I don't recognize this man. One guard swings with a beating stick directly at my Dad's head. Rather than blocking or dodging it, he holds out his gloved hand, catching it. It's as if the guard hits a brick wall. Another guard goes low to tackle him, and they end up on their ass. My Dad has counters and maneuvers for every blow. For a moment, it seems like he is going to save Niklas.

Out of nowhere, a loud voice rings out from over-head, saying their false god's name. "In the name of Tyren, Henry, stop this madness. You, of all people, are familiar with our laws. They will take your farm, your family, and your life," Mr. Brookshard exclaims.

Niklas looks at my Dad with no fear, shaking his head no. The emotional torment in my Dad's eyes flashes to ours and our dear Mom's. Four guards pin him to the ground, quickly binding my Dad with rope.

An executioner in black raises the axe high into the air. I pray he swings with conviction and ends my brother in one swift motion.

My brother Niklas, the one who taught me how to fight and how to argue, is about to meet our maker. He made friends and enemies everywhere he went, but I never imagined that would get him killed.

While the executioner's axe is frozen in the air, I make eye contact with Niklas. There are no tears in his eyes, so why should I have tears in mine? His stare pierces me. With confidence and conviction, he yells directly at me.

"Good or evil, everyone dies. I'm innocent. Amis, set men free!"

The dueler's axe strikes true in one stroke, and Niklas' living example is no more. I don't dare to turn my head, not even to avoid the traumatic scene. Cheers and roars rupture my eardrums, cutting through me with a wave of dismay. My poor mother screams with her head on her knees in absolute devastation. Nathan and Sofia drop down to counsel Mom. I am stuck, frozen, immovable, staring at my lifeless brother's body.

Why did he say my name?

Mr. Flemming tries to yell over the crowd. "Your son's body is ours now!"

My father's eyes briefly meet mine, and then he glares at a balcony across the courtyard, toward Mr. Brookshard.

They unbind my Dad. He is broken. His eldest son is gone.

The pain. Why do we have to experience so much turmoil? This life is full of good and evil, moral and immoral. How can mundane actions be so costly?

Niklas never did anything but harm the bugs in the fields and let loose with a little puff here and there. Could he recklessly kill another?

As the courtyard dispersed, my family and I were at a loss for words. We followed my father as he walked toward the provincial building.

With pain in his throat and a broken heart, he roared to the political leaders, "Cower and fear, justice will be thrust down upon you by the edge of a sword." The officers pushed him back and directed us away, as fear engulfed their faces.

My father walks us through the crowd, parting the sea of people who now stare at us in horror. We thought they were our friends, or at least fellow countrymen. Stuck in the same oppressive society. These uneducated peasants believe that when one fails, everyone else can succeed. Little do they know, Athren will punish anyone who gains too much power. Niklas, the Loyalist champion, is the perfect example of that.

I notice Nathan's girl, Trisha, giving him a peck on the cheek as we pass by. She is a stunning blonde with a surprisingly bulky build. At least he has her… She's the cream of the crop when it comes to Lyon girls... Although her family is as poor as ours. She is the perfect flower in the field of weeds. She is ideal for Nate.

I have a girl whom I love, and I think she loves me. Mariam, where is Mariam? I need her to make this go away, to take my mind somewhere else.

I hung my head as my Dad directed us out of the crowd and onto the walkway home. I glanced up at the road, and on cue, Rupert appeared. He caught up to us. I wonder how much worse his view was from the balcony. Our family is together again, but now there will be a gaping hole.

Silence built within our chests; the burning tension of Niklas' death has charred our insides. The picture of him being beheaded will forever be imprinted on my mind.

All at once, the tension snaps like a strained rope, and Rupert's dull voice echoes in my melancholy soul. "Are we going to be able to bury Niklas on our land?"

Dad's glance and shaking head tell me he has no clue. "What type of question is that? You heard Mr. Flemming!" Mom admonishes. I shift in fear, worrying bystanders might overhear. The last thing we Hastings's need is more judgment and public shaming.

"The clouds are building on the mountains. They are going to give us some much-needed moisture; let's get home before it falls on our fields." Dad responds, changing the subject from the terrible events.

"The only thing you worry about is that damn farm!" Mother exclaims.

Before anyone could even remotely process what she said, she was already running up the road to our home. Sofia the evil duckling followed close behind.

That's not true about my Dad and the farm; he pushes his emotions away by keeping busy. That's not healthy by any means, either. The next few days, he will work himself to death. I can only imagine the shame, guilt, and despair stirring inside him. He is our protector, our provider, and he blames himself for Niklas.

Changing the subject, Rupert's plain voice utters again. "Did you see how the Jasper boys were looking at us? Their scowls... I, I, would kill them in a duel right now if I could. They're pests and need to be squashed," Rupert gestures with his two bear hands.

"And you're the one to do it? You sound like a child!" I critique.

"Did you see Harry Jasper's eye? It was swollen! Looks like someone beat you to the punch, Rupert!" Nathan remarks.

I feel more mature than my brothers; they banter like school kids.

"Well, someone else needs to stand up for our family. Niklas is dead. He was our best fighter!" Rupert rambles.

"I already lost one kid; no one else is dueling. Niklas tried that route, and you saw what happened to him. Focus on the here and now. Right now, I need you all to get into the house and comfort your grieving mother!" Dad interjects.

We enter the large fields in front of our home; in good years, they're full of corn, wheat, and potatoes. We live within our means, but somehow we have gained the reputation of being violent duelers. Well, now I'm sure it will be murdering cowards.

As Niklas said, "Other people's opinions of you are irrelevant; only your own matters."

I already miss my brother.

Chapter Two:

Unwelcomed Visitors

I can only imagine the pain my parents must feel. Even for me to know this is the finality of never seeing my brother again, our family will never be whole again. How do we pick up the pieces and keep moving forward? I don't think my mom will ever be the same. Especially with how hard they fought for their first child. Niklas.

The day passed with quietness and depression lingering through our entire home. The only thing I could do at that time for solitude was fish at Ash Reservoir. The therapeutic repetition of casting and reeling eases my mind and brings peace to my soul.

Early the next day, Dad gathered us for a family meeting. Mom was understandably hiding in her room.

Dad spoke softly and somberly, "Easy times create weak people. Niklas was not weak, and he will not be forgotten. We will see him again."

Dad sighed longingly. "Sofia, let Mom properly school you." He put his hand up, shushing her. "Please, no rebuttal, not right now, Sofi," Dad said as Sofia vividly squirmed in frustration.

"Amis, you need to pick up more in the fields. We need to start planting corn and wheat. No more unplanned fishing trips."

"Rupert, thank you for assisting with the irrigation ditch, and wonderful job with planting the potatoes last month. I know it's going to be harder to help, given your judicial duties."

"Nate, I need you to start thinking about your future. You are 23." He does have a Trisha who is head over heels for him. At least she will follow him to the gates of hell, lucky ass prick.

I wish I could say the same about Mariam… She left me for a piss posh Loyalist life in the capital. Politicians are scummy rats.

Nate stuttered as he tried to find his words. "This place? This farm!? Our bodies are abused and treated like-"

Nate paused, as if the earth were still, and we heard what sounded like hooves and a wagon. The blue heelers began yapping wildly. I saw out the window three men in their black robes, getting off their horses, and a fourth halting a wagon to an abrupt stop.

We greeted the men outside. Parley and George were among them, and two nicely dressed men I did not recognize. The golden eagle pin on their collar indicated that they were with the Loyalist party of Athren.

Parley held his hand out to my father. "I'm sorry for your loss. I know you want clarity; that's why we are here."

My father directed the four men into our already small home. We were all sequestered in the living space like a bunch of rabbits; so close to each other that I could practically taste Rupert's raunchy body odor.

Staring awkwardly at one another, I immediately spoke out of turn, "Holy Harwen, what the hell are we doing here? Niklas' cold body lies dead in your wagon! He was your champion in your guild and risked his life for your gain. You Loyalists weren't even able to defend him!"

The eyes of the Loyalist widened in confusion. George replied, "We are here to ask Mr. and Mrs. Hastings if we can bury Niklas with our other fallen duelers."

Nate stammered, "Isn't that just for those who die dueling?"

George, with his black robe draped over his knees, replied quietly, "Some may say Niklas did die in a duel."

What the hell does that mean, I think to myself.

"Regardless, Niklas was scheduled to duel Harry Jasper tomorrow over Mr. Brookshard's purchase of land north towards Havensburg. The Federalists think it's a promising investment; they believe Mr. Brookshard will cultivate the land and provide resources back to our community. We Loyalists would like to keep the land whole." George sighed.

Countering, I asked, "Why would Loyalists care what Mr. Brookshard buys?"

One man I don't recognize, who looks like an asshole, began to utter, "We don't owe you, boy, an explanation. Mr. Hastings, your kids have a knack for interrupting." My Dad's eyes narrowed as they focused on the stubby man's head; this politician was obviously new to Lyon. The Politician Loyalist continued, "As Loyalists, we hold allegiance to Athren, completely in all things. We hold such obligations over individual or economic interests. At the same time, Federalists seek power for the Provinces and the nation by any means. Even if that means filling another man's pockets."

Who is this capital aristocrat? What a bitch! I grumbled to myself. I'm reminded again never to get into politics. Why would Niklas murder Brookshard's daughter? It makes no sense.

Nate quickly asked, "Who will fight for the Loyalists tomorrow, if Niklas is not there?"

Parley then smiled, "Tomorrow's fight was cancelled, and the Brookshard deal is off due to his daughter's death. We aren't sure why, but it's a good thing; we don't think we'd have a strong enough dueler to fill in. Niklas was our best fighter, which is another reason we came. We need you, Nathan; it runs in your family's blood."

Dueling is so twisted and evil. These men kill others for their cause, but why? Because they are too stubborn to agree. Or is it really Athren's foundational teachings? 'Choose to fight, if you live your right.'

My mother ripped open the bedroom door, anger steaming out of her nostrils. "You already took one of my sons; I will not give you a second. Find another to die in his stead!"

Mom is right, and the silence is now deafening in the confined room.

"Well, there you have it, you cannot have another," My Dad said, backing up my mom. Dad then changed the subject. "Parley, please give us the details of Heather Brookshard's death."

Anticipation fills the air as we each seek to find a hole or a crack in Parley's regurgitation of a story. Niklas couldn't have killed her.

"It was two days ago, the sun only had an hour left of life. Mr. Brookshard noticed Niklas waiting in the courtyard through the window of his home. When he realized who he was waiting for, it came as a surprise. Heather quietly closed the door of the home and, with hurried steps, wrapped her arms around Niklas, embracing him. Mr. Brookshard noticed Niklas planted a kiss on his daughter's cheek as they walked away hand in hand."

I look at Nate with my eyebrows raised. "No surprise there, they are too posh for us. Out of all the girls, why did Niklas choose a ritzy Federalist like Heather?"

Parley paid no mind to my comment, continuing, "That's not the confusing part of it. When the two left the square, they passed by Mrs. Fray's shop. She said she saw Niklas unraveling a pipe, and they each had grins on their faces. She also said they had walked farther down Gambetta Street toward the forest. So they were going to smoke or do some lewd behavior? Many people reported hearing an argument in the street around the time they went into the forest."

With confusion lacing our faces, Rupert asks, "What part of the forest did they go to?"

Parley's response was not surprising. "To the boulder behind Matthew Stone's house."

Nate and I look at each other, trying not to laugh, remembering the cheeky saying:

'Behind Mr. Stone's home,
lies a big black stone comb,
concealing a stoner's smoky biome.'

That's what we would say to Niklas after Dad caught him there, but that was years ago. Niklas did tell me that once you're hooked, you're never physically free. Maybe he never did get free, and he was taking Heather down the same path; she did have the money for it?

Parley continues, saying, "The events next were left unclear. When we found Niklas, his back was to the curved portion of the stone, with his head in his knees. Heather had been struck by Niklas three brutal times with an axe. Once directly in her back, when Niklas dislodged it, it pulled her down. He swung again, nicking her right thigh and again planting the axe directly in her chest. It was a bloody mess."

"That doesn't sound like my brother!" I roar.

"Honestly, if Niklas was your best dueler... Why would he roll over and let you capture him?" Sofia mocks with her arms folded.

"She's right." Dad shrugs.

"He wasn't his normal self. He had just killed an innocent girl." Parley stammers while he lays out the facts.

Silence pierces the air as tension rose in each of us, Hastings, and then it was cut like a dull knife by Rupert.

"Whose axe was it? Who found him?" Rupert's eyebrows raise.

"Oddly enough, it was Mr. Stone's axe, from his backyard where he splits his firewood," George quips.

"A firewood axe?! That's dull as shit!" Mom cries out. "And you executed him with that?!"

"Mrs. Hastings, sadly, we were not in charge of the execution. Mr. Stone found him there, right before us, and it was sadly obvious. Dueling can change you." The rude new Loyalist aristocrat from earlier said quietly. He appears to be in his forties and has a receding hairline of a rat.

"Couldn't it have been one of the Federalist duelers, like a Jasper boy, or even Mr. Stone?" Rupert presses more.

"No, Son, it was obvious. That's why Niklas was immediately executed." The new Loyalists stated factually.

"Who are you?" My Dad asks, squinting like he vaguely remembers him.

"I'm Rasmussen Minfree, and this is Jaden Daughtry. We got in from the capital, Harpstedt, last week. We've heard of all you Hastings, and after seeing Niklas in Harpstedt, we had to come see your family for ourselves."

I shook my head, and words gushed out of my mouth like poop through a goose, "We know why you're here, always looking for duelers to fill your aristocratic prick pockets. I don't trust you, because I don't know you. Niklas would never have struck someone from behind and then rolled over like a dog so you could execute him."

"Watch your tongue while you speak to Rasmussen. He is the leader of the Loyalist party." Parley admonishes me.

Jaden and Rasmussen look into each other's eyes in shock. Rasmussen (AKA Rass-hole) is short and already balding, very much past his prime. His mannerisms are prim and proper. Jaden looks like a much kinder soul.

"I'm sorry for your loss. I think we'd better be going." Parley mutters, realizing my family's disdain.

As we walked them out the door, Rasmussen slyly turned to Nate and softly spoke, so my parents couldn't hear. "You know, the best way to redeem your brother is to fight for us. You are old enough to make your own decisions. There's more money and fame than you could ever dream of. After all, we all die at some point."

Nate nodded his head in agreement.

He may have agreed to disagree. He can't join them; it would break Mom even more.

When we got to the wagon, we didn't dare look at Niklas' body. This mutilated form is no longer the person we want to remember. While saying goodbye once more, it dawned on me. Maybe wallowing in his death isn't the right thing; living with his memory is.

As Jaden, in his Loyalist black robe, hurdled his way up the wagon, he reached for a cloth sack and handed it to my Dad, saying, "These were your son's items."

My Dad turned to Jaden boldly saying, "I'll take my son's body too, he's mine and does not belong to any political guild."

We ended up burying Niklas near the eastern field under an apple tree. The view there is magnificent. A grassy meadow leads up to the thick pine trees, as they continue up to the large jagged white capped Oquirrh mountains. The March air is still cool, but I know spring is coming soon, and when it does, flowers will blossom every inch of the field. Niklas will be among the beauties in the array of colors. He was the first to die and be buried on this farm; he may not be the last.

Back inside, we discovered Niklas had left letters addressed to each of us, like he knew his death was coming.

One was addressed to me:

Amis,
There's so much you need to learn.

I knew that this letter was crucial for me, and it was meant for my eyes only. I concealed it away in my wool coat pocket for safekeeping. There must be more to Niklas' execution than we know.

Chapter Three:

The Letter

That night, I woke to the creak of a floorboard and the soft squeal of the front door opening. That had to wake someone else, I thought to myself. Who was that?

Lying silently, conscious of my dark surroundings. Moonlight peered through the window to my bed. To my relief, no other squeaks or creaks occurred in the old rickety house.

Another early morning came; Nate was indeed gone. Not even a note or a goodbye was issued. My parents' reaction was as expected. There's no joy or love in this house anymore.

Unless you are Sofia, she was all smiles when we gathered in our quaint living space, eating eggs and toast.

She joyously exclaims for all to hear, "Two more to go, and I'll have my room!"

Rupert's mouth opens in utter disgust, looking like he was trying to find the right words to trump hers. Instead, my father budded in, "You have to stop joking like that, sweetheart."

She sasses, "Oh, I'm not joking!" A huge smile engulfs her face.

"Looks like I'm sleeping with my dagger from now on." I laugh encouragingly.

"You mean you haven't been already?" Rupert's eyes narrow on me in judgment.

Then a serious look overcame Sofia, "Rupert, you aren't a judge here! Are you worried for Nate?"

Rupert's eyes squint, pondering. "Well, for one thing, he's going to be alright. He's strong and smart. They practice for many types of dueling scenarios, and if you are good enough, they'll make you champion."

"What are some duels you've witnessed?" I ask with intrigue now. We never attend those violent events, although my Dad has practically trained us from birth to defend ourselves with all manner of weaponry.

Rupert began to ramble, "Well, I've seen plenty of hand-to-hand fights, some knife fights, and even a jousting match. Most of those were in the ring or in the field, where we had a few spectators. We don't have anything like Harpstedt. That's where the real arenas are! People die every match there. In Lyon, we get one death in four duels, if we are lucky-"

"Lucky? Whose Morbid now?" Dad quickly counters, laughing in Sofia's direction.

"Has anyone intervened?" I ask.

"Yes, I saw it once, an unarmed young man who was about to die at the hands of another with a dagger. A father threw a dagger next to his disarmed son." Rupert's eyes drop.

"Oh no." I gasp. "What did you do?"

Then Rupert's tone saddens, "That's where my job comes in; if it's not egregious, we will reset and resume. It's against the law to intervene, though. When that dad threw the dagger closer to his son, I knew… This duel is not the will of the God Tyren. The father and son both were executed."

There was a sickening silence, considering that political duels had been a practice for over a century. "I'm sorry, Rupert, it must be a hard decision." I empathize.

Rupert's response gave me chills. "Laws are not meant to be broken."

Why did I feel like that was directed at Niklas? Unnecessary bloodshed is why I never watch duels. It's disturbing and not something my God would want! To think, Nate chose to thrust himself into that world of bloodshed and violence.

"Why do we duel when we make political decisions?" Sofia questions.

"Our nation was created on the ideals of the God Tyren, who is justice and order. Somehow, our founders decided that his will would be decided through dueling." Mom interjects from the doorway.

She doesn't look healthy. Her hair is a mess and appears grayer; her eyes are puffy, and she doesn't look beautifully put together as she usually does.

Dad then quickly clarifies, "We don't teach you that, because we believe our God wants us to make our own decisions. Right or wrong. Tyren, their god of order, and Harwen, their god of love, are false."

Rupert swallows hard and walks out, like he's been given too big a pill to swallow.

"Where's he going?" Mom sighs.

"He feels guilty," Dad takes a deep, painful breath. I imagine every breath is a reminder of Niklas.

I ran over to hug Mom; she needs to know we love her. My parents are good people; they've faced many trials and tribulations.

Dad then fires an arrow at my heart as he inquires. "Have you read Niklas' letter yet?"

I pause, looking at his grey, scruffy face, "No, Dad, I haven't. Why?"

"Just curious, is all."

Immediately, I went to my new place of refuge under the apple tree by Niklas' grave. My minuscule place of solitude. I rifle through my grey wool jacket to retrieve Niklas' letter. I open it carefully, as if it were a wrapped present. Damn, Niklas' handwriting is absolute garbage, but I was immediately captivated.

Amis,

If you're reading this, that means I'm dead. I met my demise either by duel or by another evil means. Let's hope I was in control of my fate.

There are some things I don't expect you to understand at this time. The dueler's guild isn't what you expect; Loyalists and Federalists are all the same, corrupt, egotistical, power-hungry bigots. If you think you're safe dueling for one of those parties, you're wrong. Let me be straight with you, I was sober for the last three years. Once you walk the path I've walked, you must make a conscious effort every day to stay clean. The stress and pain of this violent way of life have whittled me down to nothing more than a pawn in their political game, but spiritually, I have never been closer to our faithful God.

Please go to Lyon's Library, and a librarian named Ms. Cunningham will recognize you as a Hastings. They will give you a manuscript; please read it entirely.

For your safety, avoid the Loyalist.
Love your eldest brother,
Niklas

Time flew by as two weeks passed. My daily tasks continue to mount with increasing difficulty, especially since Nate left. We were able to plant all the crops in the fields within a reasonable period.

Lyon is located in a subtropical climate zone. When spring arrives, the elevated temperatures can range from the mid-fifties to the low-sixties. We get a good amount of moisture for our part of the country, which helps. I only irrigate our fields once every week. The soil is also clay-rich, which helps retain moisture. What I like about our farm is that it's only around three hundred acres in size. It's big enough to put food on our table and support Lyon.

Diverting water from the ash reservoir into our canal can be a challenging task. The corn fields tend to require more water, at least until they reach a height of six inches. The stage we are in right now for the plants can be very crucial for our year.

I have not yet found time to travel into town to visit the library following Niklas' directions.

As my Dad and I walk into the house, with dirt on our clothes and calyx on our hands, I ask in an annoyed tone, "Nate just left at the optimal time, didn't he?"

He laughs. "You are free to make your own choices, just like Nate. Just know your decisions impact others' lives."

We both glance up, when we saw the burly Rupert running up the dirt road like his ass was on fire. "Dad! Dad! Nate has a duel tomorrow."

"A damn duel already? He's only two weeks into the guild. What law is it over? Can they mediate it?" I ask quickly.

He responds, "No, they can't. The Havensburg Federalists are in disarray. They want Ash Reservoir to release more water downstream throughout the year for their crops."

Dad scrunches his eyebrows, clearly not agreeing. "There is no need for them to have more water. The snow melts, and precipitation from the Sevier Ocean is plenty."

Rupert interjects, "I know, I know. Anyway, it's going to be at midday tomorrow at the Ash Reservoir."

"A water duel?"

Chapter Four:

Watery Grave

Looking onshore, there's the round fellow Mr. Flemming, Mr. Brookshard, and a host of military officers, including the senior officer who knocked so impolitely on my family's door the night before Niklas' execution.

Nate is in the Loyalist boat on the water with an oversized coat over his broad shoulders. His blonde hair is already wet; he must have assessed the water.

Damn, out of all the challenges, this is not his strongest. He's not a bad swimmer by any means, but looking at the Federalist dueler in the Havensburg boat, they are built like a sea creature. He has long limbs, broad shoulders, and likely practices his endurance in the Sevier Ocean. Since Havensburg is a coastal city, how is a challenge like this remotely fair?

Nate is surrounded by the four men who were all at our house. Parley, George, Rasmussen (aka Rasshole), and Jaden. Their robes billow and their bodies sway due to the unsettling wind whipping continuously across the surface of the reservoir.

"Choppy water, even better!" I say sarcastically to Trisha, who came along with my Dad and me.

My Mom and Sofia wanted nothing to do with this duel. In my Mom's words, "I will not witness another son die." And Sofia is indeed a bloodthirsty evil child… Except she's mortified of the open water. Guess I know what I must do to keep her in line.

Rupert, who is in his nicest shirt, managed to help row a flat-bottom boat between Nate and the other dueler. Rupert's boat consisted of a bunch of judges. Once he positioned them, a provincial judge began to holler as loud as he could across the rocky water.

In the name of Tyren,
The Province of Murcia hereby declares it,
The duel of Ash Reservoir Water Rights,
Nathaniel Hastings of Lyon,
representing the Loyalist.
Vs.
Addison Mueler of Havensburg,
representing the Federalist.

"On my whistle, you will swim to the barge. On the barge, there is one weapon. A trident, the last man standing, will be declared champion." The provincial judge declared.

Looking intently, I saw the barge was at least a fifty-foot swim from where Nate stood. I felt sick to my stomach. The trident, which is supported upright, on the 10-foot by 10-foot flat barge, features a golden eagle signet representing the Loyalist and a red, three-headed serpent representing the Federalist. A bejeweled death weapon, mind-boggling, but not surprising given Athren's track record.

Nate's face looks focused as he braces for a long swim and possible death. He's calm, shirtless, with his feet staggered, ready to launch himself like a projectile into the chilling water. The recent snow melt could easily take his breath away.

The judge reaches for his whistle; I tense my muscles in anticipation. Then the judge bellows out, "Ready," and blares the squealing whistle as loudly as humanly possible.

Both Nate and Addison jumped as far as they could, headfirst. Stress surges through my body, making it difficult for me to breathe.

Trisha, anxious herself, yanks my arm almost out of my shoulder socket. That's oddly physical of her. Her boyfriend, the man she would gladly die for, is currently on the chopping block, and there is nothing she can do.

After three long seconds, Nate still hadn't surfaced. "Where is he?" I exclaim.

Addison is practically one-third of the way to the barge. Like a shark in the night, Nate rose. He gasped for a longing breath, dropping back under, pulling and kicking as much water as he could on his way to the barge. Again, we lost him under the unsettled rough water.

Addison, now fifteen feet from the barge, is as fast as an arrow. Stroke after perfect stroke, he seems to glide across the water.

Nate rose once more, taking in his course, lowering his head for another decent. His speed is that of a turtle compared to Addison's.

"The other guy is going to beat him there!" Trisha's voice cracks with evident emotion.

Addison's hands reach the barge, propelling his body up and taking hold of the trident. He doesn't even seem fatigued.

Where is Nate? My insides convulse with anxiety.

Addison stalks the side of the barge, waiting for Nate to surface. He doesn't seem to see him through the stormy, murky water. Nate finally appears on the opposite side, behind Addison. He must've swum underneath the barge.

It looks like Nate is going to sneak up on him, but then Addison whips around with serpent reflexes, catching Nate off guard. Instinctively, Nate grabs hold of the side of the barge and jostles it hard in the already choppy water. Addison became visibly off balance but still managed to strike the trident aggressively at Nate. To our amazement, Nate was able to dodge the blow directed at his head.

The barbs of the trident impale the barge with such force that it penetrates the wood, jamming it. Addison, being off kilter from the swaying barge, loses his footing and staggers backwards.

Nate did not have time to yell, but from our vantage point, it seemed like he was in distress. Then the realization came. One of the barbs of the trident is lodged between Nate's pointer finger and thumb on his left hand.

Gut-wrenching pain seared my insides as I thought I was going to witness another brother die. I'm sure everyone would learn of my torment if they looked upon my face.

Before Addison could react, Nate grasped the trident with his good right hand and lifted his feet to the edge of the barge, pushing off the force of a swimmer; he and the trident broke free. His left hand must be entirely ripped to shreds.

Nate and the trident are now out of sight under the untamed frigid water. Addison, in disbelief, leaned over the edge, looking for any sign of Nate and the trident.

In one fluid motion, Nate, with his injured left hand again grasped the side of the barge and with his right, thrusted the trident up, plunging it under Addison's ribs and impaling the Federalist dueler's heart.

An audible gasp sounded through the air. Addison freezes with a blank stare and falls face-first into the water, dead.

Nate slowly climbs up the bloodied, wet barge and stands to a height, taller than I've ever seen (still not taller than me). He raises his red, meaty fist in the air, and he shouts for all to hear,

"I will not die! Not today nor ever, I'm the champion!"

He is a champion, and to the Loyalist, a hero. Suely, he's fit for this way of life. Cheers and applause echoed across the water.

A loud noise screeched over the celebration, Addison's mother. She came from Havensburg to witness her son die over some stupid law. Alongside the grieving mother, I notice a stunning brunette attempting to help. She must be from Havensburg as well.

Breaking my gaze, Dad says sternly to Trisha and me, "Let us get to shore and away from this. We will wait for Nate there."

Oddly, I didn't catch an ounce of satisfaction in his tone. Was it because Nate didn't show mercy?

Once on solid ground, we waited off to the side. I glance over at the crowds of people on the dock, congratulating Nate. I couldn't help but notice Mr. Brookshard looking visibly upset. Odd, did he have a wager on this event?

As my brothers, Nate and Rupert, approach us, immense joy laces Nate's face! He won. For that sliver of a second, he is on top of the world. Trisha runs to Nate, closing the gap with impressive speed. She hugs him closely and kisses him longingly. Nate's uninjured hand brushes Trisha's hair away from her ear, and he whispers something sweet to her.

What I would give to have a moment like that with Mariam. My eyes shift searching for the Havensburg brunette, but she is gone.

As if I were doing something wrong, my Dad shoved me slightly with his elbow. "Stop staring, weirdo."

I smirked a little too much, saying loud enough for them to hear, "It's not my fault they are all lovey-dovey in public."

Nate finally acknowledges my existence, hugging me and saying, "Amis, I almost just died. Have you ever been stabbed? Cause I have!" He points to his bandaged hand, which was poorly wrapped. Was Rupert his nurse? Blood is still seeping through.

"It's a mere flesh wound." I grumble and continue, "You should probably get home to Mom and get it fixed up."

Nate pauses, "No, I need to get a proper nurse at the guild. I hope no tendons or ligaments were severed."

Rupert remarks, "You should've seen my viewpoint, it was wild."

"And it looks excruciating." Trisha voices concern.

"Nate would never admit that, though, he's too proud," I add.

"How much money will you get from the duel?" Rupert eyes him curiously.

"Someone just died, lay off!" Trisha sasses towards him.

Is this way of life worth it? I could never kill for sport, and that's what this is, even if it's for politics. It's entertainment for people of all kinds. I saw others exchanging money, as if they had just watched a horse race.

"When will you come home to visit? We don't see you like we used to see Nikl-" I stammer off. Nate's face is now visibly upset.

"Again, Amis, lay off! It's only been two weeks." Trisha lectures.

I shake my head in annoyance. I don't think he will ever come home. The golden eagle pin on his black jacket symbolizes his new home. An awkward silence falls.

Trisha pipes up again, "Guess what, Henry? I'm going to join the Loyalist guild with your son!"

She is all smiles, and Dad does nothing more than give her a side hug as a sign of support.

Good, I hope she dies, so the leash around Nate's neck is removed! I subconsciously pushed the dark thought about Trisha away. She is fast and has a strong build; she might make a good duelist. I wouldn't want to duel her; she's bloodthirsty.

I walked home with Dad and Rupert, excited to share the news with Mom and Sofia. I know exactly what my vicious sister's reaction will be.

Chapter Five:

Four-Legged Beasts

When we reach our dirt road home, I feel my mother's eyes piercing through us, looking for Nate. The pain she must be feeling.

Dad greets Mom, immediately calming her concern with his soft voice, "Nate did well, it runs in the family."

My Mom looks like a ghost, frozen with fear and heartache as she responds, "Well, why didn't he come back with you?"

That is precisely the question I have! Why does it feel like he's pushing us away?

"He loves us, he just feels guilty." Dad sighs.

"He should; the little bastard deserves to be punished." Mom staggers back, leaving my Dad's embrace.

Sofia enters the room and immediately chimes in, "He's 23, Mom! The person whooping his ass now is Trisha!"

Rupert and I roll with laughter. "Whooping his ass in another way!" I blurt out.

I turn sharply to the freckly face of Sofia's, "Guess what! You missed some blood. Nate almost lost his thumb, and he stabbed the Havensburg man under the ribs!"

My Mom strides away, shaking her head in disbelief. "Please spare me the details! I've seen enough fighting for a lifetime." She exclaims, holding her own lifelong injured hand.

I broke down the fight in detail to Sofia. She is much smaller than Nate and me. Being the bonus baby, as my parents would say. She's only 14 years old; she may still grow to Hastings' height. I know, as I share the events of the lake, she is visualizing it, as if she were the one fighting. She's always wanted to be older than she is; most teenagers do. I love her for that.

We finish the chores we had missed earlier in the day. My last chore was gathering the eggs from the chicken coop out behind our house. The coop borders the forest that leads up to the mountains. It can be an intimidating place as the sun sets. Even in my adulthood, I still have childish fears, and for that reason, I made my gathering quick. I unpack the wooden door and spot our one nasty rooster, Leo. His giant talons seemed always sharpened, ready to spur me to hell. That's one devilish bird!

I hate Leo; he'll chase you down when you aren't looking and strike with his claws. He's a cowardly little shit; I bet the hens aren't even fans of his male-dominating ego. I'd skin him and cook up his chicken breast if my Dad would let me! Luckily, I was able to gather the thirty eggs with haste. I ran into our home just before it was pitch dark, and only the moon was out.

Mom cooks supper, which luckily includes chicken, bread, and potatoes.

"Why the good meal, ma?" Rupert examines casually.

"I didn't lose another son; I think that is a good reason to celebrate." She replies.

Niklas's letter has been on my mind; I haven't had a moment to breathe with all the work in the fields. I need to get to the library and learn whatever Niklas wants me to know.

With a quick change of subject, I ask, "Hey, Sof. Would you like to go into town with me tomorrow? We may be able to find Nate and look at his puncture wound. I bet it is festering already!"

Sofia drops her spoon and shrugs her shoulders, "If you insist."

Good, now I have someone to back me up in case things go sideways. She's so small, I could throw her at any problem that arises… That would give me time to get away.

Another day ended as I lay on my intolerable mat. My mind races with the events of today. How many more duels will Nate have to survive? I'd like to know what type of contract he signed.

I wake to the sound of a wolf's cry as it pierced the night sky. Grey wolves here? I think to myself. The dogs begin to howl and yip. Dad yells, "Get your asses up, and get out back, with your bows at the ready."

Rupert practically jumps out of bed fully dressed, his arrows all quivered. I stagger back in disbelief. Did I forget to close the gate to the chicken coop? After grabbing two hatchets, I ran out the back door. Dad and Rupert were ready to lose their arrows as they faced the chicken coop.

To my dismay, two wolves were inside the coop feasting on the chickens. All we could see were their back legs. Our blue heelers could do nothing more than bark from outside.

Without thinking, I move directly towards the action. My Dad yells, "Where is your bow?"

"I'm a terrible shot and you know it." I refute, as if I were some hero.

Hero of the chickens…

The wolves must have heard me coming because they stretched their hind legs out of the coop, turning to face me. Their bare teeth show their massive canines ready to devour me whole. I remain still and immovable, being just as aggressive. To my relief, my Dad and brother had not released any arrows; they feared hitting me. I don't trust Rupert's shot any more than mine.

The wolves' hair stands straight up in their snarling, bloodstained stance. They were ready to prowl.

My animal instincts took over; I threw the Hatchet in my right hand with all the tenacity I could muster. It felt like slow motion, watching it barrel towards the wolf on the right and nailing the wolf right between the eyes. I watch as its body goes limp. Dead.

The second wolf ran at full speed towards me. I was not prepared. I somersault to the right, rolling away. The wolf catches my pant leg in the process. I turn to see one of my dogs barreling towards us. Their jaw opens wide as it clenches tightly around the wolf's neck. It was not enough, as the wolf viciously shook my dog away.

The wolf's primal instincts are on full display, and so are mine. I managed to get to my feet, facing the beast just a few steps away. Holding my last hatchet at the ready, the wolf lunged, missing me as it clanks its monstrous teeth. This time, instead of moving, I stood my ground, slamming my sharp Hatchet into the side of its head. Falling backwards, I lost my composure.

With my ass in the dirt, I swivel to face Rupert, ready to brag. Instead, I hear another wolf running at lightning speed towards me. I close my eyes, frozen in terror, waiting to be consumed. My two hatchets were already planted in the other dead beasts next to me. My heart stops as I hear the greyback's steps getting louder, pounding the earth. I feel a whoosh of air pass by me, and hear a tremendous 'thud' that vibrates the ground next to me. When I open my eyes in the moonlight, I find the third wolf on the ground. Dead, with an arrow in its heart.

A relief washes over me. Rupert's eyes widen so much that I could see the whites of them from where I sit.

A familiar voice rings out, my Dad's. "Get your ass up, Amis! Do more of that hatchet shit, and you'll be the one I'll shoot with an arrow. Listen to me when I say grab your bow."

"I killed two of them!" I yell in revolt.

"Amis, if that were a duel, we'd both be dead because you made me intervene. How would you judge that, Rupert?" Dad says, doing his best to prove his point.

"Agreed, execution on the spot for both of you. Dad saved you." Rupert then continues in a light-hearted manner. "Amis, how did you not see that third wolf's glowing red eyes in the bushes?!"

I'm flustered, as these playful attacks start to feel personal. "At least I did something! Look how many chickens I saved!" A partial smirk forms on my face.

I walk over the dead wolves to the chicken coop. Seven out of our thirty-one chickens are chewed to bits; feathers are everywhere. It's my fault, and it pains me even more to see Leo the Rooster still cocking around.

"Thank you for saving me. It's my fault the wolves broke into the coop." I say with a sincere look.

"Don't worry, son, I'll always be there to save you. Next time, don't be so quick to correct your mistakes. Rash decisions have consequences. Believe me, I know." Dad breathes deep with more pain.

I check on my poor dog, who attempted to save me. She is okay; I'm grateful she didn't get hurt because of my mistake. Our dogs aren't just working dogs; they are a vital part of our family.

Rupert and I salvage the chicken meat the best we can. We don't dare save the wolf meat. It's too gamey and greasy. We aren't starving enough for that. The wolf pelts may be worth some money if we can clean them up, or they could be a ferocious cloak to wear. I hate the killing, especially when it's not necessary.

I finally get back on my mat, looking at Sofia and wondering how she can still be asleep. Violence must make her sleep peacefully.

All the adrenaline that was rushing through my veins finally subsided. My restless body will finally give in. If I must fight to survive when at home, I should fight in a ring. Life is nothing more than a duel. The Athrenian people were aware of this early on, which is why duelist have become such a staple. There is good and evil in every decision, which is why they created their false gods, Tyren and Harwen. There's less guilt if it's not your will.

Chapter Six:

Librarian

The meadow is a tapestry, with vibrant colors springing up from the ground. The flowers glisten bright and new, capturing the sun's lustrous light of life, as they persistently pursue.

Suddenly, there she was, and my heart began to race. In the middle of the clearing, between the tall evergreens. Her long brown hair followed the flow of the trees, with the coming and going of the soft, cool breeze. I begin to move at an impatient pace. When I walked, she jogged. When I decided to run, she began to sprint. I could not catch her, no matter how hard I tried. Breathlessness, she made me breathless. My heart will never be complete without hers. One last time, she turned so slightly to tempt me onward. And then she disappeared in the blink of an eye.

My eyes awoke, solely alone. She was not Mariam, but I recognized her. I do not care; she was beautiful and perfect. I closed my eyes tightly, begging to dream of her again.

Sofia yells with a terrible screech. "Wake up, Amis, or I'll annihilate you and leave your body to be gobbled by the scary grey wolves." She mimics a crying baby.

I moaned while stretching limb by limb. Again, she screams, "Get up! We need to find Nate!"

My body quickly contorted, rising taller than the day before. "Let's get to Lyon then," I said with a smirk.

As we left out the back door, we saw the massacre from the night before. I thought we'd cleaned this up much better.

Sofia's eyes widened as she uttered, "Holy Hell! I heard what happened, but-"

She trailed off as I began to recount the chickens. "Twenty-three, that's good, ahh, twenty-four if you count Leo…. Screw Leo, he doesn't count." I laugh at Sofia, "Are you sure you want to feed me to the wolves? It can get hairy."

Straight-faced, she responds, "No, feathery."

I squinted; my eyes judged her. "Whatever you say, sis."

We begin our two-mile walk into Lyon. The colors of the meadow from my dream imbue my entire surroundings. Is this real life? Why am I being tortured?

The farms become smaller as we approach town. More structures emerge, ugly brown cottages and townhomes with their timber framework and woven twigs. It's every fire's aspiration. Just one wrong spark and this town would be nothing more than ash.

The Soldiers' barracks aren't even made of stone. There are only five notable stone buildings in Lyon: The church (now known to my family for improper worship), the provincial building (a former King's castle retreat overlooking the courtyard), the library (where books burn easily), and, of course, the Loyalist and Federalist guilds. Each massive on its own, but I never dared to venture there out of fear that I'd become a cold, callous monster. Not that Niklas and Nate are such beasts. Duelers either become killers or corpses.

The cobblestone roads seem rougher than usual as we turn onto Lewis Lane.

There are only three directions a person like me can go in this town. I need to decide soon… Seeing, I'm at my peak of eighteen years, and Mariam is already making a name for herself in Harpstedt.

I could be a Soldier: Always stuck policing peasants and collecting taxes. Not to mention being sent to war with barbarians in the northwest.

Maybe a Dueler: Begging to die.

Not a Politician: Judging duels or trying to pass laws… That's an analytical profession perfect for Rupert and Mariam.

There is a fourth option…. I don't desire it; I'm not like my Dad, a peasant.

As we reached the large, carefully fitted stones at the base of the Loyalist guild, I was awed at how incredibly breathtaking it was. They must have hauled the carefully chiseled stone from the Oquirrh Mountains, located to the east of us.

The large wooden front doors look incredibly thick and secure. We slowly push one of the doors open and immediately walk into a warmly lit, circular-shaped foyer. A few chairs were positioned against the walls, and on the floor lay a giant golden eagle rug. Immediately down the hall, an older, muscly man approached.

He held out his hand to Sofia and me, saying, "I'm Mykel, how do you do?"

I feel as if I've met this man before. His voice was surprisingly gentle and polite, but he'd seen battle. Scars crossed his face and forearm, and his enormous stature was intimidating.

"Hello, sir, my name is Amis-"

He abruptly caught me off guard and blurted out, "Hastings. Your Henry's son and Nate's brother? And you must be the delightful Sofi."

Sofia, looking offended, fired back, "Delightful!?"

Mykel laughs hysterically with a smile grinning from cheek to cheek. "I'll get Nate!"

I whisper to Sofia, "Doesn't he look familiar?"

"Not at all, he looks like a typical dueling prick to me." Sofia flexes her biceps, unafraid of prying eyes.

We sat down and waited, as I intentionally did not want to walk any further into the dungeon. Surprisingly, the guild is nicer than I thought. I suppose luxury comes before violence.

Nate and Mykel approach; Nate has a giant grin. There was a sparkle in his blue eyes; maybe he was just excited to see us. Then I heard a little patter coming from the hallway. It was Trisha… She's starting to annoy me. Maybe because she sees Nate more than I do, it'll only get worse.

Sofia began to pester Nate, asking him a barrage of questions about his first duel.

I turn and ask Mykel curiously, "What is your exact position here?"

Mykel answers respectfully, "Well, I bounce from guild to guild assisting with training the duelers, ensuring each side is getting fair and adequate representation."

"Sooo, you're the one making sure no funny business is going on?" I add.

"In a way." As he shakes his head. "I'm not allowed to have favorites, but if I did… your brother would take the cake."

"Nate is a flawless specimen," I express sarcastically in an envy-riddled tone.

"Nate is dependable, yes. Niklas is the one I'm referring to; he saw things through a different lens."

"Niklas was." I correct.

"No one truly ever dies; they live in here." Mykel taps his heart, winking, and pacing away.

Mykel is genuine and, in some strange way, reminds me of my Dad.

I turn my ears back to Trisha, telling Sofia, "The nurse got a little too handsy with Nate; she even tried to rub his abs."

"Sure…" I started with an accusatory smile.

"Hey Nate, how's your hand? Can I see it?!" Sofia asks excitedly. Nate unravels his bandage.

"That's gnarly," Sofia exclaims.

"You should see the other guy," Nate says, raising his chin a little too proudly.

This championship is getting to his head. Now he's bragging about killing someone.

"The nurse told me that the space between the index finger and thumb is called the thenar, that's where the trident barbed stabbed me. Luckily, the tendons and ligaments are all intact." Nate informs us.

Looking at his hand, I see the skin gruesomely split. That's enough to make me queasy. "Sofia, we'd better be on our way. I'm sure these two have important matters to attend to. It's good to see you, Nate. Trisha, please humble him."

"Don't worry, Amis, Nate is just as terrible with the bow as you. I whoop his golden prick scuzz all the time." Trisha teases, elbowing Nate.

I raise my eyes at Sofia... "Awkward."

I go in for a hug and head towards the giant doors to leave. I can't help but think how much our relationship has changed, and Trisha keeps him on a tight leash.

Back onto Lewis Lane, an awful aroma fills the air. The nasty cesspits carved into the street with bricks remind me why I never want to live in the city. Peasants dump their human waste in the gutters… I need to decide my fate quickly; becoming a night soil man would be a shitty thing to be.

Holding our breath, we raced to the library. Suffocation was just seconds away. A few merchants are out selling goods such as fruit, silk, fur, and a variety of spices in these nasty cesspit streets. I'm sure their products are all crap. Sofia leans in as we approach the quaint but beautiful stone library.

"Amis, what do you think you'll find in Niklas' book?"

"I don't know, but it has to be important."

I push the door open as softly as possible, doing my best to be quiet. The less attention, the better, I thought. The dark, birch-wood bookshelves that lined the wall were all taller than us. I've never spent much time in the library… The smell is like old paper, making it very musty. Tables lay up in the center of the room, and light broke through the multi-colored stained-glass windows.

A little old lady, dressed in large tan robes, approached us.

She babbles, but articulates her words clearly, saying, "What can I help you with today?"

Before I can respond, she continues, "I see you scrunching your nose, don't worry, you get used to the smell and come to love it. The scent is due to the lignin aging in the paper. They say it's bibliosmia."

Sofia's face was straight as she appeared concerned for the older woman's mental state. I abruptly elbowed her.

"Wonderful, we are looking for Ms. Cunningham," I say politely.

Immediately, her eyes widen, saying, "Niklas said you'd come. Young Mr. Hastings, I didn't expect you to take so long." She smiles enthusiastically.

As she walks away hurriedly to grab the text, I scan the shelves. There are scriptures of all kinds; some seem incredibly old. I wonder if any of these have my Dad and Mom's belief in an almighty God? There are also philosophers' texts, manuscripts, and secular literature. My curiosity piqued when I noticed a whole section dedicated to the historical accounts of the war with the barbarians. I don't know much about the Barbarians, other than they are ruthless beasts that want to destroy Athren.

This work is ancient. I'm curious how much of the literature is censored by Athren. They want you to know only what fits their narrative. Many of these texts appear to be bound in some animal skin, and the pages are sewn together. "History only lives on when we write it down," that's what Dad used to say.

Ms. Cunningham returns rather quickly for being an old lady. She states while carrying a delicate, quaint book rather tightly, "Most books are made by us physically traveling to Harpstedt, to scribe with a quill. This book was given to me a quarter of a century ago by a young man much like you."

I paused, squinting at her, trying to understand. I must have wrinkled my face too much.

She picks right back up with speed, "Honestly, child? Have you ever been in a library?"

Sofia let out a boisterous laugh. As she attempts to steady herself, she responds quickly, "Sorry, Ms. Cunningham, he's a bit weird sometimes."

Ms. Cunningham smiles genuinely. "It's okay, my dear, we are all weird in our own way. That's what makes you, you."

She then presented the book, holding it out with both hands, as if it were a sword made of pure gold. I took it in graciously.

Then she adds quickly once again, "I have protected this book for many years. It's not transcribed from the capital; having this is a capital offense." I exhale like she has placed on my shoulders. Do I want to be executed for this text?

Ms. Cunningham enunciates again swiftly and quietly, "This book is not yours; it's mine. Niklas's large down payment has allowed you the chance to borrow it."

I start to open it. In another relatively quick motion, she pushes my hands together around the book, closing it. Mouthing, "Not here!"

I shook my head in understanding. I conceal the book in my cloth sack, saying, "Thank you, Ms. Cunningham, for your kindness!"

Sofia and I turned and walked out the wooden door we just passed through. I'm eager to get home to read the mysterious book Niklas has left for me.

"What did he get you into?" Sofia voices as we commence our journey home.

Immediately, I correct her, "What did he get US into?"

Suddenly, I'm shoved as a physical presence pushes me off balance; the force causes me to stumble off the street into an alleyway.

Gathering myself, I clamor, "Get your hands off my sister!" It is too late; we are trapped.

Chapter Seven:

The Book of Gentry

My eyes stare like daggers at Zander and Harry Jasper as they detain my sister and me. I just got Niklas's illegal book, and now I'm going to lose it.

Zander, with uneasiness in his voice, says, "We need to make this quick, Harry."

Interjecting, I blurt out, "If you are going to kill us, better do it quick!" I place my gaze past their shoulders, praying and hoping someone will notice us.

Harry says sternly, "We aren't going to kill you; we just want to talk. We need to tell you something. Meet us next Wednesday at midnight by the dock at Ash Reservoir. The moon will be just a sliver then."

Blinking, confused, I retort, "Why should I trust you?"

Zander, who's scrawnier and younger than Harry, pipes up. "Please. My brother will be dueling Nate soon; he will likely die in the ring. We need you to listen to us when we have more time and fewer possible ears." As he looks around suspiciously.

How do they know about a duel this far in advance?

They clear the walkway, letting us pass. Harry then fires off, "Bring your little sister along if you want."

Causing Zander to chuckle sharply. Sofia turns around on one foot, as fast as an eagle striking its prey, she raises her leg, slamming her foot into Zander's nuts. He sinks low into his knees in agony.

Once we made it home, I found a nice corner to read in. Scanning the room, I saw none of my family was near. I promised Sofia that I'd tell her the contents of the book. Until I know what is inside, I do not want to drag anyone else down this hellhole.

Opening the book, I found another letter! Niklas, you genius! Then I read his horrendous handwriting, I might have to take that genius thing back.

Amis,

Thank you for following my instructions.

Either way, I couldn't be straightforward in my previous letter. Over the last year, while I've been in the Loyalist Guild, I've learned many things.

Becoming a dueler is more than training. They require an initiation ceremony. If you fail, you're dead. It's not common knowledge; duelers are sworn to secrecy. Each person faces a different challenge. They left me stranded in the Oquirrh Mountains for an entire night, and it was February! Good thing I know those slopes like the back of my hand.

I participated in duels across all of Athren. West to Blanding and south to Lansing. Rupert knew I fought; did he tell you? The last fight I had was in Harpstedt, where I learned later that I was supposed to die.

Be careful of both guilds. They may claim to stand for Athren, but they have their agendas. In Harpstedt, I was poisoned the day before a duel. Somehow, they learned of my allergies. I believe it was the Federalists, but I couldn't confirm.

Don't trust anyone working in the government. When Nate joins a guild, they will groom him to be my successor. Be cautious and watch what you say.

They are going to kill me; I can feel it. Champions can gain too much power, power they can't control.

Read the book, be secretive, Amis. Don't tell Dad. I believe in you, make the right decision.

Goodbye Brother,

Niklas

I'm too distracted to read the book; I need to find out who framed Niklas. I compiled all my findings.

Mr. Brookshard saw Niklas and Heather leave.

Mrs. Fray saw Niklas and Heather pass her shop.

Many reported hearing an argument or fight before they entered the forest.

Mr. Stone found Heather dead, followed by Rasmussen and Jaden.

Niklas' last words: " Good or evil, everyone dies. I'm innocent. Amis, set men free!"

They were able to communicate between Harpstedt and Lyon.

Niklas was poisoned in Harpstedt.

Just like that, my privacy at home was abruptly destroyed. Rupert sat next to me, giving me a puzzling look. I quickly put the book and letter away. Rupert can't know; he wants to ask what I'm doing, but to my relief, he doesn't.

Rupert looks the most like me out of all my siblings. He's a little shorter than I, but he has a similar muffled voice, hazel eyes, a freckled face, brown hair, and even a hint of red in his beard. He has always been a protector, to my annoyance… Sometimes he tries to be a second dad.

Niklas and he weren't the kindest to each other; they were amiable at best. If we weren't bonded together by blood and forced into an unwanted family contract, I don't think any of us would be friends. Mom and Dad have always emphasized the importance of our family unit. Unfortunately, our unit has entered uncharted territory. Niklas is gone, Nate is in the guild, Rupert is a judge, Mom is broken, and Dad is working harder than ever… Sofia is the only one who remains normal. Is Sofia normal? Did that really cross my mind? She's her usual morbid self.

Frustrated, I have to wait till tomorrow to be able to read through the book. I need to avoid prying eyes.

In the morning, I grabbed a quick breakfast, getting out the door faster than the rest of my family. I know where I'll need to hide this book. I run across the dew-laced field, getting my pant legs so wet that I feel like I stepped in a puddle. Hurrying, I shuffled through my cloth sack and sat under the apple tree where Niklas is buried. There are no apples yet, but the tree has flowered. To my astonishment, the flowers are brighter pink than usual. When the apples do grow, I bet they'll be firm, crisp, and have a sweet smell.

I rest my back against the soft tree. I can see Sofia in a far-off field gathering water from our well. I need to tell her what Niklas wrote. I need her help.

Opening the precious tan book bound in animal skin. There's nothing special about this book; the pages are sewn together, indicating that an amateur likely bound it.

The words on the first page read:

An account of Gentry A. Saunders

The Noble Red Warrior

In the words of Gentry A. Saunders,

We live with key fundamental truths. These truths cannot be changed or manipulated. Life is precious and should not be trifled with. God will not be mocked.

My life's account is relatively simple.

I was born on the 17th day of September, in the town of Eagle Valley, province of Langley, Nation of Athren. My father, Herald A. Saunders, and mother, Daphne R. Witmore, raised me with an understanding of the concepts of good and evil, right and wrong, and moral and immoral.

East in the foothills of the White Mountains, I learned many skills in weaponry, including archery, battle strategy, survival, and pure brute strength. My body was a machine equipped with fortitude, chivalry, and size. My life's purpose here is to correct the wrongful deaths of those put in political duels. These were foundational skills that enabled me to become a champion of the ring and a leader of the insurrection that overthrew King Harper VI.

I know the last king was a quarter century ago. I never knew why they abolished the monarchy; it was one of those things Athren didn't teach. Harpstedt's monks and Librarians could be censoring Athren's education. It wouldn't be hard to do, given that every book is reviewed there. Taking my eyes off the book, I surveyed the farm to make sure my surroundings were still clear. No one was in sight, so I continued my perusal of the book.

At the age of eighteen, I joined the Federalist guild. I didn't realize what anguish that would cause for my parents. Growing up in Eagle Valley, no one liked change, and everyone was predominantly Loyalist; that's why they wore the golden eagle pin on their robes. The community turned on my parents when I joined the one guild. They'd lost their son, were *blocked by their community, and eventually tried to leave Athren altogether until they met their demise.*

The Loyalists passed all the laws in Eagle Valley due to the Federalists' insufficient and poorly trained duelers. Surely, my parents thought I signed a death wish.

My initiation was brutal. Federalists seek strength and power. For my initiation trial, against my will, I was thrown into a pit of Vipera Aspis. I hate snakes. God cursed the vile creatures by removing their legs. Their entire existence is to cause humanity suffering. Indeed, one may say I have Ophidiophobia.

Pulling away from the book, I paused in disbelief. That's the main reason I've always loathed the red three-headed serpent Federalists! My eyes again focus on the parchment paper pages in my hands. Reading again:

When I was tossed into the pit, I was lucky not to land on a venomous rope. Quickly, my eyes scanned the room, taking in its entirety; approximately ten vipers surrounded me. My first instinct was to back up and do my best to keep slithering beasts unprovoked. That task proved to be impossible. There were too many. I swear they could sense my heart beating out of its chest. I slowly dropped to my knees, praying... trying to steady my quivering body. Thinking to myself, be still, be calm, be immovable. These hissing sticks have no power over me.

Opening my eyes slowly, I looked down past my knees. Yes, there was a Viper there. Yes, it was facing me. I followed its body from its small, pointed tail to its scaly, triangular head. Its pattern was wavy, with dark and pale stripes. It was coiled up like a switch-back trail, ready to strike. Looking past it, I saw a wooden stick. Slowly leaning forward, I reached my arm out, having to pass to the snake. Grabbing the stick courageously, I used it to flick the Vipers' tail. Causing the Viper to move. But it only moved closer, filling all available space between us. Like lightning, the snake coiled and struck me in my right forearm. Pain exploded in my body, causing a quick sting. I couldn't react; I couldn't move in fear. I could incite more strikes from the snakes around me.

Slowly, while kneeling, I shifted all my weight from my knees onto the heels of my feet. Again, I became completely frozen. My eyes sealed shut, I knew I was dead, but I would not let the fear of the vicious ropes constricting around me decide when I'd succumb.

Again, a shock occurred, causing all my muscles to twist and spasm. I pried my eyes open, ready to meet another vile hiss. Instead, I found a real rope swinging back and forth in front of me. In one swift motion, I leaped up, climbing out of the hellhole.

An instructor immediately hugged me and laughed hysterically, saying, "You aren't going to die today, you didn't let the fear overtake your emotions. You passed the test!"

My eyes watered as I proclaimed, "But I got bitten, one of those vipers bit me!"

Another laugh greeted me, "Don't worry, my son, we

milked all the snakes of their venom, you will not die."

I was evaluated; I passed. Control, they need someone who won't quake in fear. Dueling for the Federalist in Eagle Valley is asking to die. It's like being thrown in a pit of Loyalists. You cannot show fear.

I'm Amis Hastings. As I put the book down, I did so with a sense of disdain. I'm not some snake gypsy named Gentry. I'll find time tomorrow to read more.

I grabbed the shovel I had brought with me and began digging a small hole. I placed large stones along the sides of the hole and positioned a flat rock at the bottom, putting the book in the center of the little chamber. Grabbing a large stone, I carefully placed it on top of the opened hole. That should keep the book safe as long as it doesn't rain too much!

I completed my chores for the rest of the day. I haven't seen Sofia yet. I need to tell her everything I've learned, especially about Niklas.

$$\infty$$

A week has passed, and not a lot has happened. Each day, the spring temperatures continue to rise slightly. I have had a chance to read the book some more. To my satisfaction, it rained two days ago, and the book was still in its normal condition. The stone catacomb is secure enough to keep the moisture out for now.

Sofia and I have been bouncing theories off each other about who set up Niklas. She thinks it's Mr. Stone because it's the most logical. He did find him first and probably didn't like him because of all the puff puff going on in his backyard.

I'm more of a theorist. It was something bigger, maybe Mr. Brookshard? He seems diabolical enough to kill his daughter to stop Niklas from destroying all his Federalist dreams in the dueling ring.

While Sofia and I are walking to get water out of our well, I remind her, "It's Wednesday, you know the plan. Are you sure you're up for it?"

Reaching for the bucket at our well, Sofia responds, "Ready? Please, I was born ready. The hard part is going to be getting us both out of the house completely undetected."

I stop to think, "You are right. Let's get out of the house stealthily, and who cares if they catch it on the way back in." A mischievous grin flushes my face.

"Oh, and Sofi, did you put the bow and arrows in a safe place where no one will find them?"

As she pulled the rope with the bucket full of water, she said confidently, "Of course, right by Dad's odd pet pigeons' cage in the woods."

"Dad has a pet pigeon. That's interesting..."

"How do you not know? The pigeon is rarely home, but when it is, Dad sneaks to its cage. He thinks he is sly, but no one can get past me."

As the day shifted to night, I lay awake waiting for complete silence. We need to make sure that everyone is in a deep sleep. I hear a rumble followed by a whoosh from my parents' room. Good! Dad is snoring. His snore rumbles through the whole house, and it's hard to miss. Now Sofia and I have to worry about being quiet enough to sneak past Rupert. If he wakes, we are in a world of trouble. Having a rule follower and stickler like Rupert in the house makes us walk on eggshells as it is.

When you become a judge for the duels, you have to make decisions without letting your emotional conscience get in the way. He's been very apathetic and distant. I guess I would be, too, if I had to watch violence as the norm.

I quietly roll out of bed, trying my best to avoid any significant movements. I walk on the balls of my feet and grab my wool coat and hat. I opened the front door, and there was no sound. I whip my head back into our dark home. No one is stirring, but where is Sofia?! I can't go back inside for her.

Pivoting back outside, I closed the door as quietly as possible. Then I heard a whisper, "Boo!" Startled, I almost slammed my back into the closed door.

"Sofia!" I gasp softly, pushing her shoulder. "Why would you do that!?!"

Her response is no surprise: "Eh, I saw the opportunity." I laugh silently and grin, hugging Sofia.

Looking at her in her dark eyes, I ask, "How'd you get here before me? Are you some silent killer?!"

She shrugs her shoulders, "You'll never know… let's go, I already have my bow."

We walked in the lightless night west towards Ash Reservoir. There was no sign of life, but we cannot be so sure. We cleared the tree line and looked at the dock jutting out onto the reservoir.

I whisper, "Perfect, no one is there yet…"

I look at Sofia and point to another line of trees along the shore. "Hide in there and keep your bow and arrow ready to fire. Please tell me that you practiced aiming."

She just beamed, her mouth open so I could see the whiteness of her teeth in the dark. Then she positions herself out of sight.

I walk onto the dock and wait. A full hour seemed to slip by. I caught myself gazing up at the star constellations in the moonless night when I heard the crunching of rocks. It's Zander and Harry Jasper, given all I can see are shadows.

One of them speaks, but I don't know who it is. "Where is that feisty little sister of yours? I thought you'd bring her to protect you?" The other brother chuckles.

"She's not here, lucky for you two. How are your nuts anyway?" That didn't come out right.

"Zander, did he just ask you about your ball sack?" They both giggle like schoolgirls.

"Ok, you incompetent bastards. Why are we here?" I question, positioning one hand behind my back, my hatchet in my hand.

I turn to circle the Jasper boys, to position Harry on the left for Sofia in the woods. Just in case she needs to let loose an arrow. I hope she's paying attention right now.

Harry's raspy voice states, "I'm going to die tomorrow in the courtyard. I know it, Nate is just too strong to duel in the ring." He trails off, looking out at the placid water.

Zander quickly continues, "We need you to know, Niklas was set up. They wanted him dead."

I press them, "I know, but who set him up? Who killed Heather!?" Eagerly, I wait for their response.

Harry again says, "Niklas came to us when he got back from Harpstedt. He told us he was poisoned, and someone was trying to kill him."

I shout, "I know all of this!"

"Calm down, we are trying to help." Zander retorts.

"Niklas was our friend; he was not loyal to either guild. We will never know exactly why, but he gave us helpful fighting tips and techniques."

Then Harry sighs with a mellow tone, "Before Heather and he went into the woods, I stopped him in the street. I don't think he cared for me talking to him in public. I was trying to talk him out of throwing the duel against me; he wanted me to knock him out, not kill him. Then he got upset and yelled, 'Knock me out in the ring, just like this!' and punched me in my eye."

A rapid flush of details shot through my mind. I put my head into my hands, dropping my hatchet. I remember:

Parley said there was an argument in the street before Heather was killed.

After Niklas' execution, Nate said he saw Harry with a black eye.

The day Heather died, Niklas said he had to go because he had a date.

"I believe you." The words mumble off my lips in pain. "Did you guys see who entered the woods behind them?"

Zander shot off with a side-eye, and his head waved side to side, indicating no.

"But why would he throw the duel against you, Harry?" I mull in my head.

"Because he loved Heather." He says somberly. "Mr. Brookshard wanted that land just north of us. If Niklas threw the duel, he was going to endorse their relationship."

Grabbing my hand, Sofia gives me an empathetic half-smile. "Niklas was in love?"

Both the Jasper boys smile, not seeing or expecting Sofia to show up.

"Yes." Zander exhales. "Were you planning on shooting us?"

"It's still an option." Sofia teases.

"We'd better be going; I want one last night of sleep while I'm living," Harry says with depression riddle words. "Amis, you can be just like your brother, maybe even a better duelist. Help Zander and join our guild." The Jasper boys turn and wander away.

"I like Zander… That dude from the rustic book was a Federalist dueler; maybe you should be too." Sofia voices.

Her opinion matters to me more than anyone else's. I've grown to enjoy my little sister's company. We walked with a hurried pace back home; we don't care who catches us now.

Chapter Eight:

Brothers

I informed Dad that Sofia and I would like to go into town with Rupert, to be with him while he judges Nate and Harry's duel. Dad isn't coming this time around. He didn't seem to be worried about Nate in this one, and Mom is still grieving. She shouldn't be left alone.

Niklas' death has put a dark sadness in her soul. I don't think anyone will ever be able to make her whole again. Mom has always been the one to support and encourage us to do more. She's been my nurturer and tender heart from the moment of my birth. She needs our support and our unconditional love now.

Sofia and I stood outside waiting for Rupert. The Stable door opens, and Rupert emerges with one of our horses, saddled up. He hands Sofia the reins, and I hold out my hands halfway up the horse, giving her a foot-rest.

She sprang up onto the horse, saying, "Very chivalrous of you, Rupert!"

Rupert responds in turn with a big grin on his freckly face. "Just following Dad's orders is all."

When we reach town, we head directly for the courtyard.

"Maybe we can see Nate before the duel," Sofia says with excitement.

"I bet if you get there early enough, you can. So, it may not be ideal timing, but would you be okay if I swung by Mrs. Fray's shop? I want to see if she has any herbs." I say, winking at Sofia, doing my best not to signal Rupert.

"Okay, I'll save you a spot up close to the ring." She replies.

I pick up my pace, trying to get to Mrs. Fray's shop with as much haste as possible without drawing any unwanted attention. As I open the door to her shop, I do a brief scan to ensure no one else is there. Mrs. Fray was busy putting something on the shelf behind her.

Saying nonchalantly with a slight head bow, "Hello, Mrs. Fray. I was curious if you had any herbs that could help with numbing pain?"

Her look and response were something I wasn't expecting. "You're a Hastings boy, right? Your older brother used to come in here all the time asking for similar things."

I quickly interrupted her, "Oh no, I know he had his issues. It's not like that; my other brother Nathan has a bad laceration on his hand."

She gives a pitied look, "You know your brother is a good guy. I think he made too many enemies."

"Ya, Nathan is one of the best!" I say with a smile.

"No, not Nathan. Niklas is, or I mean was, a stalwart individual. He always cared about the little man. On the day of sweet Heather's murder, they stopped in my shop. He was talking with such charm and charisma. Telling Heather all sorts of beautiful and affectionate things. I could tell they were in love." Mrs. Fray says this with a longing look, as if it were something she has always wanted.

Before I can think, I blurt out, "Wait, they came into your shop that day hand in hand?"

She nods her head yes and says, "Don't be so trusting of people's stories. Being gullible can get you killed."

"Thank you so much for your kindness." I swivel and walk to the wooden door from whence I came.

A voice trails off from behind me and grows louder. "Amis, my boy, don't you need these herbs?"

I stuttered, saying, "Uh. Yeah, thank you." I reach into my pocket for some coins.

Old brittle Mrs. Fray handed the herbs over. "It's on the house."

My perception of people to this point has been unbearably wrong. Mr. Parley lied to me about the events leading up to Heather's death. Why?

Knowing that I can't be late for Nate's duel, I race up Gambetta Street. I need to talk to Mr. Stone now.

Reaching the fence line outside of his home, I carefully opened the white picket gate. Knocking on his front door, I listen intently for footsteps; there is no movement inside. Instead, I hear what sounds like an axe banging into wood. Is he splitting firewood in the backyard? How fitting.

I take courageous steps toward his backyard and see the cranky old man there. Swinging tirelessly at chunks of wood.

Cautiously, I approach. Stone could be Heather's murderer, I think to myself. "Hello, sir."

He looks disgruntled and annoyed, with sweat dripping down his old wrinkly face. "What do you want, Hastings boy?"

"I was hoping to ask you some questions about the day Ms. Brookshard died."

"Well, get on with it, boy! And no, this isn't the same axe used to kill your brother! I had to get a new one because of him." He says in an aggressive tone, dabbing his salty face with his stained cotton shirt.

Confidence in me grows because of his rude demeanor. "Did you see who killed Heather?"

"Son, there are some things you don't want to know, regardless of the truth."

"Well, if you won't tell me who, can you tell me if you were the first person to arrive at the rock to see Heather dead?" I question, knowing Mr. Parley said he was.

"No, son. I was not. I don't know why the champion of all the land would just let Heather die." He responds mockingly, but I sense a hint of skepticism.

"I've been wondering about the same thing. Thank you." I turned and left, not waiting for another word to spew out of his piss ridden mouth.

The truth behind Niklas' execution is painful. Mr. Stone knows who killed her but won't say! And Parley lied again, but why? Is he just busy doing his Loyalist master's bidding?

I walk with a pep in my step towards the courtyard, looking for Sofia. As I pass by the large stone provincial building, I remain in awe of the magnificent structure; an extensive amount of labor must've gone into it. I bet every building is like this in Harpstedt.

Right as I turned the corner into the courtyard, I felt a hand brushing my shoulder, and the snakelike eyes of Rasmussen gaze upon me.

"What do you want?" I ask impatiently, looking over his shoulder to the hordes of people gathering for Nate's next successive triumph.

"My, my, you are as repulsive as your dead brother." Rasmussen sighs. "I'm not here to share pleasantries or to persuade you to join Nate in the Loyalist guild. Instead, I want to offer some advice..." Rasmussen trails off, viewing my annoyed body language.

"What advice could you possibly give me?" I laugh; I can't keep my eyes off his receding hairline and short stature. Everything about this ass-wipe screams annoying.

"Well, son, I see you are envious of Nate and eager to prove Niklas' innocence. Let me share with you a story."

"Please don't." I retort.

Rasmussen spews his story anyway. "Envy does a funny thing to a man's heart. There was once a young man very much like you. He had everything he could ever want. A house, an income, and a wife, but it wasn't enough. You see, the man had an affair on with his beautiful wife. When she discovered her husband's secret, she mistakenly confronted him alone. Gruesomely, he killed her and buried her body not far from their home. One morning, he woke and found her grave disturbed, and her body mangled.

So, the husband dug a deeper hole in the earth. Praying that whatever beast came before wouldn't smell the new tomb.

Again, the next morning, her grave was unearthed. Being devoured even more than the day before.

A third time, the husband dug another grave and waited patiently in the night for the wretched beast to arrive.

The beast came back once more, only this time to consume the pitiful man."

I raise my brows at Rasmussen with a perplexed expression on my face, wondering what exactly he is referring to.

"Oh, my dear boy, you are too similar to Niklas. I can see by your blank expression that your brain isn't adept enough to understand this story." Continuing, Rasmussen rambles. "Here's the thing about secrets. No matter how deep you try to bury them, there's always someone else who will come along and dig them up."

"Are you trying to say I have secrets?" I asked, shifting my weight antsy.

"Yes, but it's your family's big secret I'm referring to." Rasmussen hisses in reply.

"My family? My family has nothing to hide. We are peasants, farmers."

Rasmussen smirks, showing his yellow teeth. "Yes, it seems so. Maybe there's more to your family. Ask your mommy, didn't you say everyone has secrets?"

I responded unhinged. "Mr. Minfree, I'm not your pawn. If what your story says is true, you'd better be careful of what you're hiding inside your stubby, shrouded head."

"If someone learns your secrets, it's best to kill them. It's even better to eliminate them while they try to dig." Rass-hole hisses once more.

"Speaking from experience now?" I ask accusingly.

Interrupting us, a politician I recognize far too well. Parley. "My liege, we must be going if we wish to witness the duel." Parley locks eyes awkwardly with me.

That explains everything; all the Loyalists are pawns to a higher power. Is it the cold-hearted serpent Rasmussen?

Sofia saved me a spot next to Trisha. She appears larger and more muscular since joining the Loyalist guild. Nate and Harry were already up in the twenty-by-twenty-foot ring. Nate's left hand is bandaged tightly. This fight will require him to favor his right hand entirely. Both duelers wear only a breastplate, each with their guild's symbol. A sizable crowd gathers for the duel.

"The only person I see from Jasper's family is Zander," Sofia voices softly.

"They all probably didn't want to watch Harry die. I don't blame them." I say just as softly, so Trisha doesn't hear.

"Look, Judge Rupert is ready to speak!" I holler with glee.

"All hail!" Sofia quips.

In the name of Tyren,
The Province of Murcia
hereby declares that this is a duel of taxation,
Nathaniel Hastings of Lyon,
representing the Loyalists,
in favor of tax cuts by two percent.
Vs.
Harry Jasper of Lyon,
representing the Federalist,
opposing tax cuts.

Harry and Nate stand back-to-back. Rupert instructs each of them to walk ten feet and not to turn around.

Rupert proclaims, "On my whistle, each of you will face and fight!"

Silence and anticipation fill the air. Harry firmly gripped a throwing knife in his hand, while Nate had a throwing knife sheathed on his breastplate and his hand clutching his sword.

What is he doing, I think to myself. It is a bold move by Nate not to have his throwing knife out. Harry could kill him! My legs are restless, and I wish I could do something to intervene. I clutch Sofia and Trisha's hands tightly in mine.

"Relax, Amis, breathe," Trisha says in optimism.

I glanced at her, and she stood calm, confident, and upright. She cut her long, blonde hair, and I noticed a scab running across her chin. She must've passed the initiation for the Loyalists.

Rupert's squeal of the whistle blares, lasting longer than it should.

Nate and Harry both turn quickly to face one another. Nate pulls out his sword, holding it high, ready to strike.

"They're twenty feet apart!" Sofia says with her eyebrows rising.

Harry probably thought he'd already be greeted with a knife to his head. He took his throwing knife and, with his right hand, brought it back behind his head. Moving his left foot forward, his feet now stagger. In one fluid motion of precision, Harry swings his arm forward, releasing the knife. It rotates swiftly towards Nate.

Is this how Nate dies? In the same place as Niklas.

As the knife spins, rotating end over end at Nate's head, he reacts in the nick of time. Swinging his sword with full force across his face and body. Metal on metal collides, causing a splintering, ringing noise. Shards of Harry's knife fly across the ring. My eyes follow a giant shard rising high in the air.

Something, no, someone catches my attention from the balcony above.

Mariam?

My heart erupts in confusion along with a dull ache. She's here?! But not here with me. She stands with the Loyalist Rasmussen and Parley.

Harry runs at full speed, closing the twenty-foot gap. Nate drops his sword, pulling out his throwing knife. Quickly, he whips it in the direction of Harry. Harry stumbles, falling to the ground like a boar shot with an arrow and thumping and skidding across the dirt. Within the dust cloud, I saw Harry reaching for his leg. The knife was sticking out of his thigh, and blood began to seep through the cut.

Zander, in complete anguish, cries, "Get up, Harry! Fight!"

Nate approaches at a steady pace with his sword at the ready.

Harry rises to his feet, wobbly as he rips the knife out of his thigh. He doesn't scream; the pain has to be excruciating. Again, Harry raises the throwing knife in position. Nate unexpectedly covers the ground between them.

Once again, Harry hurls the knife that drips with his blood towards Nate. This time, Nate was only ten feet away. With his speed of light reflexes, Nate held out his left hand to cover his face. The throwing knife penetrates Nate's left hand, stopping it inches from his face. The blade protruded into his hand in a nasty fashion.

Nate, with an intense fury of emotion, took a few more long strides, wielding his sword in his right hand. In a forceful motion, he rams his blade through Harry's neck.

The crowd erupts in cheer as Nathan is crowned champion once again. He's building quite a reputation.

Looking at Harry's body, a crushing pain resonates in my stomach. How many times have Nate and I had imaginary duels? How many times has he stopped at my chest with a dull practice sword?

Killing another cannot be suitable for the soul. We don't require death in our duels in Lyon, not like in the capital, Harpstedt. Where is the mercy!

Zander rushes the ring. Hugging his dead brother, while he sobs in a familiar remorseful way. I know this pain; I still feel it.

Trisha rushes to the ring, hugging and examining Nate's new wound. The throwing knife was still dangling in his hand; the blood soaking his bandage meant for his previous injury.

I turned to Sofia. I can see she wants to help Zander. "Go to Nate, Sofi. It would be telling if you don't." She nods, rushing to Nate.

I walked to Zander. "I didn't see your parents here. I have a horse you can borrow if you need help with Harry's body."

Mykel intrudes, saying, "I'll assist you, Zander."

Mykel's grey head turns to me. "Amis, go be with Nate. I appreciate your concern." I seal my lips and nod, striding away.

In earshot of Nate, I hear Trisha gawking over his skills. "What made you swing your sword at the knife?"

Nate's response was not surprising. "It was instinct, I know my strengths and throwing knives are not them."

Sofia laughs, "Clearly! You hit Harry on the thigh!"

Nate shook his head with pride, "I know, I was aiming for his head!"

I snort, "I guess that's one thing I can best you in!"

Reaching into my wool jacket, I pull out the herbs from Mrs. Frays. "Here, you'll need something to numb your hand; you might as well just cut the whole thing off, considering that's the only thing you seem to hurt."

"Nate, we need to get that knife out. While you still have some adrenaline in your blood!" Trisha orders.

I see a host of Loyalists on their way to congratulate their champion. Mariam is among them. I want nothing to do with her at this moment. She had every chance to find me before this.

Turning to Nate and Trisha, I say with a jolt of uneasiness, "I'm needed at home. Nate, you are amazing! I'll see you soon. "

I slick my brown hair over, check my attire to make sure I'm somewhat presentable, and strut past Mariam on my way home.

114 | Page

Chapter Nine:

Mykel

Soft rain from the clouds over the harbor bombards my face. Waves from the gulf swash, as the ebb and flow of water washes up and down the bank. The sound of waves crashing brings me a sense of peace. A voice, not a whisper or a wail, reaches my ears. Wiping my eyes, I look out over the harbor at a pier. At the end of the wooden pier, a girl bids me to come. I walk slowly and gracefully, doing my best not to startle her into another run. Her beautiful hair shifts in the wind, and the striking features of her face make my soul ache. She acknowledges my presence.

I shout, "Who are you?"

She smiles widely, her voice echoing back, "Everyone dies. Set men free."

In a quick and precise motion, she hurdles over the railing, into the rolling wake. I peer over the edge to see where she's gone; there is no sign of her within the deep blue.

That's the last thing Niklas ever said. "Set men free."

A loud voice echoes through the house. It was Rupert screeching at my Dad, "This isn't fair! Why would they do this? He should remain here!"

My Dad's soft response diffuses the conflict, "This isn't about us or him. This is what the Loyalists want for Athren. I have contacts there to watch over him."

Rupert, again in pain, says, "This is why I became a judge; I don't want any part of their political games."

I walk out of my room into the living space. I see my mom sitting upright and looking relatively put together.

"What's going on?" I mutter.

"After yesterday's duel, I overheard the Loyalist Rasmussen Minfree remark that Nate was being sent to fight in Harpstedt for the Loyalists' and Athren's national interests." Rupert slumps in a chair in disappointment.

"Is he really that strong a duelist? He almost died in both his fights." I add incredulously.

"Dad, I did what you said, and I told him to fight softly so he wouldn't stand out so much. It seems like he did. He got hurt in both of his duels." Rupert scoffs.

Dad puts his eyes down and mutters, "It will be okay, Niklas survived in Harpstedt, so will Nate."

In an uncontrolled display of emotion, I blurt out. "We can't trust the guilds! They tried to poison Niklas when he was there!"

Rupert's jaw drops in shock, and his Dad shakes his head in disapproval. Dad knew they were trying to assassinate Niklas. What else does he know?!

Mom chimes in. "We all need to breathe. If it's one thing I know about the Hastings, all of us know how to fight."

"She's right, and don't go saying things like that, Amis. If the wrong person hears, our whole family could end up on the chopping block." Dad admonishes me.

Observing his scarred, bearded face, I know he meant it. "Yes, sir, I misspoke."

The sun pierces through the scattered clouds, warming the day. I walk east, away from our home, towards the apple tree, and uncover the stone block where my new-found treasure is hidden.

I rest against the tree, gazing at Niklas' mound of dirt for a brief moment, and read.

Upon completion of the initiation,

I started the groundwork of my champion mindset. What I've learned from my father as a boy: The foundation you build on will significantly impact your future. I trained my body and mind harder than I ever had before. I exercised my body to achieve an untouchable level of stamina. I repeatedly loosed arrows until I shot the bow with perfect precision, and I fought until I knew how to counter every single blow. All brain fog was eliminated, pain in my body subsided, and my confidence conquered all.

Eagle Valley was a minor war town in the Langley Province, which gave me the chance to exercise mercy and not kill. My first duel was against a Loyalist man named Mykel. He was a brute, known for the ability to subdue anyone with his mere fists. Being in the ring with him, I knew the only way I was going to win was through energy exertion. The dueling ring was inside a great hall of a war fortress built for the King's.

We were able to bring the weapon of our choosing forward, with no armor allowed. Mykel chose a hammer; if he lands one correct swing, he could shatter every bone in my body. I couldn't hesitate; I decided on two lightweight daggers.

The match commenced as expected. Mykel swung his hammer mightily to and fro, but with little success. Every swing he took failed, but he knew one partial hit could end me and make him champion.

With my two daggers, I focused on ducking and dodging. After a few minutes of success, Mykel started to slow. Each heave of the hammer caused him to grunt loudly and breathe heavily.

I saw my opportunity to strike when he brought the hammer from behind his back, whipping it forward and plunging it into the ground at my feet. I jumped and shot my right foot down, landing with such force on the end of the hammer that the blow caused it to become dislodged from his grasp.

With my feet grounded, I sliced deep into the tissue of Mykel's dominant left arm, making it immobile. Quick on my feet, I side-stepped out of reach of his right hand, resetting the base of my posture with my gaze directly upon him.

If I could eliminate his right arm, the duel would be over. Charging him, I jutted my left arm out to push away his right. His strength was apparent, as I failed to anticipate Mykel grabbing hold of my neck. My wielded right arm plunged my dagger forward, penetrating his right shoulder, severing all its functionality. The blade must have damaged enough of the nerves and tendons in the joint, as evidenced by Mykel's swift surrender. I spared his life and displayed mercy.

Dueling is a barbaric way to introduce laws into society. It must be condemned, eliminated, and forsaken. We all look at the world through our own eyes. Our perception of reality is based on our unique surroundings. We could argue for change all we want, but nothing will change. If we look at society through another's eyes and change our perspective, we might learn something. Even better, if we can physically stand in someone else's shoes, we will change our environment enough to think like them.

That is why I became a duelist: to see through their eyes. To find vulnerabilities within the current establishment.

I now know what I need to do. Become a dueler for the Federalist.

Suddenly, Dad roars like a lion across the field, alerting me. "Nate is here!"

With expedient haste, I grab my cloth sack, wrap the book carefully, and put it back into its stone home. Nate, Trisha, and Mariam are with my whole family, walking towards me. I'm in my sanctuary under the apple tree. Oh shit! Sofia is the only one who knows what I have hidden here. Act natural…

Nate's clothes are nicer than when he lived here. I can tell the money he's winning makes him feel like it's worth it. His lovely, fancy felt hat and his high-collared, fur-lined over-gown make him look like royalty.

Now within earshot, Nate shouts out, "Amis, since when do you spend time here on a Friday morning?"

Laughing nervously, "Since one brother died and another up and left me, now I have no friends!"

Sofia and Rupert, in unison, exclaim, "What do you call us!"

Dad sits on the rock concealing my treasure, and I almost gasp in fear that it's going to cave in.

"Nate, I'm sick of asking… But since you keep injuring it, how's the hand?" I ask.

Nate's smile is enormous and toxic as he says, "The doctor thinks I'll get all function back in it. He doesn't want me to duel for a few weeks. I guess the journey to the capital is a good thing, since it'll take three days."

"When do you guys leave?" I curiously asked, trying my best to avoid eye contact with Mariam.

Mariam pipes up, "In an hour."

My face forms an impressive frown, one that was obvious enough for everyone to see.

Rupert then suggests, "Maybe we ought to let these two have a moment alone."

Please no, I think…. I feel guilty having dreams of another girl, and I'm upset she didn't seek me out when she arrived in Lyon.

Sofia, being her wretched self, proclaims, "Awkward…." causing me to shake my head in discomfort.

"Now that we are alone, how are things?" I ask.

That's usually something I would say to a stranger, being polite. Mariam is no stranger. We are supposed to be in love. Since school, all we thought about was running away together and eloping. Why'd she leave me?

She responds cautiously, "Things have been different for me. Harpstedt is nice, but you aren't there."

"I feel the same way. There's definitely no YOU here." I grin. "So why are you here?"

"The law Nate just fought for. I was the one who presented it! People in Lyon were suffering because of the taxes. I also had to relay vital information that a pigeon couldn't carry to the Loyalist leader Rasmussen."

"Oh? Rass-hole… 'ahem' Rasmussen is the Loyalist leader for Lyon?" I stammer, correcting myself.

"No, Rasmussen Minfree is the leader of the Loyalist Party for all of Athren."

Shock is evident on my face as my mouth is stuck gaping open. Another awkward silence slices through the air.

Changing the subject, I quickly spouted off a random question. "Was this your first law you presented?"

I tuned her response out, pondering... Stupid Rass-hole.

What a corrupt system. There are two sides to every situation, and Mariam's law got Harry killed. Was it utterly worth it?

Again, she speaks, and it brings discomfort to my ears. "I heard about Niklas. I'm so sorry, Amis. I should've come. When Rasmussen informed me, my heart broke for you. I know what he meant to you."

Anger burns in my ears, "Thanks." I say dismissively.

"Honestly, Amis, I'm sorry. Niklas was our best champion. He was the best dueler I had ever seen."

"You saw him fight?" I pressed in shock.

"Yes, in the capital, a week before his execution."

She reaches out her hand. I take it, intertwining my fingers with hers. Her skin is soft, a quality I have missed. I've forgotten her touch; I desire her. I want her lips on mine; I want to feel the warmth of her skin.

I kiss her on her forehead and give her a long hug. Her embrace makes me feel whole. Mariam places her head perfectly below my chin. I missed the way her hair smells. I don't dare let her go.

"Was he sick during his capital duel? Niklas said he had food poisoning before that fight." I say casually.

"No, he didn't seem sick to me."

"Oh, that's good to hear. I was worried someone had poisoned Niklas. How is that Rasmussen fellow, anyway? He came to Lyon around the same time as Niklas, right?"

She inhales deeply, preparing to respond. "Ya, he's a great guy, we used to work together a lot in

Harpstedt. I collaborated with him for a while, and we would bounce all sorts of questions off each other. He knows more than anyone I've ever met. He did ask often about the people in Lyon."

I pushed her away and stared longingly into her eyes. "What questions did Rasmussen ask about my family?"

She steps backwards. "A lot, I can't remember any specifics."

"Mariam, did he ask any sensitive things about us, Hastings. Like Dad's farm, or Niklas' allergies?!"

"I, I don't remember." She stammered.

"Mariam, I know you call yourself a Loyalist and all. Athren first…" I mock. "Please listen to me, they want control. Don't listen to everything they say, don't be gullible!" I rambled, coming off a little too strong.

"Amis, I've got to go. I think it's best for you and me-" She begins to say.

"To take a break, I know." I finished for her rudely. "Mariam, I'm joining the Federalist guild."

Her face is laced with utter disappointment. "Be safe."

I follow far behind her; we should never talk again; I consider to myself. I'm not going to tell Nate I'm joining the Federalist. I can't, Mariam will have a three-day ride to the capital to tell him everything.

I need to talk to my parents.

Chapter Ten:

Epiphany

Mariam is already on her horse, galloping off my family's property.

Rupert pulls me in for a hug as he rubs his fist through my hair like I was a child. "Why'd you break that girl's heart?"

He smiles a little too happily. "I never did like Mariam, you know?"

I shook my head, pretending to find it amusing. "Well, what girls have you liked?"

Nate approaches, "Thanks, Amis, for making my trip to the capital ultimate hell!"

I gave him a big hug. This beat of time could be the last one we share as actual brothers. "Don't die out there, don't hold back, and please don't let them control you."

His eyes radiate, and he grasps my left shoulder with his good right hand. "God may be my creator, but the devil will be my caretaker when I'm dead. I'm not ready to meet that sadistic bastard. I won't die, join the Loyalists, and meet me in the capital, Amis."

"God loves you, brother!" I say providing unwarranted affirmation.

He says goodbye to all my family; my Mom was holding back her emotions. She has regained her strength.

"Nate and Trisha must be saying their goodbyes in private." Rupert sneers as he trots away.

"Must be," I chuckle. "To be honest, it's refreshing to see Nate without his master around."

"For real, that bat is crazy controlling!" Rupert's freckled cheeks and red beard beam brightly.

The day carries on; chores are all the same. I keep myself busy, not wallowing in despair. Mom makes a wholesome supper: potato soup and chicken. Our conversations around the dinner table are modest and small. Two brothers are now gone, and the family dynamic has undergone a dramatic change.

After dinner, I sat quietly on the porch. Nature has a way of comforting my body and easing my mind. I revisited the list I made after Niklas's last letter.

- *Mr. Brookshard saw Niklas and Heather leave.* **Niklas and Brookshard had a deal: Niklas throws the duel against Harry; he gets the girl.**

- *Mrs. Fray saw Niklas and Heather pass her shop.* **Parley lied; they went into her shop.**

- *Many reported hearing an argument or a fight before they entered the forest.* **Niklas punched Harry.**

- *Parley said Mr. Stone found Heather dead, followed by Rasmussen.* **Mr. Stone said he arrived at Heather's body last.**
- *Niklas' last words: "Good or evil, everyone dies. I'm innocent. Amis, set men free!"* **The exact words that Burnette echoed in my dreams. What the hell does it mean? Set men free?**
- *They were able to communicate between Harpstedt and Lyon.* **Rasmussen Minfree arrived from the capital within days of Niklas.**
- *Niklas was poisoned in Harpstedt.* **Mariam accidentally divulged Niklas's allergies to Rassmussen?**

That last one feels accusatory, but is it true? Mariam was so defensive when I asked. Or was I just rude?

Thoughts race through my mind. Until. My heart twists and wrenches in utter turmoil. The answer was in front of me the entire time.

Niklas's last words right before he died.

"Good or evil, everyone dies. I'm innocent. Amis, set men free!"

The last conversation with Rasmussen replays in my mind:

Secrets.

Rasmussen **Minfree** = Set **men free**

I wail in frustration, loud enough for everyone to hear.

I'm an idiot! The Loyalist scumbag sat in my house the day after he killed my brother. He weaseled his way behind Heather and axed her right in the back. Why didn't Niklas kill him where he stood? Why!

My Mom bursts outside, breathing heavily, exclaiming, "What's wrong, Amis?!"

All I could do was stand up and put my head on her shoulder. Water floods my eyes as tears rush down my face.

"Mom. I need to talk to you and Dad."

Mom's soft, concerned voice says, "Okay, let's talk." And then she screams, "Henry, get your ass out here!"

His steps pound the floorboards as he runs out of the house. "What's wrong?"

"Let's walk." I point to the east field, where Niklas and the book are buried. The sun is setting softly over the trees.

Mom asks rather curiously, "You didn't get Mariam pregnant, did you?"

"No, Mom." I roll my hazel eyes. "The truth is, I found out who framed your son."

"Was it that bitch Mariam!?" Mom roars.

I batter my long lashes in confusion. "Rasmussen **Minfree** killed Heather and framed Niklas."

Silence falls upon my parents. I feel the cool breeze and hear the whooshing through the trees. I explain everything I have uncovered, unsure exactly of Rasmussen's true objective.

Dad replies monotone, "I would decimate that waste of life if I could, but we must do what's right. We cannot risk any more Hastings dying in his name."

Mom says rapidly, "You don't think Rasmussen is-"

Dad puts his hand over Mom's mouth and hushes her. Confusion grips me, and my fingers clench.

"No more secrets! Niklas is dead, and Nate will likely die if we don't help!" Frustration steams through my ears, making them ring.

"Amis, enough. Not now, but soon!" Dad admonishes.

"I'm joining the Federalists guild!" I say like a child.

"Good choice," Mom says softly. Catching me completely off guard.

We fall into silence, looking at the dark silhouette of the apple tree and Niklas' grave. What a terrible, yet beautiful sight, seeing the leaves bloom so transcendentally over my brother's tomb.

"There's one thing I don't understand. Why didn't Niklas stand up and fight? Why did he cower away?" I ask seeking understanding.

"Niklas could've been protecting us. The Loyalists would've executed all our family if he'd reacted." Dad responds, clearly pondering.

"Secrets. Rasmussen said WE have a family secret?" I say skeptically to Mom, trying to get her to reveal her sentence from before.

Dad's face looks concerned. "He's bluffing. He thinks something about us but isn't certain of it just yet."

I nodded, not daring to pry.

Dad says rather proudly, changing the subject, "Joining the Federalist is different, but the better option."

Mom gives a heartfelt stare. "Amis, I cannot lose another son! Be merciful, and don't die."

The next few days passed in a blur. I told Sofia everything. From Rasmussen, to updating what I've learned in the book, and the juicy gossip about Mariam, she was shell-shocked but expressed her happiness with my messy love life.

"Mariam should have known Rass-Hole was acting fishy. There's no way you could fight for the

Loyalist, not after what Rass-hole did to Niklas. I want to put a dull axe in his head right now!" Sofia speaks loudly as she braids her brown hair tightly.

"I want Rass-Hole to die a slow death," I say with a low grumble.

"Agreed, let's slow cook him in a cauldron. I worry about Nate; he has no clue about the truth. It's not like we can send a letter stating Rass-Hole is a sneaky backstabbing hoe bag!" Sofia says rambunctiously.

All I could do was laugh. "If we could get our hands on a pigeon, we could?" I pose the question as I brush an itchy beard hair away from my nose.

"Nah, Nate isn't worth the trouble." Sofia shrugs, flipping her now perfect braid to her back.

I grit my teeth in shock. I'm going to miss my little sister.

The guilds only take recruits at the beginning of every week, and that's tomorrow. I need to become a champion; I need to follow Gentry and destroy the guilds from within. Dueling has to end; Sofia can never have the chance to consider joining.

"Amis, when you see Zander. Could you tell him I said hi?" Sofia asks with a nervous smile.

"Do you like him? He's an adult and four years older than you."

"Age is just a number, Amis!" She counters and kicks a rock along the dirt.

"Is it? The bigger the gap, the grosser it gets." I say, holding my hands far apart.

"Amis!!! Ugh, you are so nauseating!" She says while giving me a giant shove.

"By the way, tell Mom and Dad I'm going fishing on my last night of freedom."

"I'll tell them! You know, Dad is going to join you," Sofia says factually.

I kick another rock along the dirt, farther than hers, and walk away with my eyebrows raised.

North, just past the reservoir and below the dam, I found a secluded fishing spot along the cold Ash River. The river has a continuous pulse, with a life of its own. Parts are whitecapped and churning at tremendous speeds; other parts move gracefully around bends and over rocks. I looked for smooth reflective areas where there is a mellow current within the flow.

I attached my handmade fly lure to the end of my heavy silk line. My fly is a perfect combination of feathers and fur threaded together. It doesn't take a lot to imitate a bug.

With each fluid cast I made, I did my best to mimic insects, pulling and whipping my line back and forth along the water's surface. A rainbow trout finally took the bait, coming to the top of the water with a swift bite. Excitement and thrill rush through me, like a bolt of lightning. I hand-reeled the fishing line around my wooden block. The fight of a trout wasn't much, but it's enough for you to be cautious with how aggressively you reel it in.

The beautiful fish finally breached the water and landed on the shore. I tied a rope through its gills and allowed it to swim in the water. That's going to make for a delicious meal; trout isn't known for its taste… You have to learn how to cook it properly.

A rustle through the trees draws my full attention. Two dark figures emerged from the shrubbery; it was Dad and Rupert, each with rods of their own. I wave and continue finessing my rod.

Rupert asks, "How's the fishing? Have you caught anything?" He preps his rod and lure, getting ready to cast out himself.

"Ya, I got one just before you guys showed up."

"Nice man! So, are you ready to join the Federalists tomorrow?" Rupert says in excitement.

"Ya, I think so. I'm not sure what to expect." I say lying, I know there's an initiation of some sort in the near future.

"Well, so that you know, we aren't supposed to talk about this. You will face a trial of some sort. I wish I knew what the Federalists do. Niklas was left stranded on a Mountain overnight, Mykel pushed Nate out of a boat in the middle of Ash reservoir, and Trisha was placed in a cage with a honey badger." Rupert spouts off nonchalantly.

"A honey badger? Those things are aggressive as hell. That explains the scar on her chin. Why are you telling me this? Can't you get in trouble?"

"Ya, technically, I could be executed for intervening in guild practices. Blood before guild, though, right?" Rupert smirks.

I saw my dad crack a slight smile. Perhaps I can trust Rupert; Niklas was wrong about him.

"Well, I don't want to kill unless I'm forced to. Dueling has become too much of a sport, not politics." I say with a factual tone.

Rupert's response again surprises me, "I'll do my best to support you in your endeavor. Killing isn't necessary and shouldn't be the goal. Just know, if you become a champion and get shipped off to Harpstedt, there will be killing, and I won't be there to help you."

"Fish on!!" Dad proclaims. Time seems to stop as we watch him reel in. His trout is enormous, almost twice the size of mine. He carefully took the fish off his hook and released it.

"What the heck? That fish could have fed the whole family!" Rupert's face is riddled with confusion.

"When you get so big you champion all others, I think you deserve a life of peace. Don't you?" Dad says in a puzzling way.

"I suppose," Rupert replies in disbelief. "Amis, what are you going to do if you have to fight Trisha?"

"Try not to kill her! Nate would castrate me if I did." I imagined myself facing off against her in a duel.

We fished for the rest of the day, catching plenty to the point that we started letting them all go.

When we got home, I noticed that there was roughly an hour of daylight left. I dropped my pole and quickly gutted the fish, then hurried to the east field, where Niklas' apple tree stands.

I pulled out my book in a hurry, knowing I was on a tight deadline.

The last time I read, he fought in his first duel against Mykel and saved his life. He also discussed dueling as a means to change his perspective. I opened the crisp pages and read faster than I ever had before:

After I sparred with Mykel, he changed his life. He left the Loyalists guild when his contract expired and chose not to re-up. He built a life as a trainer teaching both Loyalist and Federalist guilds better dueling practices. Mykel's friendship and change of heart were a testament to me that I could have an influence, even if it's one dueler at a time.

I eventually moved from Eagle Valley to other towns throughout Athren. I ended up in Blanding and dueled there for a few months. Each fight was more of the same: dominance and then mercy. I traveled to the palm trees of Lansing and to the desert of Federale. Everywhere I showed my strength, power, and mercy.

I'm still unsure of every law enacted in my name, but I was truly the champion of Athren. That is, until the Federalists sent me to the capital, Harpstedt, the city of King Harper VI.

When I arrived at the tall gates of the white walled city, I was intimidated by its magnificent architecture. Within, there were luxurious homes with beautiful gardens. Castles rose tall from every corner of the capital. White stone structures with intricate carvings and large, spacious market buildings were scattered within the glorious city. It was so impressive that the engineers had thought of everything, including secret tunnels to maneuver troops rapidly.

Tall towers all around protruded up into the sky. In the center lay a grand arena like no other, positioned low into the earth. Seats for spectators circled the perimeter, completely encasing the ring within a breathtaking castle, the king's castle set at the far edge of the ring. You could watch the duel from every possible angle. The arena wracked my stomach with fear. There is no simple elimination of dueling, unless the king is eliminated.

I have to stop here, I thought to myself sadly. Placing the book back within its stone home.

When I got back home, Mom had the wood stove burning and was wearing her apron, ready to cook. We saved the fish guts to cook and feed the chickens.

Mom hates fish with a passion. She is kind enough to cook it for us, though; she's practically the only person who knows how to do it right. I know my Mom didn't grow up around fish. I honestly don't know much about either of my parents' upbringings; they tend not to reflect much on the past.

Another day came without permission, and I was up before the sun had a chance to rise. I suffered from a severe lack of sleep; that was expected, considering what I'm about to put my body and mind through. I know I'll be required to sign a contract for at least two years. To some, that may seem like a long time; to me, it'll pass like the blink of an eye.

I packed my bag with only a few essential items. I don't have a lot. I strapped my hatchets to my waist, and throwing knives are sheathed in my trousers.

I gave longer hugs than usual as I said goodbye to my family. I know I'll see them more than Nate did. I have to come home; Niklas' book is here.

I set out on the routine walk I've made a million times before to Lyon. This journey never gets old. I reached the main road, taking a deep breath. The air feels sharper this morning as it stabs my lungs with each inhale.

You are smart, you are strong, and you are capable. I told myself over and over before reaching the big wooden doors of the Federalist guild.

Chapter Eleven:

Initiation

When the massive doors of the guild finally gave way and began to open, I found myself in a dark circular foyer similar to the Loyalist guilds. On the ground was a red three-headed serpent rug with only natural light from the windows illuminating it.

In the center of the room stood a pedestal. A piece of parchment paper, ink, and a quill lay on top of it. I cautiously walked forward, as if someone were going to jump out and scare me. Sofia isn't here; I told myself. Uneasiness and a sticky nervousness raced through me, as my heartbeat pumped in rapid succession, so much so that sweat dripped down my legs, making my leather pants stick to my legs.

Reaching the center of the foyer at the pedestal, I saw a disclaimer:

By signing below, you agree to join the Federalist Guild. The expectations are as follows:

Whatever is ordered, you must submit to and obey. For the good of Athren and the power of its people, you may face certain death. Insubordination of any kind is punishable by execution. You will represent the Federalist of Athren in all its glory for a minimum of two years. The Federalists will provide food, housing, and livelihood during this time. Each duel or task completed will be compensated fruitfully.

Sign below if you accept these terms:

I saw no other signatures. I must be the only one here. Looking around side to side, there was no sign, no sound. Looking up at the single dark hallway, I notice it's empty and bare. The dreary walls of the guild felt like they were closing in on me. Suffocation is imminent.

Am I in the right place? Should I do this? I could leave as if I hadn't been here. What would Dad and Niklas do? They would sign and risk certain death. Niklas and Nate did precisely that. Then I thought of the book. Gentry, the champion, signed his own life away. So, will I. The quill was luxurious and ritzy. I signed Amis J. Hastings in ink, on the massive blank spot below.

Quickly, I sat it down in a chair against the circular wall. My legs quivered, waiting for something significant to happen, like the floor below would open and gobble me whole. Everything remained the same, quiet and dark.

Time passed, and I was left to my own destructive thoughts. An idle mind only leads to depression; so, I've always been told. An hour passed, and I was left shifting my weight back and forth within my seat in complete anxiety.

Footsteps approached from the hallway, and the hair on my neck stood straight up at the disturbance. My nerves were reaching their pinnacle. My head shifted as I peered around the pedestal in the center of the room. I saw three individuals. A woman and two older men approach. The woman quickly grabbed the parchment paper and read my name. The older men look at me in utter disbelief.

"Mr. Hastings, are you lost?" One of them asks.

"Isn't your family Loyalist through and through?" The other person says.

I respond as respectfully and clearly as possible, "One of my brothers is loyal to them. I'm not so sure about the rest of my family, sir. I trust the Federalist."

The woman looked sweet and kind while she softly said, "Young man, that must have taken a lot of courage. We are glad to have you in our guild. My name is Janice, and these older gents are Tarron and Isaac." She then opens her arms to hug me.

Oh, she's a hugger, and I don't know her. Well, I just signed my life away to these people, and I took a few steps into her embrace.

"Not so fast." Tarron growls. "He needs to prove his loyalty to our guild first."

"Yes, that's right. Son, sit over here a little while longer." Isaac's weathered voice says ruggedly.

Here comes my initiation. Will it be a pit of vipers, being stranded on a mountain, left to tread water in Ash Reservoir, or thrown in a cage with a honey badger?

Half an hour passes, Mykel and two other ragged men in tattered clothes enter through the large guild doors.

"Amis, leave your sack and come with us. That's an order." Mykel commands.

I can do nothing but obey, especially if this is the same Mykel from the book.

We hop in a wagon and leave Lyon. The weather is sunny and optimistic. Rays glisten on the pine trees and sneak through the branches, illuminating the ground. We head west toward the Oquirrh Mountains, climbing the slopes to higher elevations. The temperature grows colder as a swift breeze passes through the trees. Leaves and branches brush against each other, creating a beautiful melody.

As we traveled to my trial, I couldn't help but imagine what they would put me through.

Turning to Mykel, I ask abruptly, "Are you by chance from Eagle Valley?"

He gives me a death stare, saying, "Amis, we will now blind fold you. Utilize your other God given senses."

Mykel places a thick cloth tightly against my face and ties it to a painful extent.

I hear a whisper in my ear, "Yes, I'm from Eagle Valley, now pay attention."

Thoughts began to race. What are we doing up here? Will I experience the same thing as Niklas, but it's too warm now that it's spring?

The wagon stops suddenly; hands direct me down to the solid ground. That's rock under my feet, not soft dirt. With a man on both sides of me holding my arms, I'm steered fifty feet or so away from the wagon. I hear the sound of a stream with trickling water.

A stern voice orders, "Lower your head." I obey.

Each man changes position, now one in front and one behind. The air feels incredibly cold and stale. A soft breeze splinters my skin as it blows ragefully from behind. The air smells musty, like mildew or damp earth.

The man in front of me shrieks, "Blimey! My fat noggin!" His cry echoes off the walls right as I step into a puddle of stale water.

The other from behind blares, "Shut up!"

We trek longer, but I don't know the exact length. I lost count of my steps the moment we walked single file. There are ups and downs, twists and turns, highs and lows.

I took a deep breath, noticing that it was harder to breathe. There must be less oxygen here. I know where we are.

We stop, Mykel says with a heavy voice, "This is the place."

He places his arm around my neck and explains in another whisper, "This won't hurt a bit. Just relax, search the ground when you wake."

I take one more breath, and he squeezes his bicep and forearm muscles into my neck. Fading, I see black in my brain, darkness deepens more than the blindfold that is knotted around my eyes. After a few heartbeats, I was no more.

Regaining consciousness, I found myself lying on my back. Pain rushed up my throat; he must've cut the blood supply to my brain longer than necessary.

I clawed for the bandana around my eyes and gasped for air. Where is the air? The bandana finally let loose, and I could see.

Nope, I couldn't see. I laughed to myself, "I'm stuck in a tomb!" Not just any tomb, but the Devil's Cave. If it's the one I know, it kills those who venture too deep. Maybe the toxic gas levels are too high here, or perhaps a beast lurks in the dark abyss.

I sit on my ass completely still. Mykel said to search the ground. My butt stays where it landed, so I don't lose my place in the darkness. My hands brush along the dirt near my sides, in search of an alien object not native to these dark cave floors. There was nothing but rocks and soil; is Mykel playing a dirty joke on me?

While sitting on my butt, I stretch my legs to their full length. Swiveling around, dragging my feet as I go, I finally kicked something odd. It was longer than your typical rock. I reached out my hand and found what felt like a stick with a cloth wrapped around one of the ends.

The cloth was damp, soaked in a liquid that was hopefully animal fat. I reach for my side and, surprisingly, find one of my hatchets. Thank the Lord, I'm not defenseless.

Examining the torch with my hands, acting as my eyes, I uncovered something that did not belong. At the very end, a small string dangled from the end of the torch, leading to a hard, skinny rock. Mykel left me flint! I joyfully exclaim in my head. Very carefully, I undid the knot on the string so that I wouldn't drop the flint onto the ground. Surely it would be lost forever in the dark abyss of the cave.

I placed the torch between my knees, holding it steady, and struck my hatchet carefully against the flint. Sparks flew with each strike. It was nice to see some colors other than thick darkness. Strike after strike, I began to sink into despair. I'm not going to get out of here. Again, I struck, praying for a flame to ignite.

A tiny flickering flame began to grow. I tried my best to hold my excitement, letting the chemical reaction in the torch take its course. Fire bloomed and light danced across the jagged cave ceiling. My eyes were functional again!

I studied the cave chamber before me, noticing there were four hallways I could take. I'm glad I'm not claustrophobic, unlike my Dad.

Immediately, I acquired two considerable-sized rocks, stacking them on top of each other. Marking this space as a place I've been. The chamber is slanted, with two hallways leading down deeper and two leading up. I think long and hard about the steps I made before entering this chamber. We were traveling downward; common sense would say that up is the way.

The rocks were loose, making it a steady incline; I had to remain mindful of every step I took as I encountered another troubling decision. Which tunnel do I take? Right or left. As I tried to search my memories, I recalled the maneuvers I was required to make at this junction, blindfolded. My memories blended, making this an impossible decision. Screw it, choose the right.

I moved slowly into a new chamber. Again, I marked this one, but this time I stacked three stones into a small tower. This chamber has two possible paths. I saw water along the far side, and it appeared to be stagnant; my foot is still damp.

Nothing like another decision that could easily end my life. I chose to go left, following the water puddles. Soft water fell from the icicle-shaped stalactites on the ceiling into the puddles below. The constant dripping noise made an eerie feeling. I continued up the passage, which was narrowing steadily, ducking and squeezing into another chamber. Again, I grabbed rocks this time, stacking them four high.

While I observed the chamber, I saw something dark lying in the corner. Is that a black bear? Slowly, I walked backwards, one foot after the other, heel to toes. He is sleeping; I can get out of this. I'm in his home, I'm the intruder. It's clear now that this isn't how we originally entered Devil's Cave.

Walking backwards, my shoes softly hit the gravel, causing a quiet crunch. Heel to toes, my foot suddenly hits the four-high stone tower I had forgotten was behind me.

"Amis, you stupid imbecile!" I mouth in anger. The stones created a loud crash, reflecting throughout the bear's chamber. Airborne, like time froze, I slipped and fell directly on my back.

A loud noise boomed with a deafening roar, resonating off the chamber walls. Goosebumps lathered my arms. Shit! The bear sees me, and his eyes are much better in the dark than mine. I stood up to meet the black bear, waving my torch high above my head, yelling as loudly as possible.

The bear, on its hind legs, lunged toward me, whacking the torch out of my hand. I ran back to the narrow path. The bear lunged at me, scratching my leg with its claw. I flail and slip through the small opening from whence I came. My torch is gone. The light dissipated completely, returning to darkness. This is my dismal fate, death in Devil's Cave.

The bear claws angrily at me, but the opening I maneuvered through is too small for its giant frame. It has another path; I must flee now.

My hands found the wall on my right. I limped as fast as possible in the pitch dark, following the curve and jagged cave wall with accelerated haste. If I'm going to escape this, luck and God both need to be with me now.

My hands are my eyes as they discover the wall receding into another shaft. That hallway has to be the way I originally came.

Again, I walked straight, proceeding on, sliding my hands every step, finding the other wall of the uneven cave. Hurriedly, I continue, finding the next hallway relying solely upon my hands. My foot splashed into water, and I hit my head hard. Words come to mind, "Blimey! My fat noggin!"

Rushing through the narrow hallway, a soft breeze of chilly air blows, and I hear the sound of trickling water. This is the way!

My pace quickens with confidence, and I see the pure natural rays of light shining into the cave. I've never seen such beauty. From behind, I hear another roar, like thunder rumbling from under the mountain. My bleeding leg is in extreme discomfort; I can't think about it. The adrenaline-riddled will to survive pushes me onward. The bear's giant paws are right behind me; they're much faster than my own.

I was almost out of the dark abyss of the cave. Mykel and the others scrambled as they were waiting at the entrance of the cave.

"Amis, jump!" Mykel bellows.

With all my remaining strength, I propel myself into the stream beside the cave opening. The bear sees the other threats as they emerge; they are more frightening.

In the natural outdoor setting, I crawl on all fours along the shallow spring, splashing madly as I try to gain my composure. At any moment, I expect to be snatched up and devoured.

I turned around to see Mykel standing his ground, yelling loudly, and raising his axe ready to strike, but instead the paw of the beast whips him across his chest, knocking him away. The two other men run for the wagon. They are attempting to unhitch the horses and escape.

Drenched and cold, I shot up and ran for the wagon as fast as I could muster with an injured leg.

The bear ran at full speed after them. Chasing one of them down like he was easy prey, mauling the man, and ripping him to shreds.

I made it to the wagon. The other man unhitched a horse, riding swiftly away. I released the other horse before it could flip the wagon. The bear's eyes latch onto me once more.

I jump in the wagon, rummaging as fast as I can. Searching for any weapon bigger than my mere hatchets and daggers. Looking back, I see the bear rushing towards me. He's going to kill me; Dad will be so disappointed.

'Amis breathe, don't let fear overtake you.' Dad's words pierce my mind.

My hands continue to rummage, and I find a bow and arrows. Quickly turning around and rising tall in the wagon. I release an arrow that hits the bear's side. Not a damn critical shot; the bear is even more pissed. Reaching for another arrow, I quickly notch it on the string and pulled it back.

To my astonishment, the bear rises on its hind legs, meeting me at my height. It lets out a massive roar as it swings a paw in my direction. Not gain you big bitch. I stand firm and loose an arrow, hitting the bear directly in its mouth.

It sways like a tree before going down. The bear crashes to the ground, causing a dust cloud. I immediately shot another arrow into its chest to confirm the kill. Surveying the bear, it was bigger than I initially thought. It was not a black bear, but a brown one! What's that old verbiage, 'If it's brown bear, lie down. If it's a black bear, fight back.' I handled that downright wrong.

Surveying the horrific scene by getting off the wagon and walking up to the man's body. It's gruesome and mangled in the pathway. What a bloody mess. Skin hangs off his face, and his clothes are ripped to shreds.

That could've been me… Nate and Rupert will never believe me. Niklas would never believe me. Good thing he had a front row seat.

Continuing up the trail, I look for Mykel. I couldn't see him anywhere from where he was hit and blown backwards. I looked down into the stream I had previously jumped in. His body is there, looking lifeless. Carefully, I drop down next to the water, trying not to fall in again. I place my hand on Mykel; he's just unconscious. I need to get him away from here.

The sun is going down soon. We are going to be stranded up here in the mountains. I need to build a fire. With all my might, I tugged Mykel's big body up out of the creek bed onto drier land beneath pine trees.

I cleared a space on the ground and gathered kindling to start a fire, finding bark, sticks, and some dry wood to give more fuel for the fire. Taking the flint out of my pocket, I grabbed my hatchet just like before in the cave and struck the kindling, lighting a fire.

First step in starting a fire. Ensure that the fire is contained and there's no sparse vegetation that could ignite a major forest fire. I went back to the wagon and found some food, warm clothes, and some alcohol.

Pouring the alcohol on the cut on my leg, I felt a nice zing, reminding me I'm alive. I made sure the unconscious Mykel's bundled up next to the fire. If only I had to book to read.

156 | Page

Chapter Twelve:

Bear Skin

The smell of smoke permeated the air. Opening my eyes, I find fire consuming the entirety of my surroundings. The flames scorched my skin as the blaze grew bigger and bigger. I don't want to burn alive, not in this fiery tomb. A hot wind breezes overhead, as sparks and ash spread like a disease. Something burns far off ahead of me; it's my sanctuary, my place of peace. My apple tree. I'm stunned by the burning mayhem, as I prep myself to be engulfed alive.

"What are you doing?" I shout in frustration as I'm startled awake.

"Mr. Hastings, I'm sorry to wake you." A voice whispers.

You're alive!" I yelp, lunging towards Mykel, going in for a hug.

Mykel jerks away from me. Clearly, he isn't a hugger. "What happened to the bear?"

"It's dead. One of the servants was mauled, and the other prick fled on a horse."

"Well, you, my boy, just had one of the best initiations any guild has ever known."

The sun is just about to rise. The birds chirp, and the bright rays of sunlight scatter through the trees. Mykel surprisingly shows no sign of further injury. I wrap my leg in a cloth. Two cuts run pretty deep vertically along my calf. I hobble back to the wagon, seeing the big mound of a bear.

Mykel admonishes me, "Son, you'd better save the meat and skin it. That would make a fine rug!"

I responded, looking longingly up the path. "Do you think they'll come back for us?"

"Oh yes! You're a Hastings, fighting for the Federalists. You are more valuable than you know!" Mykel smirks with a mocking tone.

"If I'm so important to them, why would they almost kill me in a cave?" I retort.

"Hastings, the bear wasn't part of the plan!"

We roll the bear on its back. It takes both of us exerting all the strength we had left. Making cuts along its belly, I discard all the guts. There's a lot; once I finish with the mess, I make careful cuts all around its body to pull back the skin. He was an awful beast, but I did intrude upon his home.

I turn to Mykel, who has more skill at skinning than I. "Since you're from Eagle Valley, do you happen to know a man named Gentry?"

His eyes grow big, blurting out in rage. "What do you know? Son, be careful! That could lead you and the rest of your family to the chopping block!"

That's a yes, being more intrigued. "Whoa, okay, I just read something about him, is all."

"You need not ask things like that of others, or you'll end up just like Niklas!" Mykel lectures.

"You want to know why we prod where we shouldn't?" I ask argumentatively. "You old folks always tend to leave us with damn riddles. I'm sick of riddles! Just give me the truth!"

"Fine, have it your way. G-Gentry was my best friend and the only one ever to defeat me in a duel. He sought to eliminate dueling from society but ultimately fell short of his goal. In turn, he eliminated…"

His words trail off as he looks past the wagon, down the beaten path. "Horses are coming. To the trees, go!"

Mykel proceeds to drag my hobbling ass off the dirt path and into the trees. "Just as much as the Federalists want you alive, the Loyalists now want you dead. We need to be sure they are friendly." Mykel insists.

Horses pound their hooves closer, and I see the servant who escaped, Mr. Brookshard, and two others. Their eyes are awestruck, looking at the carcass of the now mutilated bear.

"I thought you said the bear mauled everyone. Clearly not!" Mr. Brookshard yells, peering into the trees looking for any trace of life.

"It's okay, we can trust them," Mykel whispers in relief. He raises his hands and shouts, "Over here, Charles!"

The men pin their gaze on us as we move from the tree line.

"Mykel, did you do this?!" Mr. Brookshard exclaims.

"No, sir, it was all Amis. He saved my life." Mykel says humbly.

"Mr. Hastings, I'm surprised to see you alive." My Brookshard's cold, calculating voice is clear for all to hear.

"You don't have to make it so obvious that you don't like him, Charles." Mykel harshly criticizes.

Charles is Brookshard's first name. I chuckle slightly.

Then my gaze meets that of the man who escaped unscathed. Rage fills my heart as the image of the cowardly man fleeing, leaving us to die, crosses my mind.

I can't control my frustration. My legs force me forward with a limp towards the servant who ran. His eyes grow wide in fear, and he attempts to turn his horse around to flee again. I'm no brown bear, but I am pissed. I latch my hands on his shirt, hugging his torso and ripping him off his horse to the ground with all the momentum I can muster.

The servant is smaller than I, weaker, and oh so fragile. My fist meets his face, breaking his nose in one clean blow. Blood runs down the side of his dirty face.

Laughter boisterously sounds. "You think I don't know pain, given my terrible fate as a piss poor dueler? A coward I am, but no murderer like your brother Niklas." The servant smiles, showing his bloody, broken teeth.

"Amis, do not kill this man or you'll end up just like my daughter and your brother, dead." Mr. Brookshard speaks with reason.

My hand remains balled, ready to strike. This barbaric coward deserves death.

A bear-like claw shoots out, pulling me in. Mykel whispers in my ear. "Show mercy like Gentry would."

Reality sets in, and I'm already less of a man than Gentry. Gentry would never have been driven to the point of no control.

There's nothing but an awkward silence for a time as the tension subsides. Mykel helps me load the bear skin into the wagon. We depart and begin our descent from high elevation. My lungs experience relief; I survived my initiation.

When we finally reach the cobblestone streets of Lyon, en route to the Federalist Guild, I realize this part of my journey is the unknown. Mykel branches off from my wagon on a horse of his own.

Leaning in, he mutters, "Would you like me to gift the bear to your parents?"

I nodded my head in gratitude. "Thank you! Do you know where they live?"

"Of course, your Dad and I are good friends." He winks.

I enter back through the Federalist guild doors. This guild has to accept me now, whether they like me or not. I'm now under contract, punishable by death, to serve their party in any way they see fit for the next two years.

I glanced swiftly to my left to grab my sack, where I left it last.

"It's gone," I whisper under my breath.

In the center of the circular foyer stand nine individuals in black, each with red serpent pins, shoulder to shoulder. The old, grumpy man I recognize from before my initiation speaks, Tarron.

"Well, it seems you have passed your trial with a little extra excitement, becoming a member of the prestigious guild of power and glory." His disturbing voice crackles with each word.

"I should not have to remind you that we do not kill outside of duels unless ordered otherwise. Given your brother's recent death, I would think you'd have more control than to assault one of our servants."

My tired eyes drop to the floor in embarrassment for my rash emotion. I just fought a bear, so old man Tarron can screw off!

"Now that you are vetted as one of us, you must spar with our other three duelers for your positional rank. The highest rank will represent us as Lyon's Federalist Champion. As a Champion, you'll duel for the institution of laws and make more money. Stay at the bottom too long and you'll become a servant to the guild. Just ask our lifelong servant, Bruce." Tarron points to a crooked man on the side of the room.

Thoughts scatter through my mind; I'm left completely at a loss for words. None of this was part of the contract. I guess it doesn't need to be… My body is theirs for the next two years.

"Where are my things?" I spouted off. What a stupid question.

The crooked servant jerks to the hallway. "In your room, young dueler Hastings." Bruce's voice sounds dark and deeply disturbed.

"Tarron, stop being a sadistic bigot." The sweet woman, Janice, states, and continues, "Mr. Hastings, we heard about your bear excursion. Everyone believed you to be dead."

Zander, in the center of the room, nods his head wildly in confirmation.

"We are so glad you survived. The Federalists are fortunate to acquire Hastings to our guild. Yes, Tarron is correct. You will have to fight for your place in the lineup. That is a worry for tomorrow, not today.

As you know, we lost young Harry last week to your brother's sword. He was our best Dueler." Janice says, sighing, cupping her hands at her waist.

I see Zander's eyes drop down; the knowledge of his loss still stings. I share empathy with him.

Janice breathes deeply, carrying on. "We need to spar to determine our new champion to represent us. We only have four duelers now: Zander, Xavier (a short, thick man with a goatee and salt and pepper hair), Veronica (a natural, tall brunette with toned, long legs), and now you, Amis. This is our guild's instructor, Kilroy." Janice points down at a relatively short man with slick-back, dark, wavy hair that touches his shoulders.

Stern, but steady, Kilroy speaks, "Enough of the pleasantries. I'll see each of you tomorrow morning at dawn. Be ready to fight and don't be late." Kilroy doesn't lack confidence and authority, given his petite height.

The politicians and our one instructor filed down the long hall. Leaving the other duelers and Bruce, the servant, with me.

Zander quickly greets me, shaking my shoulders rapidly. "We heard you killed a bear! How? Was that part of your initiation?!" Zander asks, interrogating me profusely.

I laugh, "It sounds much cooler than it actually was. They left me completely stranded in a cave, and I ran into a bear along the way!"

I told him every detail as we walked down the long hallway. Torches are lit every fifteen feet or so. There's no natural light. A long, red runner carpet extends the entire length of the hall. Its pattern displays a serpent in the center.

"Holy Harwen! Hastings, your leg is dripping blood all over the ground. Look at what you're doing to Bruce!" Xavier rudely reveals.

We all turn to see poor Bruce is on his knees with a bucket, cleaning my red-stained path.

I immediately try to bend down to assist when Veronica snaps, "Lay off, you asshat!" Punching Xavier in the arm. "We need to get him to the med bay to have the nurse stitch him up."

Already, Veronica feels like the older sister I never had, and Xavier is an audacious jabroni.

At the end of the hall is a spiral staircase that leads to three floors. The med bay is the last door before the stairs.

Before Xavier and Veronica entered the room, they agreed that they were turning in for the night. Zander stayed by my side.

I ask skeptically. "Is the nurse even here?"

Zander responds, "Oh yeah, she always is." He screams, "Carrie, we have some blood in here!"

Behind the double doors, a woman with messy blonde hair walks out disheveled, as if we had just woken her from a restless sleep.

"Blood again? You've got to be kidding." Carrie says, exasperated.

I raise my pant leg and expose my blood-soaked bandages. "A bear clawed me pretty good."

"A bear!? Why would you fight a bear?! You duelers, I swear, you do nothing but find new ways to make me work. Xavier seems to rupture his hemorrhoids daily, Zander is riddled with depression, and now you. Bleeding?! My Veronica is the only strong one." Carrie says, smiling to herself proudly.

Zander's lungs swell huge as he laughs wildly, "Xavier's Hemorrhoids."

Carrie sewed me back together. She said, "I'll live for now," but frankly, since I signed my life away, I feel like I could easily die at any point.

Zander escorted me up a set of spiral stairs towards our rooms.

"If you rank at the bottom, do you really become a servant?" I casually ask Zander.

"Yes, but you'd only serve for your allotted contract. The guild will never do that to you, Hastings. Rest up, you'll need it if you want to get ranked as champion." Zander then walks up the hall to his room.

Chapter Thirteen:

Rankings

Waking up in the morning feels different here. I've never had such a comfortable bed with soft furs and slick silks. The decorations are simple. My room was spacious, with dark lighting and neutral color themes. With a simple oak chair and a small table. Opening the curtains, I discover a giant window overlooking a small courtyard below. I'm guessing that's one of our training areas.

Being in a guild feels oddly familiar, but lonelier than I hoped. That's what I get for joining Nate's opposing guild.

I have never been blessed enough to have my own room. Typically, Rupert is in my business right about now. I'll miss the annoying trivial things my siblings do. I can feel myself growing idle. I don't think I'm capable of being an only child. I love having siblings who keep me constantly on my toes, giving me someone to lean on for support, and providing clear examples of how to navigate the ever-changing world. Nonetheless, I prepare for the unknown events of the day by putting on a black linen shirt and leather pants. I threw my belt and shoes on and took a wool jacket from my closet that features a red three-headed serpent.

A loud knock vibrates my room. Walking to the door, I noticed my leg felt much better. As the hinges of the door screech, shivers race down my spine when I see the frightening Mr. Bruce and his old, rickety frame standing hunched inches from the door's opening. He hands me a small parchment paper, grunting, not saying any audible words. Opening it with hesitation, I see a particular broad list of rules written by old man Tarron himself:

The Federalists Guild Code of Conduct

1.   *You must represent the guild in all your words, actions, and deeds by displaying chivalry and allegiance to your title as a Federalist dueler.*

2.   *You must be on time and present for any scheduled activity. Failure to comply with this may result in adverse action such as flogging.*

3.   *Living spaces in the guild are not your own. You may be subject to random searches and seizures. Any illegal material or propaganda will result in criminal prosecution and or death.*

4.   *No outsiders are allowed.*

You are a representative of the Federalist. Failure to comply will result in imprisonment or the death penalty. If you are unable to fulfill the dueling contract, your body will belong to the Federalists, and you will do as we desire.

A loud gasp in annoyance escapes my lips after reading such stiff rules. No way my brothers haven't broken these rules. Niklas had his puff, puff, and without a doubt, Nate had Trisha hanky panky-ing in his room. I raised my eyes to Bruce. He smiles widely, exposing his broken, rotted black teeth again, remaining mute. He turns promptly and hobbles down the hall.

Leaving my room, I immediately stumbled upon Zander in the hallway, waiting for me. His pasty face has definitely been washed, and his dark hair is perfectly parted down the center of his head.

I point to his superbly finished hair, "That's going to get ruined quickly."

Zander jabs back, "At least I don't have dirty wavy ass hair like you!" He slaps me square on the back. "Let's get something to eat. Veronica and Xavier are already in the mess hall."

We hustle up the spiral staircase, taking us past the med bay to the mess hall. Sure enough, Xavier and Veronica are sitting down in leather chairs at a table. On the side of the room, a whole row of food is laid out.

"Is that free for the taking?" I ask with pure excitement.

"Of course, nimrod." Xavier snarks.

"Xavier, have you looked in the mirror? Your jagged beaver teeth and grey hair make you look stupid." Veronica says, smirking.

Xavier purses his lips together. "Grey hair at an early age runs in my family! It's a sign of wisdom."

We all laugh. Wisdom.

I get some toast with apricot jelly, just like my mom used to make. I sit down across Xavier, staring at him as I do. Taking a bite of the sweet jam, I ask, holding up the parchment. "Xavier, you don't seem like a rule follower. Which one of these have you broken?"

He stares blankly back at me, "Like I'd tell you, Hastings!"

I smile, "Let me guess." Laughing slightly. "You've let a few floozies sneak into your room?"

"No, just your mom," Xavier says with a smug look.

Veronica squints hard at Xavier. "Who pissed in your mouth last night?"

Damn, Veronica is fast with insults. "I was just looking at these rules, and there's no way my brothers were sticklers enough to follow all this malarkey," I say.

"Listen, Hastings, don't trifle with the guild. They are watching and waiting for us to screw up." Veronica says with her eyes, pacing across the room.

"And be punctual!" Zander adds abruptly.

"If you make me have to do any extra conditioning, I'll come into your room and-"

"And do what, Xavier?! Make love to him?" Veronica giggles.

"Seriously, Xavier, you really want to challenge him? His brother just killed mine, and he just slayed a giant bear." Zander snaps rather depressively.

I respond modestly, "I'm not either of my brothers."

"Right…" Xavier rolls his eyes. "Let's get going and find out where we will rank."

As a group, we walk down the hall towards the front door. I follow closely behind as we go through a couple of doors and into the spacious indoor practice ring. The gym is lined with banners of past victories. Every champion who wins in a duel has their name stitched into a banner, and the law was over. It's astonishing to see. I look along the walls from years and years ago. I wonder if Gentry's name is here from when he fought in Lyon years ago. I wonder what happens if you die?

"Hastings! Are you going to join us?!" Instructor Kilroy asks impatiently.

I filed in, trying my best to be attentive amid my rising curiosity.

"Each of you knows that our politicians create the laws we are so blessed to die for. They identify a need of the people, present it, and attempt to compromise with the Loyalists. The opposing party always denies the proposal because they are a bunch of hard asses, which forces us to duel. They tell us how we need to prepare."

"That's the only thing these political puppets can agree upon, how we kill each other," Zander mumbles softly.

Veronica shoots her hand up rapidly. "Yes, Veronica," Kilroy grumbles.

"Sir, how are we supposed to be ready? The last three duels were jousting, swimming, and a standoff?!" Veronica questions.

"Great question. The best duelers are those who are balanced. Regardless of the circumstances into which they are dropped, they are well-versed enough to succeed. Which is why we will be ranking you based on three aptitudes: Strength, Speed, and Improvisation. Jousting duel was mainly about strength, the swimming duel was about speed, and the standoff was about improvisation. However, improvising can be useful in all situations."

"Today, I will rank you on a scale of 1-4 points for each of the three separate tests. The dueler with the most points at the end is our champion." Kilroy gasps for air after his long speech.

"Someone needs to hit the gym. The goal is to be in the middle of the pack. That way, you never have to fight, and you don't become a servant. You just ride the guild life for two years." Xavier says as quietly as possible.

"Until they call you up to fight for a law they don't really care about, just so they can kill you off," Zander says with a grin.

"As you know, the last rankings were:

Champion- Harry
Second- Veronica
Third- Zander
Fourth- Xavier."

"So much for the middle of the pack…" I mutter Xavier's way.

Kilroy continues, "We will start with speed. Meet me out front in five minutes. We will run to Ash Reservoir and back."

"Damn it," I say.

"Are you going to be okay with that nasty bear wound?" Zander asks with a concerned-laced face.

"I hope so. The bandage on my leg is still in decent shape." I say nervously. The compression and support of the wrap help me walk, but there's no way

I'll be able to run. Not yet, Kilroy has to know this. I just survived the bear's assault.

We walked onto Main Street in front of the guild. The nasty smell from the waste gutters running in the cobblestone streets almost makes me hurl. We lined up for stretching. Peasants fix their gazes on us. They know who we are and keep their distance.

"Holy Harwen, I hate it when people stare; they need to keep to themselves. Move along!" Xavier directs the onlookers. He's always so loud and rambunctious.

Kilroy arrived on a horse. "I'm not running with you, so I'll ride instead. None of you has integrity, so here I am micromanaging." He says begrudgingly.

We lined up, staggering our feet. Ready to abuse our knees and bodies. "This will be a three-mile run, starting downhill and finishing uphill.

At the ready, go!" Kilroy exclaims.

My legs churn one after another. I stay right behind Zander, trying my best to keep his pace. This run will require an elevated level of endurance.

I notice Veronica breaking off from us. Her long gazelle legs should be considered cheating! It's not a bad sight watching her legs spring off the ground one after another in perfect unison.

Zander is pretty fast himself. I turn around and see Xavier staggering behind. He's a little shorter, and his legs have to move twice as fast to keep this pace.

Once out of Lyon, we continued up a wagon-tracked road. Sweat accumulates on my head, dropping into my eyebrows. The salty water slightly irritates my eyes. I have to focus, as I whip away the sweat-driven tears. I pick up my pace, passing Zander by. I see Veronica up ahead. I can catch her; I'm faster, taller, and stronger than she is. I tell myself out of pure confidence, forgetting the throbbing numbness of my leg.

She isn't slowing, but my determination and willpower are taking over. I'm now right behind her pounding feet. With my legs blazing across the ground, hands and feet pumping wildly, I'm finally able to pass her right before reaching the Ash reservoir.

I touch the dock post at the reservoir, springing off with force. I'm halfway! I'm going to be first; that's an easy four points.

Out of nowhere, I collided with Veronica, the jarring impact was so sudden that we both ended up on our asses. She quickly rises to her feet and carries on. Did she run into me on purpose? The thought crosses my mind, and I swiftly push it away.

Zander then passes right behind. Attempting to get up and continue striding forward, my injured leg is weak and pulsating wildly. My stitches are busted open from the collision. Blood seeps down my leg.

Xavier now sees me as he touches the dock. When he comes back around, he stops, puts his shoulder undermine, attempting to support my hobbling ass.

"You're going too slow. You can leave me; I'll crawl back if I have to." I say, feeling guilty.

"No, I was going to be last anyway. Don't worry, once I see a glimpse of the guild, I'll leave you to crawl the rest of the way." Xavier says, with a laugh between his wheezing breaths.

As we enter town and get closer to the guild, there's quite an abundance of peasants in the streets, walking and pushing carts. I was one of them yesterday; I am no better. Again, they look wildly at Xavier and me as blood drips on the street.

"They're watching us again," I chuckle.

"Stop staring, you hob knockers!" Xavier screams.

We finally reached the guild; to my surprise, Xavier didn't finish before me. For being a little bitch, he actually has some honor.

"That's great teamwork. As a guild, you need to collaborate and build camaraderie. Excellent job, Xavier, you still finished last!" Kilroy smiles.

We filed back into the guild. I headed straight to the med bay. Carrie, our nurse, cleaned the wound and restitched it for me.

"Don't let anyone hit you there again! If they try, I'll kick their asses myself!" Carrie says in a serious tone.

"I promise that next time I see you, it'll be for something different," I smile, thanking her.

Walking back into the practice ring, I notice Zander's jet-black hair is completely disheveled, Veronica seems content and focused, while Xavier rubs his lower back. He must be sore from supporting my heavy ass.

I approach my fellow duelers with a noticcable limp. Veronica apologetically says, "I'm sorry for running into you. The race would've been yours if I didn't do that."

"It's all good, I pushed my calf too hard while running anyway." I try to say in humility.

Kilroy strolls in, taking over the room. "Everyone! Splendid work out there. I'm impressed by you four. We have a long way to go, though. I don't think any of you are adequate for a real duel at this very moment. The current rankings are:"

Veronica: 4
Zander: 3
Amis: 2
Xavier: 1

"We can count, sir," Xavier outbursts.

"Don't be frustrated, son. The next challenge is right up your alley, Strength." Kilroy says excitedly. Kilroy continues, "For this challenge, I really considered having you wrestle for it. But we do enough of that as is."

Bruce waddles in and out on four separate occasions while Kilroy is talking, and each time he carries thick, long wooden planks with metal hooks screwed into each end. He attaches the first plank's hooks to a metal chain hanging from the ceiling and to a chain coming from the ground. It's designed to maintain the plank in a steady vertical position. The plank is suspended vertically through the air; the chain from the ceiling is taut due to gravity pulling the plank.

Our eyes are trained on Bruce, but Kilroy keeps talking, "One at a time, you will each swing your sword only once as hard as possible, trying to splinter the wood and plunge it deep into the plank. The person who cuts the deepest wins, and so on. Easy enough, right? We will start with Veronica since she won the speed challenge."

I quickly shot up my hand. "Yes, Hastings." Kilroy moans.

"Sir, what type of wood are the planks made out of?" I ask curiously.

"Oak, son," Kilroy says straight-faced.

Oak is really dense. This challenge is going to take more form and finesse than brute strength. I need my form to be perfect and to utilize every muscle in my body.

Kilroy hands out swords to each of us. They are worn out and old. "The metal on this sword is nothing special. When you finish abusing them here, we will have them smelted at the blacksmith and made anew."

It's heavy and definitely a piece of shit.

"How are we supposed to cut anything with this?" Zander asks in disbelief.

"Shut up, Veronica, please start," Kilroy says, completely dismissing Zander's complaint.

Veronica steps up. The sword is so big that she has to use both hands. She lines up in front of the suspended oak wood. Her eyes are closed, which is not in her favor. Twisting her body, she swings the sword with all her might. The wood shakes violently between the chains. She is still gripping the sword in awe. It's almost as if the oak caused her to rebound backward with the sword. Upon further examination, it looks like she splintered a slice, but only one inch.

Hitting a sword against wood like this only causes damage to be inflicted upon the blade. Good thing they are old swords. Veronica looks disappointed, but in retrospect, she did go first, and it does look extremely challenging.

Bruce changes out the wood planks, and Zander steps up to do the same. Zander, with his slender build, may be able to generate more torque with his arms and body to swing faster; however, his strength and follow-through will definitely be lacking. Sure enough, it seems like he made contact with incredible velocity, but the blade of the sword didn't get very deep at all. During the aftermath of the swing and review by Kilroy, Zander only managed two inches into the wood.

I can win this. Stepping up to my fresh oak plank, I pinpoint a target on the wood that I want to strike. Just like I did when I chopped wood back home. I find a good growth ring on the wooden plank and concentrate my gaze. Generating as much power as I can through my body and legs, I forcefully land a decisive blow onto the plank. I feel a vibration up the sword, and feel tiny wood pieces fly into me. The plank absorbs my blow! My hands are in pain due to the abrupt stoppage.

Kilroy measures my cut. "Four inches." He says excitedly.

"I wish we had an axe or a saw." I lean into Zander, saying. He nods his head in agreement.

Xavier steps up; he looks bulky enough that he might be able to do considerable damage. I notice he has his hands together on the hilt, looking very controlled with his eyes open. Based on the way he holds the sword, he is an exceptional swordsman. With a composed combination of motion and strength, he swings hard and true. His follow-through is more prevalent. He steps away, and we instantly see he's won.

Kilroy, with a broad smile, exclaims, "Six inches! We have our winner of this round."

"Impressive!" I say, patting Xavier hard on his sore back.

"Now that the round is over, our point totals are as follows:"

Veronica: 5
Xavier: 5
Zander: 5
Amis: 5

A straight tie. The next round will decide the champion of our guild!"

"We're all tied?! I've never seen this." Veronica, who's been here the longest, says.

"How in the hell!" Xavier says, raising his voice almost to a pubescent crack.

"It's simple math. Focus." Zander says, completely unfazed.

Kilroy starts back up, "For this last round, one dueler will go at a time. You are not allowed to talk or communicate about events until after everyone has experienced them. I want each of you to stretch and prepare your mind for whatever you may face. Remember this challenge is about improvisation."

We all sit in silence as we think about the possibilities that await us. I remain attentive. I know why

I'm here: to redeem Niklas. I'm here to discover a new perspective. I'm here to change our nation's mindset. I need to become the champion to do it.

Like Dad always said, "There's a reason for pain and suffering. Overcome trials and tribulations to survive. That's the only way we can accomplish our purpose."

Xavier breaks the silence, "I don't think I'm ready to be the champion, not after Harry."

"What would you know about Harry! He was proud to be a champion, proud to represent our guild. If you were a true dueler, you would be too!" Zander says in revolt.

I step between them, pushing them apart, "Knock it off, we'd better give this our all. Dueling isn't just about us and our fame. There's more to all of this than our own glory!"

"What would you know? You're new here. You don't know what it's like to train next to someone for months, and then they end up dead in the blink of an eye!" Veronica says, folding her arms.

I withdraw my stance, taking a few steps back. I can't tell them what I know about Rasmussen. How he got Niklas killed, or about the book Niklas left me. Not yet. The information could get into the wrong hands. My face tightens in anger as I think about slowly killing Rasmussen.

Breaking the tension, Kilroy shouts, "Veronica, you are up… Follow me."

Veronica disappears as she slips behind the door. We sat in silence again. Then, ten minutes pass by as Kilroy calls Xavier.

"How many of these rankings have you been through?" I lob the words toward Zander in hopes of a response.

"This is my second. I now know the rankings are different every time." He turns to me with a soft grin, not exposing his teeth. "Don't worry, Amis, you are a Hastings. It's in your blood." He kicks my foot.

"Zander, I'm sorry about Harry."

Zander stares silently for a minute, "It's not your fault, you are not your brother. Everyone dies; every man is set free." That's an odd phrase, I think to myself, brushing my sweaty hair back to its proper position.

Soon after, Zander was called. I'm left to myself and my own thoughts. Patiently waiting for whatever trial, they could conjure up next. I pace the room back and forth; an idle mind is the devil's workshop.

Kilroy finally peeks in, "Hastings, you're up."

I strut forward gradually.

As I exit the doors, I see a table with a variety of weapons. All training weapons. Including hatchets, daggers, throwing knives, long swords, axes, and a real bow with field arrows that had blunt tips, not meant for penetrating blows. Glad to see I won't be doing any real killing.

"You can only choose three," Kilroy says.

I strapped up my favorite weapons: hatchets, a long sword, and daggers.

Kilroy then directs me to another door. Spouting off directions fast. "When I say go, run outside, and survive. How quickly you eliminate your opponents, and if you prevail, will determine your score. Good luck."

I stagger my stance, ready to burst out the door and accelerate toward whatever danger lies before me. I almost forgot about my injured leg, but no matter how distracted I am, the pain still lingers.

Kilroy makes eye contact with me and smiles like a maniac. "Go!" The word bellows loud from his mouth.

Ripping open the door, I see the training courtyard, the one from my bedroom window. I scan the yard for all possible threats. Four Athrenian soldiers await me. Each in distinct positions, the ground is mostly clear with scattered barrels here and there. In the distance, I see a bowman on a platform. "Shit!"

One soldier from behind that I don't recall seeing hits me low with his shoulder, trying to take me to the ground. I swiftly shift my body weight and kick my legs away from the attacker, trying my best to protect my injury. Then, leaning over, I grab him by the neck and legs, flipping him hard onto his back, like a calf in the field. I take a wooden dagger and plunge it into his chest, eliminating him from this pretend game.

Getting back to my foundation, within a split second. Two other men rush me wildly with wooden swords. Immediately, I fell into a defensive stance. I whip my wrist, flinging a dagger at the closest combatant. Then, pulling out my sword, I rushed to meet the second. Relying on my quick footwork and fast reflexes, I met the soldier blade to blade for four consecutive strikes, clashing the wooden swords powerfully. Until the soldier thrust his sword forward at my stomach, and I slashed it down with such intensity that it disarmed him. In rapid-fire succession, I uppercut my sword across his chest.

The soldier who received my flying dagger parried quickly, leaving him disoriented for a few moments, giving me a chance to take care of his friend. I engaged him in a dynamic dance of strategic position and calculated strikes. Again, I eliminated another swordsman as I subdued him with a deceptive false attack, luring him in for an abrupt vital kill.

There are two soldiers left. One is nearby, and the bowman is forty feet away on a platform. Blunt training arrows begin to wiz by, causing me to roll and hide behind a barrel. Re-sheathing my sword and pulling my hatchets out, I prepare for my final assault. Sweat drips from every pore; exhaustion is causing me to reach my breaking point. My leg is stable; the pain is unwavering.

Poking my head around the barrel, I'm unexpectedly met by the other welding swordsman, readying to strike me down. I meet his sword with the gut hooks of my hatchets. Risking his sword, plunging my own weapons into me. I fire my left hatchet up, directing his sword away, and my right hatchet nimbly strikes the soldier's armpit. The soldier yips in pain, yielding.

Refocusing my attention on the Bowman, I quickly realize I'm outmatched. Unable to run as fast as usual, with the lack of a bow, the soldier will surely end me. The bowman readies a blunt arrow in his bowstring, looking for any clear and open shot to finish me. There are no structures between us, no more places to hide. Better late than never.

"I should've picked the bow!" I proclaim aloud for no one to hear.

Rising abruptly, I ran from the barrel, somersaulting forward, dodging an arrow along the way. On one knee, I raise a hatchet between both of my hands above my head, heaving it towards the bowman in the distance. The bowman evades the rotating hatchet with ease. Pulling his bowstring back, he releases another arrow, ending me where I stand.

The blunt arrow to my chest makes me wince in pain. "Hold it together," I mutter to myself...

My dad's words still echo in my brain: "Listen to me when I say grab your bow!" It looks like I still have something to learn, to say the least.

Chapter Fourteen:

Blunt

Standing in the practice ring, I look across my fellow duelers to see their faces distraught. It appears they had a terrible time as well.

Everyone stands silently. We weren't expecting the Federalist to conjure up such a terribly hard finale for the rankings.

Instructor Kilroy and the Politicians, Janice, Tarron, and Isaac join us in the practice ring.

Tarron crows at us, "My dear Duelers, there's a reason we put you through rough challenges. It tells us a lot as a guild what our focuses need to be on, where our strengths are, or if we need to eliminate anyone."

"The last challenge was indeed a testament for us that we have some of the best fighters in Lyon. We watched each of you. Yes, there is plenty to work on, but each of you was able to eliminate two of our finest soldiers before being slain. We Federalists are extra ecstatic to hear that two of you eliminated four soldiers. Mr. Kilroy, what are the final tallies?"

"Thank you, Tarron. The final tallies are as follows:"

Veronica: 9
Amis: 8
Xavier: 7
Zander: 6

"When it came to improvisation, you all impressed me greatly. Zander had speed and aggressiveness. Xavier, you held your own before two swordsmen cut you down simultaneously. Amis, your critical thinking and ability to change between various weapons was a wonder to witness. Next time, choose the bow instead of the daggers, and I think you'd win. Now, Veronica, your speed with projectile objects amazed each of us. You won because of how fast you eliminated the four you killed. Word of the wise: build your strength. You didn't get the last soldier because they physically manhandled you."

"Veronica, you are our champion and will represent our guild in our next duel. There will be one in the coming weeks. Everyone, take a load off for the remainder of the day. Mykel will be in tomorrow for more extensive in-depth training." Kilroy's words trail off.

Veronica, with a big smile, asks, "Who am I dueling next week?"

Janice, the sweet politician, speaks up. "The Loyalists champion is Trisha. Amis knows her well; we expect him to give all the pointers he can." Veronica gulps and shifts her weight in uneasiness.

My eyebrows raise with nerves. This is a scenario I never considered. Helping my guild fight and or possibly killing my brother's love.

Everyone disperses except for me. Walking the practice ring, I follow the banners looking for Gentry's name, the champion from my book. I scour the beautifully hand-stitched banners representing duels that enacted meaningless laws, causing senseless deaths. Seeing the names of some folklore and legends, but not my hero's name.

Then I noticed something odd. One name isn't normal. They had four wins in a row, taking place in Lyon by a dueler named 'The Noble Red Warrior.'

Where do I remember that title?

"It's from Niklas' book," I whisper to myself. His name literally means Noble Red Warrior. Unusually, they put nicknames on the banners. Mykel is right, the name Gentry is illegal. They've certainly done wonders to censor our history.

Four wins in a row in Lyon? Gentry said he traveled all over Athren to duel. He must've really wrecked the Loyalists' laws everywhere he went. How did he manage to show mercy? I continue to peruse through the names, and I notice one man's name near the Noble Red Warriors. Charles Brookshard. My mouth opens wide as my jaw drops in shock. He knew Gentry!

I feel a soft tap on my shoulder. Startling me as I jump out of my skin.

"Oh, hello, Janice. How do you do?" I say in a nervous surprise.

"Mr. Hastings, what are you doing?" The older motherly figure with big, rimmed glasses questions.

"Just admiring all those who fought before," I say, quick on my toes.

"Oh, how lovely. I wanted to express my condolences to you regarding the passing of your brother, Niklas. He was a terrific fighter and negotiator." She says, putting a hand on my shoulder.

"He is a good man; I think he is proud of me," I respond, feeling a pang of pain in my heart.

"Indeed, which is why I think when you are healthy, you'll become our champion. You'll be able to follow in your brother's footsteps and go to the capital as a duelist." She says, going extremely silent, with her eyes remaining trained on me.

She's trying to read me. That's why she touches me all the time. It has to be an energy or body language thing. I think skeptically.

Unemotional, I say, "Whatever the guild needs me to accomplish, I will. I'm not here for my own personal glory."

"Very good!" We will talk soon. She stalks off the wood gym floor.

I need to finish that book. I need to know what Gentry did, how he eliminated the king.

My day concludes in solitude. I'm exhausted and beaten down from the last few days. Carrie, the nurse, gave me some herbs to help numb my leg.

I was able to eat a hearty dinner, more than I'd ever care to admit to Rupert. He would indeed be jealous. Bathing in the guild is eye-opening as well, a luxury before death. There must be a bunch of servants here that they don't talk about; there's no way Bruce could manage all of this alone.

My head hits the pillow, and my eyes close tightly. If every day is like this one, it's going to be a long two years.

Rhythmic beats drum softly against my window. Rain droplets smash against the glass. Water lines streak across my window. Rain brings peace with its beautiful sequence of drops, cleansing the earth of its filth.

Another day begins.

We stretch on the gym floor; my stitched leg seems to be scabbing quite a bit. That's a good sign. I lathered an ointment across the laceration and carefully wrapped a new bandage Carrie, the nurse, gave me.

"What do you think they have us do today?" I ask out of curiosity.

"Pry footwork and conditioning," Zander replies.

"We are their violent puppets for their political games. So, whatever they want." Xavier says pessimistically.

"This again, Xavier? We are going to have to deal with you being a moody ass?" Veronica says, raising an eyebrow.

"I'm just saying, we are their property!" Xavier says, staring spitefully at Veronica.

"Property that gets paid well," I say.

Stepping into the gym, Mykel and Kilroy looked prepared. Mykel towers over Kilroy as they stand next to each other, both wearing leather jackets. Mykel's is lacking a guild symbol; he's a neutral party preparing both guilds equally.

"I heard yesterday had its heightened moments of stress. Veronica! I'm glad to see you bring home the honor of being the champion! Now we need to help you become the champion of Lyon. Follow me!" Mykel orders.

We walked out the doors into the poorly lit, dark hallway. Only to reach the courtyard. The same courtyard where I got shot by a blunt arrow yesterday.

"We don't have the luxury of Athren soldiers to assist us today. They are busy policing the streets and enforcing the laws you die for." Kilroy says sharply.

When I look out upon the courtyard, I see a table with four bows and a large number of arrows. There's also a bunch of barrels again, scattered throughout to provide cover. Off to the side, I see a narrow balancing beam.

"Something we learned yesterday is that our duelers struggle with the bow, except for Veronica. One thing we will be doing to combat this is grouping up into pairs of two. Veronica, you will be with Zander, and Amis will have Xavier." Mykel instructs.

"Oh, and please do us a favor, no shooting each other in the eyes, these blunt arrows can still be lethal. It's enough force to penetrate the goo of your eyeball." Kilroy articulates it in such a way that we all know it's happened before.

We stand on opposite sides of the yard. There has to be roughly seventy feet between us.

Xavier turns to me. I noticed a bruise under his right eye that I didn't see yesterday. His grey, buzz-cut makes him look fit for this military-style life. "Hastings, this might sound crazy. I know what we need to do. When they say go, I'm going to sprint up close to the center. I figure shooting from a closer range will give us a better chance. Amis lay down all the cover fire you can."

Picking up my bow. I note it's only a thirty-pounder. That will be easy for me to pull back; my accuracy is still awful. "I'm terrible with a bow," I say, making my cheeks go red.

"Hot damn, Harwen, we are so screwed," Xavier says, laughing.

Xavier and I are in a position and quite ready to lose. Mykel blows his whistle. Xavier sprints to the barrels lined up in the center. Veronica readies her arrow and releases it as it travels with accelerated speed, missing Xavier. I place the nock of an arrow into my bowstring, firing it off at Zander, who is dashing towards Xavier, missing him, of course. I need to shoot quantity over quality.

Distracting Veronica, I send a volley of arrows in her direction. My arm grows tired, but Xavier needs support. Xavier and Zander are stuck in a standoff of their own. Each of them bobbed up from the barrels, releasing an arrow at the other, hiding. This plan won't work.

I shoot a few more arrows toward Veronica, not getting close enough for a kill. Then I run sprinting on the opposite side from Xavier.

I yell at Xavier, "Focus on Veronica!" He nods from where he's ducking.

Veronica continues firing off arrows that are incredibly close to hitting me. Brief, whooshing sounds whizz all around me.

Xavier hesitantly relocates to a central barrel. Zander and Veronica barrage him with arrows. They pelt the barrels, causing loud thumps. Thump, Thump. Damn, these blunt arrows can still generate forceful damage.

I bolt again, running forward to the enemy side, giving myself a perfect opportunity to hit Zander across the centerline of the yard. Stopping in the wide-open space, Veronica sees me. She turns sharply. I steady myself, feet squared, both eyes open for my depth perception. I focus all my attention on Zander. The exact moment I release an arrow; I get nailed in my stomach. I don't acknowledge the pain. Reacting won't change anything; the blistering ache will subside.

My eyes are completely mesmerized by my arrow as it slightly wobbles, propelling through the air. It nails Zander right in his forehead, causing him to whiplash and fall to the ground. I'm out, and now he's out; it's up to Xavier.

Xavier watched it all unfold; he had an arrow of his own at the ready. Letting go of his bowstring, his arrow is propelled with perfect precision. Veronica is eliminated!

I raced to Xavier, cheering in joy. "You did it, holy Harwen, yes!" I exclaimed, tackling him.

Xavier grins widely, "Told you my plan would work."

We lock eyes with Zander as he gingerly walks up, holding his head, "I guess this is the only spot I gave you to hit." Zander groans, pulling his hand away from his forehead, and there's a red ring the size of a small egg.

"Nice welt! That's going to bruise for sure!" I say, laughing at him.

Mykel gathers us. Veronica is quiet; she's probably feeling frustrated.

"How many arrows did you collectively release?" Mykel poses the question.

"Were we expected to count?" Veronica snaps.

"No, but the answer is too many. The chance of living or dying cannot come down to luck. Amis shot fifteen arrows and only hit Zander once. Xavier shot eight, Zander shot five, and Veronica shot eleven. That's thirty-nine arrows in total! Way too many." Mykel critiques.

"What do you suggest?" I say, really trying not to roll my eyes.

"Amis, your Dad would only need one arrow." Mykel admonishes me, grabbing a quiver full of arrows from behind his back. "You all will shoot these real arrows at the target over there until I say stop."

"Lovely," Zander says sarcastically as he rubs his shoulder.

For the next hour, we fired arrows over and over again. I'm getting better. But I'm still not my Dad. Mykel then has us do sprints until my legs quiver. This damn cut on my leg isn't ready for this type of treatment. When will they let it heal?

Mykel then orders two of us to stand on a balancing beam. We wield wooden swords and fight, trying to maintain our footing. I do surprisingly well; Xavier is the only one to knock me off. He swings with incredible force like Nate.

After the long, tiring day, we all washed up and met in the mess hall. I load my dinner plate up with an assortment of vegetables and chicken.

"Wanna know something weird I saw today?" Xavier says, waiting for one of us to take the bait.

"What? If it's another dumb conspiracy about failed duelers being sealed alive in the walls, I don't want to hear it." Zander says.

"No, it's not! But I swear I can hear their cries from my room! I saw Mr. Brookshard's name up on one of the banners!" My eyes bore into him with intense interest.

"He must've been a good fighter, too. He has quite a lot of banners." Xavier continues.

"My Dad told me he was a duelist during a particularly challenging time in our country; around the time we lost the monarchy. He never went into detail." Zander says in a nonchalant tone.

"That's really odd. There isn't any story behind the King's rule ending. Either nobody knows, or Athren will execute anyone who talks about it." I say, adding to the conspiracy.

"Does anyone know anything about this King? Did he have a family? I want a shot at a former princess." Xavier says, daydreaming.

"I heard his bloodline continued... I wonder what ended up happening to the King's offspring." Veronica adds. She's been very distant and quiet since we beat her earlier. Maybe she's scared of dueling Trisha.

"There you go, Xavier, get your jollies off fantasizing about a princess. She's in Athren, somewhere…" Zander says, mocking him.

Then a clashing of plates makes us all jump out of our seats. It's Bruce. His back seems more hunched than normal.

"When did he get here?" Xavier whispers.

We all seem to shrug in worry.

We spent the next hour together in the mess hall, sitting on the leather couches by the fireplace. The fire crackles, and its warmth adds to the comfort of the company. Xavier and Veronica have been extremely flirty tonight. I know they constantly banter back and forth; this is on a whole new level now. Before I can see if they take it any further, I bid farewell and call it a night.

When I return to my comfortable room, I quickly get into bed. I've never been in a situation like this, with luxurious blankets, food, and accommodations I could only dream of. There's a reason they treat us the way they do, we are their gladiators. Fighting for one party's political gain. Tomorrow is not promised. That's why Mykel and Kilroy push us so hard.

My head spins at all the wild things we put our bodies through. Mentally and physically, it is easy to lose yourself and your identity. I think of Nate and how much it feels like he has changed. Dad and Mom are always so keen on us living a morally clean and right-eous life. Not so easily influenced by the temptations of the world.

Chapter Fifteen:

The King

The rest of the week flies by, and before I know it, I'm on my way back to my parents' farm for the weekend on a horse I borrowed from the guild. I'm not like Nate; he refuses to visit after he joined the Loyalist guild.

The day is beautiful, summer is almost here, and the sun continues to grow warmer each day. Riding up the dirt road, I see the fields sprouting plants all around. There is no better sight.

Dad and Rupert are hard at work in the fields. Mom and Sofia are inside the house. When off the horse, I make my presence known by causing the dogs to go wild in excitement.

"What are you doing here?" Sofia says in a dark tone, full of pure judgment.

"Thought I'd save Mom from her evil little daughter!" I struck back.

"Mom isn't the one who will need saving if you don't get over here and hug me," Sofia says, brushing her dark hair out of her eyes and grinning.

I embrace my little sister and Mom. I've missed them. Their hair is up in the same type of bun, and it looks like they've been sewing some new clothes. Sofia is Mom's little twin, except she's diabolical.

"How are things here?" I asked in a worried tone.

"Well, it's only been a week, so not a lot has changed. Your father and Rupert have been working hard. There's a lot to accomplish and not enough time to complete it." Mom says.

"Everything looks great, and the plants have definitely grown; life on the rise always is a good sign," I say in an overly optimistic way.

"Amis, Rupert has been so annoying lately. You should see how much he is trying to be Dad, literally in every way. Dad's old knees were causing him terrible pain, and the next day, guess who had the same issues… You guessed it, Rupert!" Sofia's words spit out so fast that I don't think she takes a single breath. She hasn't been able to express herself.

"Thanks for the update, Sofia! I'll watch for Rupert's bunkum too." I say with slight sarcasm. "Well, I'm going to go find the boys and help out if they need a hand."

"You'd better take your ritzy leather jacket off!" Sofia blurts.

I flip her the bird in response. I feel like I can hear Mom's gasps in disgust. I've learned a lot of rotten things from Mom anyway; she has a filthier mind than anyone I know.

I walk out toward the vast corn fields. There, they are busy applying their own makeshift pesticide, made from inorganic compounds. I see Rupert dropping every so often to pick any weeds growing near the stalk of the corn. Dad sees me out of the corner of his eye. His awareness of his surroundings is surprising to me.

"That was some bear skin we had dropped off the other day," Dad says proudly.

"Mykel brought it! Did he tell you the story behind it?" I ask in excitement.

"Nope, he said it was your story to tell. He did say you saved his life. Is that true?" Dad side-eyes me.

"Yes, but not the way you may think," I say, telling them all the details of the bear story.

"You'd better be glad you didn't rank at the top," Rupert says, egging me on.

"Why?"

"Then you'd have to fight Trisha. She'd beat your ass no problem. Trust me!" Rupert says as he grunts, plucking another weed.

"You're probably right. Oh, Sofia says you've been mimicking Dad." I say nonchalantly, trying to stir the pot.

Rupert moans.

I assisted them the rest of the day with their labor. Farmers never get a day off. When we finished, there was an hour of sunlight left. I told Dad that I was going to spend time with Niklas. Sitting under the apple tree by his grave, I took a deep breath of the fresh spring air and began to read.

The guild in Harpstedt was glorious beyond all measures, with the most luxurious clothes, food, and training facilities. The advantages of training here were insurmountable and could prepare you for anything. Upon my arrival, the guild greeted me like royalty. I expected nothing different, considering the advances I've helped with for their cause. It is easy to forget your true purpose among all the distractions; I had to remain disciplined. Focusing on my goal with a sound mind and a clear heart.

I was in Harpstedt for over a week and still had not been called up to fight. The thought of actually having to kill another still brought me pain. If it's to save others and prevent further bloodshed, it's the right thing to do.

Then a notice came in the form of a letter. King Harper VI has invited me to accompany him to a royal dinner. I'm here to fight, not to dine! There's no need for such unnecessary social pleasantries. Begrudgingly, I attended the King's dinner event.

I asked a beautiful woman from my guild to accompany me. In all the lands I've wandered. Sea to sea, mountain tops to valley depths, I never found such grace and elegance in another. I will not share her, nor her name. She is mine. I will give my life and my soul to protect her. But, for the sake of this story, I will call her 'Eve.'

The king's castle is a majestic, imposing fortress. Each room is dedicated to captivating every ounce of your concentration. The chambers were adorned with rich tapestries, stained glass windows, and lavish decorations. The main hallway led to an expansive, open ballroom with a grand staircase, lined with the most eccentric of rugs. Banners hung from every corner bearing the eagle and three-headed snake. Statues and ancient weapons are strategically placed, highlighting the history of wars past with the barbarians.

I wore my finest clothes: a bright red silk tunic, with black cotton trousers. I wished to carry a weapon on my person, but there was no way to conceal it among all the elitists. My lady, 'Eve,' on this excursion dominated everyone with her mere wits and attractiveness.

We were amongst some of the more powerful individuals in Athren. Politicians, generals, judges, and businessmen. We gathered in the grand ballroom, waiting for who knows what. I still had no idea why I was summoned. I'm grateful that my lady joined me.

The Loyalists avoided me like the plague; I've probably made their lives hell with the lack of laws going in their favor. The highest-ranking Federalist politicians had my back, escorting us around and introducing us to all those they deemed essential.

Trumpets blared a high-pitched, brassy sound that echoed throughout the castle. All eyes and attention pivoted to the grand staircase. The King and Queen began their descent down the stairs. They were dressed in elaborate clothes, rich in color and material. The Queen's gown featured an intricate embroidery of jewels. Each of them wore crowns with gold trim.

Their steps slowed as they finally concluded at the bottom of the stairs. Everyone bowed, and I followed suit. The King, with his dark beaded face, began to clearly articulate, "Welcome to our home, we are so blessed to have each of you. Each of you is a vital part of our society, and we even have two duelers among us!" Everyone's eyes peered toward us. "Now let us go eat!" The King says this while directing with an open hand towards a pair of double doors.

Then, like a blur, a teenage boy came tearing down the stairs. When he reached his Mom, he grabbed her hand. Begging, "Let me join you for dinner."

The Queen looked towards the King for confirmation. The Queen nodded her head and said, "Stay by me." The boy couldn't be more than 15 years old.

When we entered the luxurious dining room, a round table stood before us that appeared to have been crafted from warm-toned mahogany wood. The silverware was authentic, and the glass plates and bowls were skillfully placed, in perfect patterns on the table. Names were written on our seats, and I found that 'Eve's' was next to mine. The conversations were not a bit interesting.

The room was full of the biggest bigots in all of Athren. Eliminating this room would set our country on a better path. I noted that many of the military leaders were discussing the gruesome, relentless war in the northwest against the radical barbarian savages. Based on the details they were divulging, I would never want to be a soldier stuck on the front lines.

The dinner went smoothly until the end. The King stood up, clanking his drink like he was planning to give a toast. I could see his son light up in joy as his dad was about to speak.

He spoke plainly, saying, "Gentry, you are wondering why I invited you here. All these men possess some form of power and authority. You now have that similar power. The way you've conquered all your foes in the ring across all of Athren has been quite an extraordinary feat."

The King took a deep breath and bellowed. "I need your help with another matter. The Barbarians on the northwestern border have been a growing issue."

I see a general nod in agreement. "By the will of Tyren, these two barbarian spies we killed just last week. They cried relentlessly, saying they knew you from your time in Eagle Valley. It's my understanding that's where you are from?"

The King gestured to the center of the round table, where a beautiful cloth lay, clearly covering the contents underneath. A rope dangling from the ceiling was connected to the fabric on the ground. A servant pulled a lever. The rope retracted in an abrupt and speedy motion to a pulley on the ceiling, taking the cloth with it and revealing what was hidden underneath.

The heads of my lifeless parents were positioned directly towards me. My parents are dead. I wasn't there. My emotions began to stir. Pure rage engulfed every ounce of my soul. A mixture of emotions started to torture me. Shock, numbness, profound sadness, anger, disbelief, and most of all, guilt. I couldn't react; I couldn't show emotion. 'Eve' grabbed my thigh so hard it brought me back to reality. There's nothing I can do about it now. My eyes met hers, and she could visibly see I was a wreck about to explode into pure violence. She doesn't know who they are to me, but she can read my emotions too easily.

The King's cruel voice filled the air, but all I heard was ringing. "We caught these two trying to escape from Athren. When we captured them, we suspected and confirmed that they were barbarian spies. They pleaded and begged, even stating that they knew you as if you were their offspring, Gentry. That was odd to hear, spies raised Gentry? Our greatest champion. Do you know them, son?"

Taking a deep breath, I avoid my decapitated parents. "No, sir, I don't know these traitors." My heart sinks deep, "Your Majesty, whatever lies they were saying, were out of survival. That didn't work out for them." I said this with my face clearly red, as sweat began to build on my forehead. My parents were barbarian spies?

Rage engulfs every fiber of my being. I stare at the Queen and her son. If only they knew that they were going to be without their wretched King in the near future. I will exact my revenge; I will bring down King Harper.

The King responds with a mocking tone, "Great, now that we've cleared that up, please tell me what your plans are here in Harpstedt?"

"To be honest, your majesty, to further the Federalist's agenda, make money, and finish out my contract. Hopefully, giving myself a chance at a life of peace." I said rather quickly, wanting this to end.

The dinner concluded, and I left to go back to the guild in a hurry. I will spare the reader the details of my insufferable pain and the mourning of my parents' deaths. I will do everything in my power to execute my revenge. The King is scared of my power; he is attempting to keep me in check.

Power left unchecked can bring out the vilest demons. The King isn't a demon; he is the devil. And I'm going to kill him.

I put the book down. Every time I pick it up to read, I'm left with an awful taste in my mouth. The King was a horrid, evil prick who deserved to die. I want to read more; Gentry's hatred towards the king corresponds with mine towards 'Rass-hole.'

216 | P a g e

Chapter Sixteen:

Veronica

I snap back to reality from the depths of my brain. I find that the sun has now completely gone down. Quickly, I put the book away. It's become more and more sacred to me. I scampered back across the field to my parents' home.

When I open the door, I'm greeted by Rupert saying, "Where have you been?"

"None of your business, bug off!" I say back, rubbing my tired eyes.

"Sorry, Mom had supper prepared and we were all waiting on you," Rupert says apologetically.

"Oh shoot, my fault. Let's eat!" The words exit my lips enthusiastically. I'm excited about my Mom's cooking!

Mom baked a perfect loaf of bread and cooked up a chicken with some carrots and potatoes. The food here will always trump that of the guild. Fresh food out of our very own garden makes any meal taste much better. It's a reward for all the challenging work; Mom always goes out of her way for us. She has to put more effort in than most, considering her right hand is practically disabled from an injury in her childhood.

Dad seems to be noticeably quiet and focused. Right on cue, Rupert breaks the silence. "There's going to be a duel in a week and a half. It's supposedly a big one. Remember the duel Niklas was going to fight the day before his execution?"

Dad looks up from his plate with visible interest. Rupert carries on, "Mr. Brookshard is looking at purchasing that land again, just north of Lyon. Amis, do you think Veronica has a legitimate chance against Trisha?"

I squeeze my lips together, raising one cheek, pondering. "Veronica is fast and excellent with the bow. I think if Trisha gets too close, it's game over for her." The words spilled off my lips.

Rupert speaks up again, "It should be a good fight then! Trisha is amazing with the bow, from what I've heard. She's also pretty ruthless in hand-to-hand combat."

Veronica could be in a world of trouble, given Nate's history of taking his opponents out entirely. Trisha could easily follow suit.

"I sent a letter with a pigeon to Nate, so he knows the exact day. The guild in the capital might give him leave to come." Rupert continues like it's his everyday conversation.

Sofia rants at the top of her lungs, "Rupert, you are so analytical. Can you, for once, not talk about dueling?! You wear those plain black judgmental robes all the time. You aren't a judge here. You're cut from the same cloth as us; you are no better. Amis and Nate could literally die. Why would you think…"

"Sofia, enough! Rupert has done nothing but protect your brothers!" Dad raises his voice, losing his temper.

Sofia storms out of the room. There was a rather awkward silence; Rupert was clearly taken aback by Sofia's robust and brutally honest comments.

I changed the subject drastically, "You know something odd I discovered in the Federalists guild? Charles Brookshard was once a duelist. Clearly, he made it through his contract."

Dad bobs his head up and his eyes narrow, "There's a lot of information that isn't common knowledge. Athren has a special ability to hide history."

"Well, what else has been hidden? The fact that we used to have a king." I say confidently, not scared of who hears.

I see my Mom's eyes widen as she says, "Yes, that's one quite different thing. We no longer have a monarchy."

"Or that there are barbarian spies among us?" I say skeptically.

Dad looks out the dark window longingly. Rupert is entirely silent as he has his hand on his reddish beard. I'm sure he is trying to hold his amazement together as he waits patiently for more outlandish statements.

I take the last bite of potato off my plate, cleaning it spotless. Dabbing my mouth with a napkin, I think to myself, 'A week in the guild and you'd think I'd have no more fear or self-restraint.' My mouth opens again, "Why do we duel anyway. It's barbaric and a form of entertainment. A way to make men heroes and more than just mere mortals."

All these words would be a capital offense if heard by the wrong party. However, speculation on government policies and procedures fosters the best kind of conversations.

Dad takes his eyes off the window and picks up a knife from the table. He begins spinning it, twisting all his fingers in a perfect sequence and harmony. The blade starts to blur with the tremendous speed his spin has gathered. Then he drops it suddenly when one of his fingers doesn't reach the proper positioning to propel the knife on another rotation.

Dad whispers; we all tune our ears to listen. "Dueling came to be because of people's distrust of others. No one was willing to elect an official based on a majority vote. People viewed politicians as being corruptible."

"And they aren't corruptible now?" Rupert interjects.

"I don't believe human nature at its core is inherently evil. If whoever is elected has a sound mind and a moral heart, they will present laws that we, the people, will be able to vote on. Not duel and die for. Hundreds of years ago, a king and his royal subjects would present duels to appease the people. They said dueling would show us what Tyren's will was." Dad says as he shifts in his chair.

"The citizens believed that crap back then?" I say in disbelief.

"They believed their leader then, just like they believe them now. Dueling isn't God's will; every life is precious in his eyes." Dad looks down at his knife. "We need the people of Athren to step up and work in unison. That I'm afraid is an impossible task."

"Dad, when will we get our revenge on Rasmussen?" I say a little too eagerly.

"Revenge? Something I've had to learn is patience. Evil men who commit wicked acts will always face judgment and justice." Dad says, looking directly into my eyes.

The night unfolds as we clean up dinner and put out all the candles, eliminating the glimmering light. Darkness spreads throughout the house. I lay on my uncomfortable mattress; I do not miss this.

Morning light shines. I wake up to Leo crowing in an annoying row of cock-a-doodle-doos. Damn, Leo is still alive; he is the bane of my existence. He has a red fleshy comb on his head and an abnormally large wattle below his bill. I end up assisting Sofia with the cleanup and feeding of the chicken coop. Praying that today is the day I get the courage to kill that chicken accidentally.

After a few other chores, I gather my things and prepare my horse to leave. Saying bye to everyone and reminding them that I will see them next weekend or at the next duel between Trisha and Veronica.

There's no place I'd rather be than next to Niklas under the apple tree, reading. Soon, I'll find out what happened to Gentry and his 'Eve.'

When I return to the guild, I prepare for a nice workout. Wearing a tight shirt cut off at the shoulders and some breathable workout pants, along with my leather shoes. I put leather bracers on my wrists and rewrapped my injured leg.

I do a routine workout that involves push-ups, sprints, and a variety of upper and lower body exercises. Today is the only day I have to train how I want.

After completing my extensive workout, I practiced throwing knives and hatchets in the gym. Throw after throw, with various positioning and routines.

A voice echoes off the walls out of nowhere as a knife misses the bullseye by a few inches. "Is that all you got?" Zander says, trying to provoke me.

"I'd like to see you try!" As I try to hand him a knife.

"I'm okay. We are all back now and in the mess hall. Care to join?" Zander asks.

"Sure…" I say drawn out skeptically.

I follow Zander inside and see Xavier and Veronica sitting on a couch. As I approach, I see Xavier fidgeting with his hands uncomfortably; his face is flushed, and he is avoiding eye contact with me at all costs. Were they talking mad shit about me or something?

My eyes meet Veronica's. She is sad and looks pretty uneasy. There's something she needs to get off her chest. Her mouth is open, but it seems like she can't articulate exactly how to speak. I sit down on a leather couch across from her, and she looks somewhat abashed.

"What's on your mind?" I prod her for some information as to why they are acting so strangely.

"Amis, I'm not sure how exactly to tell you this. I fell off my horse yesterday and broke my collarbone. I went to the nurse Carrie immediately after, and she told me that it would take six weeks to heal and to keep it in a sling for 2-3 weeks." Veronica says, gesturing to her right shoulder.

"Your clavicle? What does this mean?" I say in shock.

"You are our new champion, Amis," Xavier answers casually, unsure of how I will respond.

I squint my eyes; my head begins to buzz like a migraine is coming on. Maybe it's the fire going or the terrifying thought of actually having to duel. I'm going to have to face off against Trisha.

The room goes dark for me, and I know someone is speaking, but I can't make out their words. I immediately rush out of the mess hall, to the long hallway, up the spiral staircase, and into my bedroom. My head hits the silk pillowcase on my bed, and I close my eyes, trying to shut the world out. Nate will watch the duel. I have to talk to Trisha to set ground rules with her. We need to ensure that we don't harm each other. My anxious thoughts dissipate, and I enter a senseless unconscious state.

When I wake up the next morning, a headache ensues. Grabbing a quick breakfast, I hurry to the practice ring and await Instructor Kilroy. Again, I'm dressed in practice attire, ready for another physical day of training.

Veronica strolls in with her sling, looking very disheveled.

"Had to do your hair with one hand," I ask in judgment.

Veronica looks down and says, "It's hard to do anything in this state. Look, Amis, I'm sorry. I know you don't want to fight Trisha…"

I cut her off, "It's not your fault. I decided I'll need to stand up and face reality. I chose this party for a reason. I knew this was a possible outcome. I'm just glad it's not my brother."

"Ok, just know I'm here if you need to talk."

Xavier and Zander walk in together, breaking the ice completely. "You two are being extra happy. Xavier, is that a smile I see?!" I say before they ask me if I'm okay.

"Yes, I decided to smile today. I am second in line now. All I need to do is break your collarbone, and I'll be the guild's champion." Xavier motions like he's going to push me.

"Lord help us all if you are the one to represent us." Veronica teases.

Kilroy walks in with a hurried pace. He approaches the center of the room with a large wooden ball the size of Xavier's head. He throws it directly at Veronica with speed to see if she is really hurt. She eats the blow to her injured right arm.

Dropping to one knee, she yells, "What the hell!" She buckles in jarring pain for a moment, but to my surprise, she steadies herself relatively fast.

"I had to ensure you were actually defective. We don't take injuries with grace in the guilds and will execute anyone faking an injury." Kilroy continues.

"You could've just asked Carrie!" Veronica retorts.

"I don't trust anyone; I've been burned too many times. Veronica, you will be a servant to the guild until you are healed. During your downtime, you are expected to condition the parts of your body you can. You will have to compete again in a new ranking process to become champion. Last thing, your compensation will be withheld until you are physically fit and able. Understand?" Kilroy recites like he's said these words before.

"Yes, I understand, sir," Veronica responds respectfully.

No pay? Wild.

"You are dismissed." Kilroy orders.

Veronica hangs her head low, walking away. Xavier leans toward Zander and me. "I hate to see her go, but man, do I love watching her walk away."

Zander shakes his head in annoyance.

Kilroy continues, "For you three, we will need to rework our focus. Amis, in one week, you will duel the Loyalist, Trisha."

Kilroy continues, "We will start today's training by running to the Ash Reservoir's dock and doing various swimming and balance exercises."

"Lovely, more running," Xavier mumbles.

"Don't worry, Xavier, I'll bring the wagon, so you don't chafe your balls on the way back," Kilroy says, grinning.

"How thoughtful of you, sir!" Zander chuckles.

The next few hours are brutal from running and swimming. It felt as if Kilroy was trying to kill us slowly. The water is still frigid as we approach May, not that the guild would care what its temperature is. The sun's rays make it a little more bearable.

Our last training session was when Kilroy had me get on a barge fifty feet from shore. The very same barge on which Nate killed Addison with a trident. Kilroy gave me a wooden shield and a long sword.

Zander was on the shore to my left, Kilroy center, and Xavier to my right. In a rapid sequence, Kilroy called out right, center, and left, directing the release of blunt arrows in my direction. My job was to subsequently respond to his directions with my shield at the ready to defend my body mass. I had to stay standing. At least that's what Kilroy demanded.

It was treacherous and confusing. I was actively adjusting my weight to meet the swaying barge. Water would wash up on the surface, creating a slick hazard. When Kilroy would yell in a direction to shoot, it was the opposite for me. He would say right, and an arrow would be soaring towards me from the left. That alone took up almost all of my mental capacity.

With practice, I was able to form a stable base in the center of the platform. Oscillating slightly with each of Kilroy's commands. In the last round, Kilroy ordered a volley. Successive arrows were launched wildly in my direction. Eventually, it caused me to fall into the water.

Circular welts littered my body, with some even bleeding. If this is any indication of my duel against Trisha, I'm afraid to say that this is the end. I need to find her before the duel, before she's allowed to beat me or kill me.

The wagon ride home felt a little empty and dull without Veronica keeping Xavier in check. Zander reminded me that Veronica will be back before we know it, but not soon enough.

The week went much of the same. Mykel taught me some unique saber stances. Kilroy spent a lot of time trying to drill into my head the importance of exploiting an opponent's weakness and trusting my instincts.

On my own time, I spent much of it nursing my sore muscles and plotting a way to talk to Trisha without getting caught.

Chapter Seventeen:

Preparation

When Friday hits, nerves grip all my muscles. Monday can't come; God, please stop it from happening. Trisha and I can't duel.

I rolled out of bed to the feeling of my muscles tightening the instant my feet hit the ground. My legs know more abuse is coming. Taking the first couple of steps to my closet is always the roughest. My body is so strained and exhausted that for my first few steps, I waddle like a duck.

Damn, I need a girl in my life. Someone I can take care of, someone to take care of me. Just a distraction from this mundane life. I miss her, Mariam, from before she left for Harpstedt. She used to be so easy-going and fun. I can't be with her now, not after what she has become, a political pawn to Rass-hole.

If only the lovely girl from my dreams were real? It's a figment of my imagination. I can see her face perfectly in my mind: her long, perfect brown hair, her beautiful smile, and her eyes that light up my world. I'm getting carried away; there's no sense of being delusional. I could spend my weekends at some pub, picking up girls. That isn't me, I'm stuck wanting something long-lasting, not temporary. Rupert says I'm a hopeless romantic.

I casually walk out of my room to the hall. Today is my last practice before this asinine duel. Trisha must be nervous, too. I think to myself as I approach the stained-glass window overlooking the spiral staircase. Step by step, down the stairs, I feel my aching body crumbling under the weight of the pressure. My knees keep my legs moving, and my heart keeps my blood pumping. So here I am, still alive. I can't forget my purpose; I can't forget my reason why.

I walk into the mess hall and grab a piece of toast with apricot jam and a huge glass of orange juice. My eyes scan the room, hoping to see Veronica assisting in some capacity. She's never around. Bruce always seems to be lurking around.

"What do you have on your list of chores today, Bruce?" I ask politely.

Bruce's moans, surprisingly, his crackly voice responds, "Just the usual, that Xavier fellow keeps me busy enough. He is a disaster."

"Indeed, he is. Have you seen Veronica around by chance?" I ask, raising my eyebrows in the hope of any detail that could direct me to her.

"Oh yes, she's hard at work in the provincial building. Being a secretary. She's sorting all the documents for us, Federalists." He says as if it's common knowledge.

"That's good to know, thank you, sir. Have a good day, and I'll tell Xavier to grow up!" I rush out of the mess hall.

I enter the practice ring ready for my last day of long labor before my first duel. I see Kilroy talking to Zander and Xavier on the opposite side of the room. I tread their way, but out of the corner of my eye, a large man snags my attention.

"Young Mr. Hastings, I need to talk to you about a pressing issue." Mr. Brookshard growls for everyone in the gym to hear. As he proceeds in my direction, I notice his belly sticking out; it is hard to believe that this man has ever been a duelist. He always has a cigar in his mouth, smoking or not, it's there. His eyeglasses dangle from his suit coat. I doubt he ever needs reading; he probably has a servant read for him. Arrogant, pompous, asshat. I'm surprised a girl would stoop down to his level to bear him a child.

"Good morning, sir, what do I owe the pleasure?" I say it in a slightly sarcastic way.

Mr. Brookshard stepped so close to me that I could smell his boiled egg from this morning's breakfast. He speaks out of the corner of his mouth. "Amis, this Monday, you are fighting for a law that will greatly impact me and my fortune. I aim to purchase a substantial portion of Athren land and cultivate it for the benefit of the people. If you win this duel, you will be a catalyst in helping fight starvation for the impoverished citizens in Lyon and all of Athren." He takes a deep, wheezy breath before continuing.

"The duel Nathan won, when he killed that boy on the Ash reservoir, greatly affected me. We needed more water to flow downstream for my potential plantation. I will have to adapt as always." Mr. Brookshard sighs.

No pressure to win or anything. I pause for a moment, tactically thinking about all the terrible things I want to say.

Then the words slip out, "The purchasing of that land. Isn't that the same duel you were hoping Niklas would purposely lose for?" I glanced at my surroundings, making sure no one else heard.

"Yes, you are correct. Niklas may have been a Loyalist on paper, but he was a Federalist at heart. The events that unfolded on the day of my daughter's death were so terrible. My heart shattered into a million pieces when I heard about Heather's murder. It shattered even more when Heather's lover, Niklas, was executed." Brookshard's voice and body language look genuine.

"You don't believe Niklas killed Heather?" I pose the baffling question.

Brookshard sighs loudly, "No, I don't think he did. He loved her too much."

My eyes widened with confusion, remembering the day of Niklas' execution; how he stood on his balcony overlooking the events. I can't trust him. The information about who killed Heather and who framed Niklas is too valuable to throw around aimlessly.

"Sir, with all respect, the day of Niklas' execution. You yelled at my father in front of all of Lyon, as Niklas was about to be executed. You told my father to 'stop this madness.' Did you not?" I pose the question, as if he is snared in a trap.

"I did tell him to stop. He could have started an uprising all by himself if I hadn't. Your father is worth more to Athren alive than dead. Niklas knew this, too."

I'm left dumbfounded, with a complete loss for words. Niklas shook his head, telling my Dad to stop too. Mr. Brookshard may be telling the truth. All I can do is shake Mr. Brookshard's hand and say, "Thank you."

I walk past Mr. Brookshard, brushing his shoulder, to my guildmates and Kilroy. Maybe that bigot Charles Brookshard isn't so evil after all.

Training was much lighter today. Kilroy wanted to ensure I was fully healed and functioning by Monday. I spent the rest of Friday and Saturday by myself. I need to get my mind entirely right. I went through routine workouts and scenarios. I was able to practice with a variety of weapons, even the bow. They haven't given me any clues when it comes to the duel details.

Our Politicians, Janice, Tarron, and Isaac, could still be in the negotiating phase with the Loyalists. Many times, duelists do not know what challenge they'll face until they arrive.

Sunday came, and I felt healthy and stronger. I decided to head home for a few hours to check on my parents. If I die, I'd hate not to at least see them again before my impending doom.

I grabbed one of the guild's horses and saddled it up. It's a strong, brown, sturdy horse with clear muscles. It definitely would be the horse I'd choose if I were jousting tomorrow. Casually, I ride to my parents' home. Passing the old librarian, Mrs. Cunningham. I do my best to blend in with my surroundings. The last thing I need is her chasing me down for an illegal book that I haven't finished yet. The horse's hooves beating the cobblestone road provide a steady noise for me to focus on, so I don't get lost in terrible, deep thought again.

The streets are littered with people. If I can win this duel tomorrow, I can change the projection for many of these poor peasants. It's not always their fault that they are stuck in poverty; in some cases, it is self-inflicted. Most of the time, oppressive societies and a lack of opportunities are the primary culprits. I don't know many of these citizens properly. I believe that, no matter how grim a situation may be, we can rise above it. All you need is the faith and will to do so. You'll never get anywhere if you don't at least make an effort.

I have the opportunity as a dueler to give back to these people, to be their voice. My perspective on dueling has changed by a minuscule amount. I want to give the average everyday person their voice back, let them choose what they want. Just like Niklas, Dad, Gentry, and Mykel want.

As I reach the outskirts of Lyon, the noise of the town fades. Wind high up can be heard whisking through the trees. Flowers have bloomed in an assortment of distinct colors. Looking west, I see an open field leading down to the reservoir with a grove of trees along the way. To the East, I see my parents' farm, and the high-rising Oquirrh peaks towering above.

On the farm, I see a group of people gathering outside. As I approach more, my eyes focus, and I see clear, distinct features of individuals I know. Nate. He made the journey back home to watch us fight. Surely when he left Harpstedt, he had no clue it was going to be me dueling Trisha.

"There he is! How come you didn't come yester-day?" Rupert asks.

"I needed time to recuperate after all the manhan-dling they've been putting me through," I respond, walking my stead right up to him.

I dismount, clasping hands with Rupert and hug-ging him, and greeting everyone else along the way. Reaching Nate, we stare long and hard at each other. There's tension between us.

I smile, "Did you hear?"

He pauses for a second, reading my face, "About what? The bear, or you having to duel my fiancé."

"You guys are engaged?! Nate, I get you have to cheer her on." I say, putting my hand on his shoulder.

"Of course I'm rooting for her. You're the dum-bass who joined the opposite guild!" Nate scowls, try-ing to make me feel some guilt.

"He has his reason; maybe if you didn't abandon us in the night, you would know what those are." Sofia comes to my defense while folding her arms. My little sister always advocates for me.

I smile widely, "It's okay, Sofia. Nate, I do need to talk to you."

Nate shakes his head in disbelief. He looks bigger and stronger than ever. He can't conceal his muscles under any of the clothes he wears. It's okay, Dad is a giant, and I'm still taller.

"Whatever you have to say, you can say it in front of everyone." Nate scoffs.

"Fine." I'm beginning to lose my patience with his moody ass. I shift my weight and continue, "You need to relay to Trisha, no life-threatening blows. The last thing I want is for some stupid duel to fracture our relationship."

Nathan's mouth drops, and his face becomes flushed. "Are you stupid or something! You better not kill my fiancé. If you do, I'll terminate you."

My eyes narrow, bawling my fists and preparing to strike this arrogant jerk. I step towards Nate, waiting for him to react. Next thing I know, I'm stumbling backwards, about to fall over.

Dad jumps between us, pushing us away. "There's something that Amis found out about the Loyalists. They may have been behind Heather and Niklas' deaths." His strong voice states it, but spares the significant detail of it being Rasmussen.

Nate walks away, screaming, "I'm so sick of this conspiratorial nut job of a family!" He hops on his horse and rides away.

"He will come around; give him time," Mom says, embracing me with a hug I didn't know I needed.

"We will all be there to support you tomorrow," Dad says.

"Rupert, do you know what tomorrow will entail?" I ask, begging for a hint.

"The only thing I've heard is that it will be tomorrow at the field." Rupert sighs with his head down. "I'm sorry, I wish I had learned more. They have been very secretive lately. They are expecting a big audience tomorrow."

I nodded, "Great... I'd better leave soon. Sofia, can I talk to you for a bit?"

I pulled her away. "I haven't finished that book yet, but if I die, I need you to read it and return it to Mrs. Cunningham," I say with a twinkle in my eye.

She nods, hugs me, and says, "Whose morbid now? You aren't going to die tomorrow! I'll kill that hoe bag engaged to Nate if I have to. She and the Loyalists have soured Nate against us."

"Sofia, please don't intervene." I laugh, never knowing when she's serious. "She has become another sister to us after all these years. I think she will ground Nate and help him see the errors in his ways." I say sighing.

"Okay! Amis, if you want to beat Trisha tomorrow, get close to her. Use your weight and strength to your advantage." Sofia stammers on.

"I will, thanks, coach!" I chortle sarcastically.

I say my goodbyes to everyone and turn away from the farm I love.

Chapter Eighteen:

Trisha

I'm drenched in sweat. The anxiety and stress of today's events are growing. I swivel out of bed and put my feet on the hard, cold floor. I go to the washroom and soak, relaxing all my muscles in a warm bath. I asked Bruce so kindly last night to prepare it for me this morning. I've been so focused on the previous few days that I've shut Zander and Xavier out completely. The last thing I need is Xavier's shenanigans distracting me.

When I get out of the bath, I dry every inch of my body. I decided not to wear any heavy armor today. Instead, I have leather pants, a cotton shirt, and a black leather vest, an elaborate red belt, leather bracers on my wrists, and a bandanna around my head.

I walk downstairs into the circular foyer and wait in a chair up against the wall. I visualize what today will be like at the field. For all I know, we are going to be jousting.

A collective group of footsteps approaches from the hall. Individuals emerge one by one. Janice, Tarron, Isaac, Zander, Xavier, and even Veronica.

I stand up, bowing my head in their direction, asking, "Where's Kilroy?"

Tarron's wretched voice answers, "He's grabbing the wagon now."

Xavier opens his mouth, "You're all kitted up, aren't you?"

"Don't bother him, can't you shut up for once in your life!" Veronica scolds Xavier. He cowers backward.

There's definitely been a void with her gone. I only shake my head, not allowing any nonsense to preoccupy me. My stomach is tightening, and I'm having a tough time moving. I need a release! I'm nothing more than a farmer's son. These people surrounding me put the weight of the Federalist upon my shoulders. I am not my brother's; my arms aren't as big, my skills aren't as enhanced. I know this, I've trained with them all my life. Disappointment will be etched on their faces by the end of the day.

Then the doors of the guild open with force, slamming against the walls. Mykel's here. Walking over to me, he slaps me in the face and yells. "Wake up. You will not die today!" His eyes are glued to mine. He winks, shifting his head to everyone in the room. "Stop surrounding him, you wankers!"

Pushing Mykel as hard as possible, I demonstrate my brawn and backbone, making him stagger away. My anxieties cease for a brief moment. I rotate my neck side to side and shrug my shoulders back, loosening up my muscles.

I stalk out of the double doors of the guild on a mission. Kilroy has the wagon at the ready. The politicians, Mykel, Kilroy, and I all load up. Xavier went to step up in the back, but his ride was short-lived.

"You are not our champion. Enjoy your walk to the field." Janice booms at him.

Veronica and Zander laugh a little too hard.

Once we arrived at the field, Kilroy and Mykel walked me straight to the field. A majority of the town is here, packed together butt to gut. I saw a desk set up for wagering, market carts for concessions, and even guild merchandise. What has this event turned into?

When I walked out onto the field, wooden stands lined one side all the way down. In the center was a raised platform for the Judge, Rupert, and all the politicians to stand. Kilroy walked me to that platform and looked me over once more.

Hugging me, he whispers in my ear, "I believe in you, stick to your instincts, and use your skills."

All I can do is nod my head. Trisha has arrived, followed by Nate and an instructor of her own. She looks stronger and has similar attire to mine. Her hair is down, flowing free, and her facial expression exudes confidence.

Rass-hole walks onto the field. I can feel his despicable presence anytime he's nearby. The hairs on my neck stand up, and I have to do everything in my power not to attack him. He pulls Trisha off to the side. He's telling her a critical piece of information.

"Amis! Amis!" Someone is calling my name from the stands. It's Sofia! My heart leaps as I see her, Mom, and Dad. Scanning the crowd, I find my fellow duelers and Mykel. 'Please don't embarrass yourself,' I think.

Rupert, above me on the platform, talks down to me. "Amis, are you in compliance with the rules and regulations of dueling? There are no hidden weapons on your person, and no tampering has occurred?"

I roar back up to him for the politicians to hear. "I comply!"

Rupert goes on to ask the same questions of Trisha.

As my eyes are fixed on the platform above me, I see Mariam. She's here?! Ugh, why! Rasmussen emerges again on the platform, standing next to her. Sickness builds within my stomach. Is this a ploy to get into my head?

Rupert's voice projects loudly so all can hear.

"In the Province of Murcia, this duel will end when the first person yields, or if death is the outcome, so be it."

In the name of Tyren,
The Province of Murcia hereby declares this,
The duel of Charles Brookshard's
Proposal to purchase 1,000 acres from Athren,
Trisha Atheby of Lyon,
Representing the Loyalists
against Brookshard's purchase
Vs.
Amis Hastings of Lyon,
Representing the Federalists
in favor of Brookshard's purchase.

"Each of you may go to your respective sides of the field," Rupert says quietly, just to us.

I make eye contact with Trisha; her confidence is gone. Something changed in her eyes. Walking in the grassy field, I feel the blistering sun beating down upon me. Looking out at the stands, I see my family sitting together. Nate is with the Loyalists, which isn't surprising. Mariam stands next to Rasmussen on the platform above, with Rupert and Tarron.

Trisha makes it to the opposite side of the field from me. She has to be at least 150 feet away.

I'm glad I wore this light vest; it'll make a world of difference in trying to close the distance between me and Trisha. Stepping up onto the wooden platform, I see to my left a bow and arrows. On my right, there's a shield and a dagger. It's like they know my weakness is accuracy with a bow!

Rupert holds his whistle steady in his hand. I look at Mom and Dad's faces. Dad looks composed and confident, while Mom is a nervous wreck, squirming in her seat. There's no judgment from me on this one.

My legs are jittery, and my hands shake wildly. It's Trisha, I tell myself. We have known each other for years, and she is in love with Nate; they are perfect for each other. There's no way this will end in death; it will just be a nice, clean knockout. I can't lose; it would be so embarrassing. Sofia would never let me live it down.

I breathe sincerely, trying to shake this gut-wrenching feeling in my stomach. Be calm, trust your instincts, and show mercy.

Rupert puts the whistle in his mouth. Time stops, I'm stuck in this position, unable to overcome the nerves that are stiffening more and more within my joints. Then I make eye contact with Trisha; she's clearly emotional, visibly upset, and dealing with the same nerves.

The whistle squeals. I see Trisha bolt for her bow and arrows. She quickly puts the quivers around her shoulder. Nocking an arrow and preparing to let it loose. Oh, is she serious? We are far enough away that she could easily miss and kill me.

I quickly rush to the dagger and the round wooden shield. I hear the crowd roar; she's definitely released an arrow. I squat low, picking up the shield to cover all my body, just like I practiced on the barge. The arrow lands a foot to my right.

I began to rush forward at full speed, keeping the shield above my head and torso. I need to protect the kill shots. Air whooshes by my right ear. It feels like she's trying to kill me. They aren't blunt arrows!

Everything turns to a blur, my blood begins to flow with intense speed through my veins, making me very aware of my elevated heart rate. Another arrow is propelled forward at a fierce speed, causing a sharp whistling sound. It penetrates my wooden shield with a loud bang! The arrow breached through the wood of the shield, splintering it. My eyes focus in terror at the arrowhead sticking through. I quickly peer over the shield to catch a glimpse of how close I am to her. Only sixty feet away now.

Trisha releases another arrow. It screams by. This has to be intentional; I thought we'd have a clear understanding. Injury, disable, or even paralyze. Not eliminate or kill! She's practically my sister. No one will die today; there has to be a way to prevent this. I think to myself in confusion. I continue to run.

Only thirty more feet to go. In pure rage, I shout, "Trisha! Are you going to kill me? Is that what you want?"

There's complete silence. I keep walking, more cautiously now. There's no other arrow for what feels like ten seconds. I don't dare peek around the shield, I can't. Looking to my left, I see the stands. My Mom's hand is over her mouth. Shit, shit, shit.

The silence quickly fades. A twang can be heard vibrating from Trisha's bowstring. Suddenly, I experience a piercing pain followed by a searing sensation shooting up my left calf muscle, as the arrow penetrates my flesh. I stumble and roll. There's no time to register the pain.

Miraculously, I end up on one knee. Trisha preps another arrow as she tries to hitch it to her bow string. In a swift motion, I grip my shield on the side with my thumb on top and fingers beneath. I whip my arm, snapping my wrist, saucering the shield at Trisha and hitting her.

It doesn't seem to inflict the pain I was hoping for. She is stunned, faltering onto her back foot, dropping her bow altogether. For a second, as she tries to gather herself, I move as fast as my leg will now allow, closing the distance to a few feet. I lunge-tackle Trisha hard to the ground, my dagger still in hand.

With my 220 pounds of weight on top of her, I physically control her on the ground. Putting my dagger down next to me, I try my best to wrestle her to submission with just my hands.

"This is over!" I sternly demand with my knee on her stomach and my hand on her shoulders, holding her in place.

Her eyes reached mine. She begins to cry. "Amis, I'm sorry. He said one of us has to die or they'll kill Nate." She whispers.

"That's not true! I'm not going to kill you!" Frustrated and confused, I shake her shoulders rapidly. "Trisha, I can't kill you!"

She sobs as tears well in her eyes. I can tell it's hard for her to breathe. "Amis, I'm sorry. He said it's the only way." She closes her tear-stained eyes.

With her eyes closed, she takes a deep breath of courage. Raising her right arm swiftly, jolting it forward, she skins my neck slightly with an arrowhead. Pulling her arm back swiftly, she tries stabbing me again. I retreated from her. Then, she slams the arrow into my right shoulder. With her other hand, she snaps the arrow stuck in my left leg. I scream, flailing completely backwards. She jumps on top of me, trying to beat my head in with her mere fist.

My left hand searches the ground in desperation; I'm alone again on the floor of the dark cave. Punch after punch, my face begins to drain blood. My left-hand searches again in the dark abyss when I feel the hilt of my dagger. Securing the dagger, I stab with one forceful blow into Trisha's lower back, near her kidneys. I push her off me. She begins breathing deeply, convulsing in pain. The tips of her blonde hair soak in her blood. It was a vital blow.

Her voice is shaky in realization. "Am I going to die? Am I going to die? I'm sorry…." Screams pierce my ears, and tears fill my eyes. My hands try to comfort her now, but this can't be real.

Trisha's breath is fading as her sweet voice says, "I need my Nate now…. I'm not ready to leave. I didn't want to… Nate... I, I, need my Nate." Her eyes blink slowly and heavily. With her last gasp, a whisper trembles slowly, "Rass…" Her voice fades in a soft exhale.

I killed her. My brother's love. I hugged her body, weeping. "Noo! Noo!"

Footsteps trample towards me. Nate picks me up off the ground and aggressively shoves me away.

He jumps onto her body. Holding her head and brushing her soaked hair, he moans. "My love. You're going to be okay. I'll protect you; I'll save you. I've got you, and I will never let you go." Tears build up in his eyes and start to ripple down his face.

Dad and Mykel scoop me up off the ground, carrying me away. "Dad, I never wanted to kill her. I wanted to show mercy like Gentry did." Tears stream relentlessly.

My Dad, with a courageous smile, says, "You tried your best to show mercy, you made me proud."

I'm fading to black. I see Mariam weeping, shaking her head in disbelief, and next to her, the man I hate with my whole soul. Rasmussen.

254 | Page

Chapter Nineteen:

Pain

Confused and disoriented, I spent the next few days in and out of sleep. Carrie came to check on me a few times. She loaded me up with herbs and ointments. She's worried that the laceration on my shoulder may get infected.

Opening my weary eyes, my head still pounds with immense pressure. I try to gain awareness of my environment. My eyes are having a terrible time adjusting. I'm lucky to have retained my eyesight; Trisha nearly beat my skull in.

Mom is with me now. I turn onto my right shoulder. I forget the hole in my shoulder, as immense pain shoots throughout my body. Trisha really shattered my body. I quickly lay flat on my back again and speak slowly, wincing between every word.

"Mom, is Nate okay? I should've let Trisha kill me."

"Amis, what's done is done. There's no reason to self-loathe; move forward." Mom comes in and hugs me. "Don't worry about Nate. Someday, he will heal and forgive. We all saw that you did it out of self-defense; you had every chance to kill her before that. You didn't; you were trying to show her mercy. We love you, son."

"Mom, where's Nate now? I need to tell him something. He is not safe!" I say in a panicked tone.

"He went back to Harpstedt. Mariam is aiding him."

My body convulses in rage and frustration. Heat rushes to my face, and the somber realization creeps into my mind. Nate, I can't protect him, I can't save him. He's in the hands of the murdering feen Rasshole. Nate is an ignorant idiot, Mariam is just as naïve, and I am powerless.

"I need you to get everyone. Can you arrange a family meeting?" I demand like an incapable toddler.

Managing to sit up straight, I need to start moving. Sofia's eyes lit up when she laid eyes on my mangled body.

"How bad do I look?" I ask her

Her response was, well, exactly what I expected. "Your face is so battered and bruised up, I don't think any girl would want to be with you any time soon. They wouldn't want to look at your swollen ugliness. Even if they did, they'd never be able to kiss you, out of fear of the bruising popping and spreading like some disease."

The only response to that is pursed lips and silence. If you give Sofi an inch, she'll take it a mile.

Once everyone was huddled in the little room, I told them why I didn't knock her out on the field when I was directly on top of her. She was saying such puzzling things until right before her final word. Trisha uttered that nasty villain's name, "Rass."

Rupert's quick response lets me know he believes me. "That explains a lot. Right before the match, I saw Rasmussen walk onto the field and speak to Trisha. Immediately after, her complexion changed... Dad, Nate isn't safe. We need to do something. We can't protect him!"

"There's only so much we can do from here. I have some friends in the capital. I will try to send them some correspondence by pigeon. Hopefully, they can decipher it and not get caught." Dad says with clear uncertainty.

"Niklas was too powerful and too unpredictable for the Loyalists. Nate is just as good a warrior, but he is easier to manipulate, especially now, given his vulnerable state." I say, looking down at my hands.

"When does the guild need me back?" I ask.

"Not any time soon. Amis, you need to continue to rest. None of these problems can be solved right now." Dad says as he gets up and squeezes my left shoulder. "Relax, son, you're safe now." Everyone shuffled out of the room.

A day passes, and nothing has changed physically for me. Rupert made me makeshift crutches, so I can at least hobble through the house in a decent fashion. The arrow went completely through my calf muscle. Trisha was close enough to me at the time for it to penetrate almost all the way through. Sofia told me it was halfway out when Trisha snapped it out of my leg.

I've been trying to help around the house so I'm not too much of a burden on them. Mom already has enough on her hands. Tomorrow I will journey to the apple tree and finish the book.

Sofia helps me get out onto the porch in a rocking chair. I don't think I actually needed her help; I need to milk her kindness while I can. Taking a small knife in my hand, I whittle a stick.

The dogs bark, destroying a perfectly peaceful afternoon. That usually means there's a visitor or another pack of wolves...

My duel-mates walk down the dirt road. I can see Xavier's face light up when he sees me rocking in the chair. His smile is infectious and radiates to me.

The moment they get on the porch, I try my best to stand up and give them all hugs. Zander practically shoves me down, smiling, "There's no need to stand for us, we are nothing special."

"So did Carrie tell you if your handsome face will return to normal, or will you look like a dumb dog forever?" Xavier asked, trying to be funny.

"Wait till you have to duel, champion!" I respond, assuming Kilroy made Xavier our new leader.

"You know, the bosses at the guild haven't said much to us on that front. They've been preoccupied, even letting us have the day off today. I know Kilroy was impressed by your performance, but he was disappointed you showed mercy and almost got killed for it." Zander rambles in a monotone as he leans up against the porch railing.

Suddenly, Zander jumps out of his skin, howling, "What the hell, ahh my bum!" He moves to the side, revealing Sofia holding a broomstick that's poking through a wooden slate in the railing.

Sofia must've heard him from inside. She giggles helplessly, "Don't get too comfortable, Zander, I know where you sleep!" She runs away giggling.

Veronica and Xavier roll in laughter, unsure exactly what just happened.

"Your sister is demented, you know," Zander says, moving back to the wall of the house near me for protection.

"She is, and she really adores you. Terrible combination if you ask me." I say, grinning widely.

"On a more serious note, the town went berserk after the duel. Many people won money gambling, and as a result, they chanted your name in excitement. 'Champion, Champion!' While others protested altogether, declaring it was unnecessary. Citizens supported the duel as entertainment or as an essential means of justice. Others denounced it, calling it immoral and criticizing the politicians for letting it occur." Xavier says.

"You should not have been expected to kill Trisha," Veronica adds, almost so quietly it's a whisper.

"I wasn't planning on ever fighting her, nor killing her. I thought we had an understanding. That is until..." I spent the next few minutes explaining exactly what Trisha had told me. Also, I believe Rasmussen has been the mastermind behind all the recent deaths in my life.

Zander did not seem surprised. "Remember what Harry and I told you at the dock! Your story backs it up."

Validating his feelings, I tell Zander that he and Harry were "Vital in unraveling the puzzle." Which is true, to some degree.

We spent the next bit talking and conspiring about what Rass-holes' motive is. I also had to lay down the law and emphasize the seriousness of what we're discussing.

I had to spare some of the details, such as the book. That is a secret known only to Sofia.

I noticed Veronica had grown increasingly quieter and less involved. She had been different since breaking her collarbone.

"Everything okay?" I ask with a concerned look.

Her eyes well up as tears streak down her face. "Since you entrusted us with your secrets, I feel like I have to tell you mine."

She began breathing heavily, unable to get the words out. Xavier rushes over and hugs her, wiping the tears from her red cheeks.

Continuing, she stammers, "I purposely broke my collarbone. I knew it was the only way I could get out of dueling Trisha. I had an anxiety attack... I didn't want to die."

The silence is deafening; I'm at a complete loss for words. Zander looks at me out of fear of what I'll do. My body is so broken because of Trish; I can't even raise a fist if I want to.

I hobbled the few steps to where Veronica is sobbing.

She speaks softly again, "It's my fault you almost died, it's my fault you... You killed..."

I grab her and squeeze tight. Her eyes reached mine. "Veronica, that's a very cowardly thing to do. I could turn you into the guild. I won't, if you keep my secret. I forgive you." I say clearly, so she hears every word, and I hug her. I know our friendship will never be the same. I can never trust a slug like her again.

Xavier and Zander join in. Xavier laughs, expressing, "My injured friends have made up."

His hug causes so much discomfort in Veronica and me that we scream. "That's it, I'm going to rip your buck teeth out while you sleep! Xavier, you hairy beaver!" Veronica shrieks.

"This is why we can't have nice things! Xavier, let go." Zander clamors.

"Do you act childish on purpose, or is it something you can't control?" I smile so hard, my eyes squint.

"To be honest, life is much easier if you're light-hearted." Xavier articulates the words as if he were a philosopher.

The day continues as expected. I offered my friends dinner, but they insisted that they needed to get back. I told them that I hope to be back in the guild next week, of course, I'm not ready to train again.

264 | Page

Chapter Twenty:

Gentry

When the sun rose above the mountains, its rays began to spread their warmth across the dew-laced fields. I decided to make a trek to the apple tree and read the remainder of the book Niklas left for me. The walk felt twice as long as I hobbled with the makeshift crutch under my armpit. Today is about productivity.

I feel stronger; my shoulder is regaining some rotation. There is, of course, a nagging pain that will reside with me for a long time. I pray it dulls after a while.

I push the stone off the tomb for my book. Every time I pick it up, I examine all the edges and pages to ensure it hasn't deteriorated further in its harsh environment.

I open to the page where I last left off and take a long look out across the beautiful farm field. Holy Harwen, my parents' property truly is majestic. The sun's rays provide an array of diverse colors that glisten naturally. The sweet smell permeates the air, creating a lovely aroma. It's a perfect setting to read:

Weeks rolled by, and I still have not been called up to fight in the capital's arena. The King himself called me the dueling champion of Athren, right around the same time he revealed the leftover contents of my parents. What a maniacal, twisted, perverted person. How could he execute such an atrocious thing?

I will get my revenge, I will eliminate the head of the snake, the King. The citizens deserve to be empowered and to have a voice of their own. Not the voice of a sword.

This limbo of constant training but not fighting has been driving me insane. I'm not a hundred percent sure the King will ever allow me to fight, out of fear, I'll become more powerful than him. Not dueling has allowed me to cultivate and grow closer to 'Eve.'

My relationship with her has blossomed into beauty I never thought possible. From the moment I met her, I was completely enamored. Our attraction was anything but gradual. The ability we had to communicate and listen to each other demonstrates our advanced emotional connection.

Then the guild informed 'Eve' that she was being called up to fight, and my heart sank. It should be me representing the Federalists. My instructor told me that the decision came from the King. The King was influencing our laws. Our Federalists guild sees it, and I know the Loyalists experience the same jaded decisions.

If duels dictated our society's laws, there should be zero influence from any outside source. The King swaying a fight and deciding on the guild's champions proves there was no purpose for dueling at all. It's just entertainment. I must eliminate the King.

My 'Eve' was being forced to duel. She was prepared to the best of her abilities; her speed and quickness match anybody's. She was self-reliant, unafraid of any challenge, and her heart was full of ambition. There was hope for her.

The King was trying to punish me. There was no way he was going to give her a fair fight. The day of her duel, she was separated from me and left to prepare on her own.

The expansive size of the arena was an awe-inspiring sight to behold. White sand was scattered across the surface. The circular walls were matte black, with sharp spikes protruding everywhere, and there were two gate entrances on opposite sides of each other. Towers rose high above, and the stands all around provided an ample opportunity to witness brutality. The far side of the ring was the King's platform, where he and the politicians overlooked the proceedings. The castle towered high above the platform. Just a block away and right next to the King's palace was the Gulf of Athren.

I developed a plan, but the execution thereof had to be precise, with each component working in harmony. I found a position close to the railing of the ring opposite the King's platform. A place I had picked out far in advance. I arrived extremely early, waiting endlessly for the citizens to come. I concealed my body completely, wearing an oversized wool coat and leather shoes laced incredibly tight. The weather conditions were clear, and not even a breeze was felt.

The arena was alive with activity as citizens gathered to witness the duel. The event was pure hysteria; the stands were packed to the brim, butt to gut. People's faces could even be seen in the windows of the tower. Spectators corralled me, but I maintained my space, so I wasn't stuck shoulder to shoulder.

On the left side of the arena, 'Eve' arose from the depths of the dark gates, which quickly closed behind her. She appeared to be in good health. She had her long hair up in a braid, a white cotton shirt as an underlayer, black form-fitted pants, a black breastplate, and leather boots. She was well-equipped, carrying a sword and two daggers on her hips.

'Eve' walked out to the middle of the arena, surveying the robust crowd. There's no way she would find me. I watched as her eyes moved to the Loyalist's dark gate. A giant of a man emerged. He was roughly 6'8" in height, dark build, bald with a bone in his nose, and a necklace of human teeth dangled on his chest. He

wore only a leather girdle, a skirt, boots, and bracers on his wrists. He was large in stature, with an enormous muscular build.

Looking upon 'Eve,' I did not see her falter or experience any doubt. Both 'Eve' and the 'giant' looked up above them, thirty feet. The politicians, a judge, the King, and his teenage son were all standing on the edge of the balcony railing.

Eighty yards was the length of the ring; 'Eve' was forty yards away if I broke down and intervened. That's a long way.

I heard the judge belt out the typical sequences of words.

Citizens of Athren, welcome to a duel of death.

I tuned the words out altogether, putting my full focus on the duelers. Suddenly. 'Eve' changed her fighting stance. With her sword drawn, her left foot pointed at the 'giant,' her right foot at 90 degrees, and both her hands on her sword.

The sound of a whistle reverberated off the walls of the arena. A mace swung violently towards 'Eve.' The 'giant' missed by mere inches. The crowd grew loud, booing. Everyone realized this could be short-lived.

I will not let her die; there's no point in living without her. Another swing of the mace, her quickness is too fast; she parried away as she rolled. The mammoth of a creature uses all his muscles and waves the *mace again, lower and forcefully. 'Eve' easily jumps over the low swinging mace and quickly plunges her sword deep into the monster's belly.*

A hush falls over the spectators, who are all stuck in absolute awe. With her hands still on the hilt of the sword stuck in the man's body, she yanked it back, trying to extract it. It doesn't budge. The 'Giant's' hands clasped around hers, squeezing hard on her hands. The beast gritted his teeth and growled.

'Eve' kicks the 'giant' in the shin, but he does not budge. He continued to add pressure on her hands around the hilt. Pop, go her knuckles. Then he swung his head forward, right into 'Eve's' eyebrow. Blood began to drip down her face in red streaks.

He continued to squeeze her hands so hard that crackling could be heard by 'Eve.' Luckily, it was her non-dominant right hand breaking into pieces. She raised her leg again and kicked with more intensity, hitting him square in the groin. He released her hands and roared in frustration. Grabbing the hilt of the sword in his stomach, he ripped it out in one fluid motion. 'Eve' retreated backwards, pulling the dagger sheathed to her. Blood puddles formed on the white sandy ground around them.

This has gone far enough. I dropped my coat, revealing a bow and arrow. The crowd, being enamored by the events on the field, gave me the perfect chance to strike. Quickly nocking the arrow in my bowstring,

I rose and aimed. I took a deep breath for half a second, then loosed the arrow, sending it spiraling towards the onlooking King.

Roughly eighty yards separated me from my target. No one in the arena seemed to notice my actions. A second later, the high-velocity arrow smashed into the chest of the King, puncturing his foul heart. The King faltered forward, falling off the side of the platform, into the dirt below.

The teenage son now looked down upon his lifeless father's body.

Hysteria ensued, spreading like a disease through the stands. After the shot was confirmed, I put the bow on the ground and covered it with my coat. Someone around me has to have noticed my actions now.

On the field, the 'Giant' and 'Eve' are so locked in on their duel that they don't seem to notice the riot forming around them. The beast hunted her like a predator stalking its prey. He follows every movement of hers with perfect synchronization. Finally getting close enough, he's able to swing the bloody sword with fierceness and malice, in the hopes of finally ending her. 'Eve' raised her dagger to meet the sword. When the two metals met, the dagger shattered, dispersing the shrapnel of projectiles everywhere.

For a moment, it seemed that all hope was lost and 'Eve' was another victim of a sadistic duel. The 'Giant' raised his sword once more and swung it down with full force. 'Eve' shot her hands out in a natural reaction of self-defense.

From her perspective, the sword was almost to her. Then, the unexpected happened, as the 'giant's arm was severed, flying away, and his sword clung to the ground.

The beast jerked rigorously, holding his chopped, blood-squirting arm, bellowing in cries.

I pushed him to his knees. "Go back to hell." I sliced his Achilles tendon on one leg. Letting him bleed out from his wounds or live with the pain always to remember.

Grabbing 'Eve,' I noticed soldiers swarming us, even with the mania that had transpired. We ran wildly to the opposite wall of the arena. Mykel was there against the railing with a dropped rope. God bless that man.

Soldiers chased us viciously; we reached the rope in the nick of time. We carefully avoided the spikes on the wall and climbed up, just as we had done many times before in practice. I gave my friend Mykel a quick nod as we ran up the stairs and out of the arena.

We made it to the paved streets; chaos encompassed the city. Some are taking advantage of the oddities and have begun smashing the windows of prestigious buildings and looting. People can be heard shouting, "The King is dead!" and "The duel was intervened!"

We quickly ran towards the Harbor. Guards are already blocking every exit of the city. If we wanted to reach our escape boat and get out of the capital, we may have to fight. Following the street next to the castle and arena, we could finally see the docks jutting out over the water. Five guards stood shoulder to shoulder, blocking everyone from leaving.

This is going to turn into a confrontation.

"Mykel, 'Eve' can hardly stand. Are we sure we want to go this way?" I said, rushing.

"No, Gentry, this is the only way. Unless you want to swim around."

"Great. I'll start on the left and work my way in. 'Eve,' you take the middle. Mykel, you start right."

We split up as we approached the capital soldiers. Our weapons were already drawn and at the ready. Begrudgingly, I raised my sword and began to strike at the officers. Two engaged me, trading blows. For a moment, the two soldiers matched me step for step. Metal clashed wildly, and occasionally sparks dashed before our eyes.

When one of the soldiers got a little too greedy, trying to jab at my chest, I was able to evade the thrust and slice the soldier in the lower ribs. The next soldier swiped at me wildly. Whooshing of air traveled fast through my hair. I met one of the uncontrolled swings with mine. Stopping its pursuit in midair. I punched the soldier hard in the stomach, causing him to lose his breath, and, in another motion, I nailed the soldier across the head with the hilt of my sword. The blow knocked him out cold.

Looking back to my right was 'Eve.' She's beaten and battered, having no place to fight. The soldier who challenged her stood no chance as she drove a dagger into him.

One of the injured men on the ground began to speak coldly, saying, "You're the ones who murdered the King. You'll pay for this! In this life or the next!"

Mykel silenced him by jamming his foot into his throat. "It's now or never!" Mykel said, exasperated.

We all turned and ran up the dock to the small sailboat we paid a pretty penny for.

Once we were out on the water, I turned, looking longingly back at the grand white walled city. The towers shot up to wild heights, and the King's castle now lies barren.

"What a perfect sight!" I said, sighing.

"Gentry, we don't look back!" 'Eve' insisted.

"You know, once the whole Nation finds out it was you who killed the King, you'll never be able to rest." Mykel declared.

The results of that fateful day changed my life forever. Athren was never the same; they abolished the monarchy after the King's death; none of the King's posterity were deemed fit to rule. Athren began relying solely on the two parties to govern. The people of Athren need to wake.

> *A society without its voice is dead.*
> *We are like a river.*
> *Some parts are rough with rapids,*
> *Others are smooth and placid.*
> *There are falls and big bends,*
> *but we continuously flow on until we end.*
> *Now jump in, tread, and transcend.*
> *Gentry A. Saunders*

Gentry could still be alive. It's only been thirty years since this happened; he is probably in his fifties or so. I close the finished book; my mind is racing with all the possibilities. The King's son may also be alive. Did the King have other offspring? Mykel, that scumbag, knew all of this while he's been training me!

I cautiously placed the book in the stone hole, carefully sliding the rock over it to ensure it was concealed. Time to heal and finish what Gentry started.

Chapter Twenty-One:

Ash

Two weeks pass by like the blink of an eye. Carrie has been hard at work visiting me often and cleaning my wounds. I'm able to stroll and put weight on my leg. I may get back to full strength after all. Being so immovable has taken a toll on me, but there is light at the end of the tunnel.

I've been doing my best to assist with the daily duties of the farm. The mundane tasks make me feel like this is my future again. Luckily, Kilroy sent a letter the other day stating, "Please, report to the guild by the week's end. There's an important matter that must be discussed."

Whatever they have to say, it can't be good. I expect to be compensated when I get back for my victory over Trisha. Accepting that blood money may evoke a range of emotions, I have not yet decided what to do with it.

Another matter I must address. Returning the book to Mrs. Cunningham. I wish I could study the words more. There has to be a hidden message within its pages. Niklas wanted me to learn something more than Gentry's story.

At dinner, the whole family gathered. Everyone, but Nate, of course. This dinner felt different. We know it won't be the same after I head back tomorrow. It's comforting to know that my support system will always be here.

Rupert started rambling about a dueler. "When I was in town today, I overheard some of the politicians talking about a girl who's being moved up with the Federalists. She's from Havensburg. I guess she has dominated three duels without killing her victim."

I put my head down, remembering the impact my sword made against Trisha. I should've knocked her out, but I was in shock.

Rupert continues, "The guild decided that they needed her talent in the capital. I guess she'll be stopping in Lyon over the weekend on her way down."

My eyebrows scrunch with curiosity, "Stopping here?"

Rupert, making an outlandish voice clearly mocking me, says, "Yes, Amis, you'll be able to meet her. Be careful, she could beat you silly."

"If she could kick his ass, what does that say about you, Rupert? You don't duel, just saying." Sofia snaps back.

"You think I'm not capable of fighting, because I don't duel? I'm just more intelligent. Look at Amis' face?!" Rupert points at me, sneering.

"He looks much better, just his nose is a little crooked." Sofia retorts.

"Hey, I'm right here, guys!" I butt in.

"Rupert, you say you're smarter. You seem like a coward to me!" Sofia says, giving an evil look.

"Enough!" Mom hisses.

There's a long silence. I'm expecting Sofia to storm off again, but she doesn't.

"Rupert, do you happen to know the girl's name?" I ask.

"Hmmm, something, Lynn. I don't think you know her."

I put my head back down and rub my fingertips across the grooves on the wood table, pondering. This rehab was nice. Now I have to go back to fighting and praying I can escape death for the next 23 months. After dinner, we all quickly clean up and get ready for bed. Finally, I'm able to close my eyes and sleep without images of Trisha dying.

A deafening crash shatters the tranquil night atmosphere. I shot awake, sitting up, uncontrolled, ready for a brawl. Again, shattering glass rips through the air above me, followed by a fiery torch. Smoke from the outside air saturates the house.

Dad barrels into our room, going berserk. "We have to go. Amis! Get your bow and arrow, try to shoot these pricks. Rupert, Sofia, give the animals a chance!" Dad darts back out of the room, just as fast as his orders.

We spring into action, but my eyes are soon mesmerized by the eerie orange glow. The crackling of a vicious fire whips wildly through the fields. The night sky is dominated by a vibrant red glow that is spreading incredibly. The firelight below dances uncontrollably, engulfing all my family's valuables.

I'm frozen in place, completely dumbfounded by the scene unfolding before me. Who would do something like this? In that exact moment, my spirit shakes my body back into motion when the roof above me is drenched in flames. Sprinting out the front door, positioning myself on the porch, with an arrow primed and ready. I see five red shadows ride horses up the dirt path, galloping fast away from the catastrophic burning.

I draw a bead as I aim the bow confidently down the path at one of the arsonists. Releasing the bowstring, vibrating loudly, and flinging an arrow at a resounding speed. I watch it travel through the smoke, nailing an arsonist in the shoulder. It causes them to jerk forward on their horse, but not fall off.

Anguish sinks deep into my soul. My Dad, standing in the yard on the right, releases another wooden missile. With perfect accuracy, the same arsonists tumbled off their horse, dead.

"Go help your brother!" Dad exclaims, piercing his voice through the ashy air.

He then shifts his gaze, running east to the apple tree. Jumping off the porch of our house, that's now ablaze, I pivoted left towards the stable. Fire rages mad, fueled by the hay kindling. Not all the animals will survive. The red and orange streaks dance rabid, high up to fifty feet; animals screeching, causing a horrific noise.

A horse shoots out of the stable in a violent fury. A flame runs rampant across its mane. The horse jerks, falling to the ground, rolling desperately, trying to extinguish the flame. Upon reaching its side, the horse whimpers and whines. I can't do anything now, but I think they'll be all right. My eyes raced perilously looking for Rupert. Somehow, he managed to prep the wagon with two well-tamed horses. Sofia was in the back, holding Leo the chicken in her arms, rocking and reciting eerie words. "Death will be thrust down upon those that harm us."

"You saved that damn rooster?!" I ask in pure rage, stopping Sofia's evil trance.

"Yes! All the others were released and at least given a chance!" Sofia hisses, still visibly shaking.

"Throw him in the fire!" I demand.

She ignores me. Mom walks briskly past me, carrying a box of sacred keepsakes, including a few high-class weapons I have never seen. Two long swords, a bow, and a pair of hatchets. Her head is held high in complete silence. We all climb aboard the wagon in utter defeat.

"We need to go before it's too late," Rupert shouts at us, whipping the reins.

"What about Dad! You can't leave." Sofia yells in defiance.

"He will be all right. Go." Mom sounds.

Rupert steers the horse-driven wagon down the dirt path that had not yet been entrenched with fire. My eyes shoot back longingly, seeking my Dad.

"Amis, we don't look back." Mom insisted, "Dad will be okay."

"But Niklas'!" I point aggressively.

"No! Niklas is in here." Mom says, placing a hand on my chest.

I shift forward, holding back my tears of pain and emotion. Niklas' grave, the book, and my family's wealth all burn by the heart-wrenching flames. With my eyes glued forward, I can still see flickering light from my peripheral vision. Our wagon jerks to an abrupt stop.

"There's a body in the road! Amis, get out and help me move him." Rupert orders.

Jumping from the wagon, my feet land with a thud. Ahead of the horses, I see the body. Two arrows are sticking out of the lifeless mass. Rupert approaches him, turning them over to see their foul face.

"I recognize this piece of shit. He's a new recruit in the Loyalists guild." Rupert mutters.

"Of course." I say, growling, "Do you think Rasshole put him up to it?"

"Most likely. Here, take his legs."

I bent down following Rupert's direction, grabbing the legs to move the dead weight off the path.

A shout comes from behind, startling me and causing me to drop the Loyalist body to the ground.

"No! Put the body in the wagon." Dad howls, running up to us. The fire is still burning, marching its way toward us.

Turning to him, I ask, "You want us to sit with a dead man?"

"If you can't manage that, you can walk! We need him." Dad says clearly, not joshing around.

Rupert and I fling the corpse in the back, and blood pools. Rupert, now back with the reins, sets out for Lyon. I walk alongside one of the wagon wheels at a steady pace. Dad doesn't seem fatigued or winded.

"Dad, how did you get to be such a good shot with the bow?" I question.

"That's just something my father had taught me growing up."

"I'm sorry to disappoint you in that regard," I say, looking into his eyes with a slight smile.

"Each of you is unique and has talents that I wish I possessed. I'm proud of you."

Silence befalls us as we continue on our journey. I look back in the direction of the farm. There's a silent crimson red ray illuminating the horizon. It's disheartening, knowing my parents just lost everything, and I lost the book. Mrs. Cunningham is going to be livid; that's a scary sight.

Dad catches my gaze.

"Son, all that stuff we just lost is temporal. If you change your perspective, you'll realize that true joy comes only from eternal things. Like family, relationships, and memories." Dad lectures.

"I know, but I'm worried I'm going to forget. I won't be able to remember every detail of Niklas' personality. Memories fade, and time keeps moving."

"Maybe you ought to journal the stuff you want to remember. Just like heroes of old." Dad says, raising his eyebrows and pulling a book out from underneath his cloak.

"How?! How do you know about the book Niklas left me?" My mouth opens wide in shock. I rip the book from his hands.

"You don't think I didn't notice you reading all the time under the apple tree?" Dad replies.

"I, I…"

"Or when Nate and Mariam came unexpectedly. Why, I yelled, announcing that we were heading to your secret spot? Or why did I sit on the large stone that housed the book? No one can find it, considering it's a capital offense." Dad squints his eyes. "Parents always know what their children are up to."

"So, have you read it?" I ask, being very curious.

"Yes, long ago I did," Dad responds in a sad tone.

"Is that where you went? When you ran off during the fire?"

"Yes, I knew how much it meant to you, Amis."

"Is it bad that I'm not going to give it back to Mrs. Cunningham?" I ask.

"No, it's not hers after all."

We reached the streets of Lyon. The rattling and screeching of the wagon bolts and wooden frame are loud enough to wake the entire town. A resounding, continuous clanging of horse hooves and the constant rumble of the wheels create a unique, but familiar sound. The streets are quiet; there's not a soul.

"Dad, where are we going?" Rupert inquires, seeking directions.

"To Mykel's, then the Federalist guild," Dad answers.

Mykel's home was nicer than I expected. He has a wooden fence lining his front yard; it appears to be handmade. Entering the fenced area surrounding his home, we walked onto a brick path, evenly spaced, that led up to the house. It looked like there was a garden mirroring both sides of the path. The house was made of timber and thatch, with lovely glass windows. It was hard to see everything in the darkness of the night.

Dad hurried to the door, pounding on it repeatedly. Mykel answered, groggy and dazed.

"Henry, what are you doing here?"

"Loyalists burnt our farm. We need a place to stay, and I need your help." Dad blurted out.

Mykel's jaw drops in disbelief. He rubs his hand across his bearded chin, "Help again? Okay, give me a few minutes. You all are welcome to stay in my spare bedroom for the time being."

"Thank you, you've always been a great friend!" Mom exclaims. Realizations sprout as I look at Mom, Dad, and Mykel in realization.

My face must look odd because Mom asks, "Are you sick?"

"Ya, I'm okay, just tired." I walk back to the wagon and sit down next to the dead body.

How am I so naive! With Niklas and now this! Looking back on the dark path towards Mom and Dad, I can never look at them the same.

The book that Dad went out of his way to save. They are the ones who escaped death, the ones who escaped dueling. Dad killed the King; Mom stabbed the 'giant' in the stomach, almost dying until Dad saved her.

There are so many moments in my life that I should've known. They are not ordinary people! Dad's extreme strength and weaponry skills. The way neither of them talks about their past! Mom's injured hand. They were the first to settle our farm. Dad became deranged when Niklas was about to die, and it seemed like he could dismantle the Athren soldiers.

Even recently, they gave me clues! Dad is shooting his bow with ease, killing this damn corpse next to me! Mom gave me the exact words, "We don't look back.". The actual words she gave Gentry!

This is what Niklas wanted me to learn for myself. Why do people always talk in code? Just be direct and honest! They are Gentry and 'Eve,' if that is even Mom's real name.

While deep in reflection, I rub my temples deliberately. Dad approaches, slapping my leg, "Time to go, we need to wake the town."

"Whatever you say, Gentry."

Chapter Twenty-Two:

Meeting

"So exactly how do we wake the town?" Rupert asks, incredulously.

"Simmer down, Rupert. We need to go to the Federalists guild first and foremost." Dad explains.

Mykel joined us in the wagon, while Mom and Sofia stayed back. The horses began chugging along. I sat in the back, hanging my feet over the edge. The distressing thoughts persist in my mind. The scrutiny of my life is ongoing, with every bump the wheels roll over. It explains everything. Mom and Dad always expressed opposition to Athren's traditions of dueling. Who else knows?

Mykel, Mr. Brookshard, and Niklas. There must be more people. Does Rasmussen know? Is that why he hates our family?

The wagon comes to a screeching halt, as Rupert howls, "Whoa, whoa."

"Mykel, awake, Kilroy. Amis, get the duelers." Dad directs.

"What are you and Rupert going to do?" I question.

"We're going to guard our dear friend?" Dad replies, pointing to the deceased body in the wagon.

When I walk up to the large wooden double doors of the guild, I attempt to push them open. They don't budge. My palms turned into fists, pounding the door as hard as possible. I stand there awkwardly looking back at Dad and Rupert with wide eyes.

"Use more force!" Rupert projects the words.

The moment I turn back, the latch jostles, and a squeaky squeal comes from the door hinges. Bruce's prominent nose and eyes appear around the door.

With a wretched raspy voice, Bruce speaks, "What business do you have here this hour? Oh, young master Hastings?" His voice was clearly in shock. "Come in." The door swings wide open.

Strutting in, I sound off, "Bruce, I need your help."

"Yes, son, what is it?"

"Can you gather the politicians here, now?"

"Yes, but it better be important." He is firm and condescending with his words. I look him over and realize he is in a nightgown, looking like hell.

Bruce stalks off up the hallway. I followed behind him awkwardly. The hallway feels so much gloomier this time of night. I reach the spiral stairs at the end of the hall. Once on the second floor, and at Zander's door, I slam my fists against the wood. A rustle stirs from within. Zander opens the door even more flustered than Bruce.

"AMIS, what are you doing?"

"Zander! I need you to wake everyone else. Now! It's important and meet me out in front of the guild."

"Is everything alright?!" Zander asked worriedly.

All I can do is nod and say, "It will be."

"Oh, okay. I heard Xavier and Veronica's loud voices in the hall a little bit ago. They might still be up; I'll get them."

"They were up at this hour?" I shake my head, letting my imagination wander. Zander looks wide awake and put-together.

I hustled back to the wagon; Dad and Rupert didn't move one bit, and I noticed Mr. Brookshard was now with them. How'd he get here before everyone else?

"Well?" Dad asks, shaking me back to the present.

"They are coming. It should be just a few minutes." I sigh.

Ten minutes passed by. A hush of silence falls over us as we wait; tension and confusion fill the air. No lights illuminate any of the surrounding buildings, and the streets are opaque. There's stillness in the air. Nothing but uncertainty faces us.

Mykel appears from the street, followed by Kilroy. I nodded to Kilroy, acknowledging his presence.

The older men gather with Brookshard, and it made me feel important, but honestly, a little strange. They are a different generation altogether, gray, grizzled, and weird.

"Hastings, you dragged us out of bed. What is the meaning of this?" Kilroy's grumpy voice sounds.

"Relax, Kilroy," Dad says sternly.

The door of the guild creaks open, and the young duelers emerge. Xavier, Veronica, Zander, and a newbie recruit I'm not familiar with. Their eyes examine everyone standing in the street. Their body language changes immediately, tightening up.

"Oh shit, this must be serious." Zander mumbles.

"Amis!!! You're alive, up and walking?" Veronica expresses joy.

Xavier runs over and hugs me and whispers in my ear, "I'm glad you are okay."

"Why wouldn't I be, okay?" I hush back just as softly.

"Uh, no reason... Please save me. The new girl, April, and Veronica keep ganging up on me." Xavier changes the subject quickly.

Veronica aggressively pulls him off me. "No secrets, Xavier." My eyes meet Xavier's as he is dragged away. Pure fear resides in his eyes.

Zander stands off to the side, chuckling, enjoying the show. I am grateful to have them as friends.

"There's a body back here?" The newbie April asks with a concerned voice, pointing to the wagon. Veronica and Xavier's facial expressions look concerned.

"Get away from there! Who are you anyway?" I snap towards the newbie.

"I'm April, just joined up."

"She's just like the month April, damp and dreary," Xavier adds with a sneer.

Veronica provides another swift punch to his arm, then asks. "You killed him?!" Her face is in shock, looking at the corpse.

From behind us in the dark, a voice echoes creepily through the dark street. "You think you can beckon us at any hour you please, Hastings's boy!" Tarron grumbles.

His unattractive frame comes into view, adorned with terrible twigs of hair and a coat. Janice, looking calm and interested, follows behind.

"My boy did not call on you; I did. You represent us, the people; it's time you start." Dad declares with pure anger in his voice.

"So be it. Explain." Tarron responds as rancid as ever.

Everyone gathered close to listen to Dad's soft voice, including my guildmates. "A few hours ago, five criminals torched my farm. Destroying the entirety of it. This Loyalist dueler was one of them!" Dad grabs the dead man's legs, yanking him out of the wagon with his brute strength. Making a loud 'thud.' "This is the only one of those arsonists pricks we were able to eliminate."

April turns to Veronica with big eyes.

Janice approaches the face of the corpse, investigating. "This is a Loyalist dueler."

Brookshard mumbles something under his breath as Kilroy is visibly upset.

"How are we supposed to believe you?" Tarron retorts.

"Are you mental? Can't you smell the smoke in the air? Are you suggesting that we burnt down our own farm just to kill this boy?" Dad, frustrated, faces Tarron with rage.

"Don't be such a senseless, dull old man." Janice stalks impressively towards Tarron.

Tarron backs down with his tail between his legs.

"What would you have us do?" Janice asks cautiously.

"Wake the Loyalists. Tell them to gather at sunrise in the courtyard." Dad demands. Janice nods in agreement.

There's an hour before dawn. Our party made its way to the courtyard. When the Loyalists arrive, who knows what to expect? If Rasmussen is among them, it'll be the first time I've laid eyes on him since Trisha died. If I could drive a sword through him, I would.

Dad said we don't seek revenge, now I know why. He sought revenge when he killed the king. It seemed to work out in his favor, though; does he regret it?

I turn to the new girl, April, while we walk. "How do you like the guild so far?"

Her soft and innocent voice begins to ramble. "Well, it's alright, considering I'm alive. The people are meh, and the food is good. I've only been in for the last week, and we haven't done the rankings yet, considering you were away. Before I joined, I heard some wild stories about your family. Making the Hasting clan seem like a bunch of mythical gods untouchable in the ring." She trails off, realizing she said too much.

"What type of stories?"

"Well, that your Mom and Dad are barbarians. That's why you and your brothers are such gruesome fighters, and no one was familiar with your family name until a few years ago. I also heard that your parents steal kids and farm out the strongest ones to become duelers. So, your parents can earn a profit through them and free labor in the fields. Or your parents used to be duelers but got kicked out for some crimes they committed." She says as her face begins to blush.

I blurt out a hysterical laugh. "I hope they keep coming up with more!" Thinking consciously, that last theory, she nailed right on the head. Turning to April, smiling, I say, "You're going to fit right in!"

We reached the courtyard. It's barren and somber. The ring I'm so used to seeing surrounded by a horde of people is empty. So much killing has transpired in this yard.

Right now, its flat brick landscape is a vast, open space amidst the tall surrounding buildings. Through an opening near the provincial building, a group of individuals emerges. It's the Loyalists, all geared up as if they are going to war.

"Why do they strut in here like they're going to kill us?!" Zander jokes.

"They are just overcompensating." Xavier makes a hand motion around his junk in response.

There's Rass-hole, sporting a smug look in a politician's robe, with his idiotic demeanor. His stupid jaw is clenched down on a toothpick. What a tool.

My Dad, Mykel, Rupert, and all the politicians are gathered around in a circle in the middle of the ring. They are having a heated discussion, but I can't make out the words.

Mykel shouts down to me, "Get the body and bring it here."

I motion to Zander, and we retrieved the corpse, which is already mangled from being handled very poorly. We drop him at the feet of everyone standing there. I raise my eyes at the egocentric maniac Rasmussen. His devilish eyes meet mine. A slight smirk appears around the rim of his mouth. What an asshole! He wants me to react, but I won't. Not here.

Zander and I turn to walk away.

"This is one of your duelers!" Janice scowls.

Looking at the Loyalist duelers to see their reactions. There are four of them, and they've been busy directing their eyes down towards the earth like they were ordered to.

Then I blurt out in uncontrollable rage, "You four over there! Do you wag your tails and follow every order your masters give?"

One of them bites back, definitely their current champion. "I trained with Nate and Trisha! I cared for Trisha until you killed her! Do you honestly think I would burn Nate and your family's pathetic farm?"

I move aggressively in his direction, losing my head. All I see is a red blur. I don't have a weapon on me; he does. I don't care. They can't bully their way around Athren. Dragging their nuts to and fro, thinking everyone has to submit to their will. It's just Rasmussen who really needs to die; whatever casualties occur until that happens is a necessity.

In the Loyalist champion's face, I whisper, "I know Rasmussen ordered you."

He shakes his head violently in denial, biting his lip.

"I kill you where you stand, you backstabbing bitch." He fires back, clearly referencing my decision to become a Federalist.

"You have the sword, try it!"

Mykel jumps between us. "Dan, Amis! Save it for a duel."

I get back to my side, shaking and antsy, adrenaline pumps through my veins. The loud exchange had ended in the ring, but it was far from a peaceful resolution.

Mr. Flemming came forward from the group and hollered for everyone to hear.

"It has been agreed upon by all individuals present. The Loyalists and Federalists will each present a dueler to settle the dispute of the Hastings fire. If the Loyalists are victors of the duel, Henry Hastings and his family will be exiled from Lyon for the wrongful killing of Bryson. If the Federalists are the victors, the Loyalist guild will be forced to compensate Hastings for the destruction of their farm, and Rasmussen will be ordered to return to Harpstedt.

"The duel will take place tomorrow at midday. An assessor will be sent to Hastings' farm today to gather an estimated appraisal for all the Hastings' losses. Guilds, please prepare a champion to come forward."

I roll my eyes in disagreement. Everything always comes down to a duel. Can anyone come to a real decision or conduct an impartial investigation? This is not justice!

Kilroy makes his way over to me. "Amis, technically, you are still our champion. I'm going to ask you, because I know you were injured. Are you still willing to be our champion?"

"Yes, I am," I say plainly, staring at Rasmussen.

Kilroy resumes, "There's another matter we will need to discuss; it will wait until after."

"After we find out if I live or die?" I say with a broad smile.

Kilroy nods and walks away.

A few moments later, Rasmussen bellows out, "Daniel will be our champion!"

Kilroy immediately followed, trumping him, "Amis will be ours."

The rest of the guild gathers around me. "You'd better get Carrie to look you over," Xavier says in a hushed tone that only our squad can hear.

"Let's get back there now, maybe I can persuade Mykel to tell me this Dan guy's weaknesses," I express, just as quietly.

Dad forcefully grabs me from behind and spins me 180 degrees. He steps away from the group, and I pursue.

"Son, I have full faith in you. The best thing you can do in the ring is find a way to show mercy. Try to bridle your anger."

"Is that what you used to do?" I ask fast, as my throat tightens, anticipating his response.

He grins, "Try to be merciful. If you lose, they say they'll exile us from Lyon. Rasmussen will try to eliminate us."

My lips grow tight; the King killed his parents. "No pressure or anything, Dad."

"Well, you're related to some infamous duelers." He smacks me on the back. "Come home today if you can, to help us evaluate the damage."

"I will, and I place the book back in the wagon. Rupert may want to read it now."

Looking at his gray hair sprinkling on his head. I'm only an inch shorter than him now; that's something to be proud of.

Getting back to the guild, I can comfortably breathe now. This place isn't a home, but it is a refuge. I paced the long hallway to the med-bay. Entering the white-tiled room, I sat down, resting on a bench. The room is quiet, no one is here, but I don't call Carrie. Kicking my legs out and putting my head back on the wall, I relax my tired eyes.

A door launches open, causing a loud 'bang', and the latch relocks. My eyes dart open quickly, scanning the room.

"You know the way you were sleeping had terrible lumbar support," Carrie expresses, rummaging through her medicine cabinet.

"Noted," I reply, rubbing my eyes.

"Honestly, I'm surprised you didn't wake sooner. When Raelynn from Havensburg showed up, I spent thirty minutes wrapping a cut on her arm. She was giggling the whole time at your drooling mouth and vibrating snore." Carrie rattles off nonchalantly.

"Lovely. Who's Raelynn?" I question shaking my head.

"Oh, she's the girl going to the capital. I would have introduced you, but she went upstairs to retire. Now let's see your wounds."

Exposing my pant leg and my shoulder, I let Carrie take a thorough examination. Her eyes gaze from lesion to lesion. She applies some remedy ointment to each of them.

"Show me how your movement feels. Start by standing on your left leg and hop, then squat with one leg." Carrie orders.

"Ok, but if this is some sick joke…" I beam and leap up and down on one leg.

"You're definitely not as graceful as a rabbit. You look a little shaky, definitely past your prime. Now show me your shoulder strength." She hands me a heavy sword. "Rotate your arm while holding this."

Holding it out, the weight feels difficult to bear. I began twisting my shoulder joint, making it complete one full circle.

"I suppose that's good enough to duel. Amis, know your limitations. Tomorrow, when dueling Dan, he will try to exploit your injuries. Please find a way to counter him, protect yourself. I swear, if I have to spend all my focus on taking care of you, I'm going to quit."

"I'm your favorite!" I smirk.

"Whatever you say." Carrie rolls her eyes.

Leaving the med bay, I feel less confident than when I went in. I started walking in the direction of the mess hall to grab a quick bite to eat. The mess hall was quiet and peaceful, allowing me to feel comfortable enough to grab what I wanted without feeling any judgment. Occasionally, I become an introvert, especially when I have a lot on my mind.

After eating, I changed my clothes rather quickly and found myself in the practice ring. Kilroy was sitting on the mat in the center of the room like he was waiting patiently for me. Walking to him, I look up at the banners around the room like I usually do. There's a new one, it's mine.

"Amis, I'm glad to see you. Look at your new banner? Your name will be amongst the others in lasting memory." No words breach my lips; I stare blankly at the fabric banner with my name stitched. What a terrible thing I did to get it there.

"How'd it go with the nurse? Are you in adequate condition to fight?"

I burst back to reality. "Carrie gave me the all clear!"

"Good, let's get to work."

We spent the next two hours undergoing rigorous training with the sword, focusing on footwork, counters, and double-handed power strokes. My shoulder held up reasonably well. All the movement and rotations made me nervous that I would stiffen up the next day. It was nice to feel needed again.

"So, I take it, will we be using strictly only swords tomorrow?" I question directly.

"You know I can't tell you," Kilroy gives me a wink. "Really, all I can tell you is that you will have to wear heavy armor tomorrow."

"Heavy armor." I regurgitate back. "Whose idea is that?"

"Rasmussen's and Taron agreed to it…"

Doesn't he know I'm weak as it is? Adding more weight will make it even harder for me. Anger and frustration build up inside me.

"Thanks, Kilroy, for your help today. I think I'd better be going, my family may need some help salvaging our farm."

I shake his hand and withdraw, heading rapidly for the guild's stable to grab a horse.

I rode the swift and agile horse at speed to my parents' devastated farm. Not a care in the world for those around me. I weave through the traffic on the street, avoiding peasants and vendors. They all know who I am, and according to April, they have absurd conspiracies.

Upon reaching the farm, I see that it has all turned to ash. The stable is a skeleton blackened shell of its former self. The fields are black waste with ashy scars down the individual columns where the vegetables grew. The worst is the house; it's burnt to a crisp down to the stone foundation. A few charred walls remain, but there's nothing salvageable. The intensity of the fire was too overwhelming. Even the steel items we had were damaged, making them ineffective.

"Amis, are you here to find your baby blanket?" Sofia asks, trying to be funny.

"This is worse than I thought," I say, frowning.

"It's just a bunch of stuff anyway. We are lucky it didn't march up the mountain." Sofia responds with optimism.

"That's true. How many animals made it?"

"A few chickens were running around, and that horse that broke out of the stable. A cow and another horse didn't make it. Oh, the dogs survived! They came running up to us as soon as we arrived this morning!"

"Where are Mom and Dad?"

"Oh, they are in the field with the assessor and Mr. Brookshard," Sofia answers. "I overheard Mr.

Brookshard say that the Loyalists think we were wrong for killing Bryson."

"Were we?" I ask, pointing my gaze into Sofia's deep brown eyes.

"Not at all. All those arsonist pigs all deserve to die."

I give my little sister a side hug and walk deliberately towards the group in the scorched field. I see the apple tree and Niklas' grave off to my left. The tree looks burnt, with scorch marks ripping vertically. There's hope it will heal and resprout. I am within earshot of them now.

"Henry, I know this place is a lot to handle, especially without three of your boys here now to assist you. I want to present you with an offer." Mr. Brookshard proposes.

"What are you offering?" Dad asks back. "I expect the Loyalist to reimburse me for my loss."

The assessor croaks, "We will see what the duel tomorrow brings. I do have a calculated estimate of damage."

Brookshard's deep voice groans, "Let me fine-tune the details. What I'm willing to present to you is a home reconstructed for you and your family; you'll be welcome to stay. I'll hire a few individuals to run the establishment. Niklas' grave will remain intact, and if it's okay with you, I would like to relocate Heather's grave next to his." Mr. Brookshard explains.

"I think that's a lovely idea. Henry and I will think it over. Please come to us when you have the official offer." Mom acknowledges.

Mr. Brookshard and the Assessor walk away towards our ruined home. Checking my surroundings and seeing no one near, clear my throat loudly. My parents immediately shift their heads.

"What do you guys think you're going to do?" I inquire.

"We aren't so sure yet; it depends solely on tomorrow. We have faith and confidence in you, and regardless of the outcome, there is no reason to be concerned for our well-being." Dad reassures.

"Son, we need you to remain focused; do not distract your mind with the issues of this family. Focus on the issue of tomorrow." Mom urges me.

"I have questions about your past. Questions I need answers to. Like, what's your real name? Mom? It sure as hell isn't 'Eve.'" I croak, hoping to prompt an honest response.

"My name has never changed. It's Sarah. We felt it was common enough not to draw any unwanted attention. Your Dad was the only one we needed to change. The name Gentry became outlawed. Your father became a fugitive throughout all of Athren overnight after the events of that consequential day."

"Good, my whole life isn't a lie!" I declared, laughing. "One more question for today. Do you think the King's son is still alive?"

"He has to be, maybe not trying to be King, but definitely looking for us," Dad says, speculating.

I give them meaningful hugs, even though that isn't my Dad's sort of thing. I think feelings have always made him feel strange. We gather back together and journey back to Lyon. This might be my last time leaving the farm with my family, even though it has been reduced to rubble.

"Do you think we will all be together again under one roof someday?" I pose the question.

"I know we will." Mom answers confidently.

Chapter Twenty-Three:

Raelynn

I found myself alone again in the mess hall, eating at a small table. Today has been incredibly stressful and taxing. My mind is focused, longing for my comfortable and utterly perfect bed. I take another bite of bread and a spoonful of potato soup. Bruce stumbles into the mess hall. I'm sure he's preparing to clean up after me. He walks directly towards me, dropping a sack on the table.

Coins audibly clang as his voice wheezes, "Master Hastings, here are your winnings from the last duel."

"Thank you." My eyes grow dull as they drift, gazing at the cloth sack on the table.

There's nothing like being paid for killing my brother's fiancée. Dueling is a sick and twisted practice; I'm going to abolish it. When I finish dinner, I retire to one of the leather couches by the fireplace. On the refectory table between the U-shape of the couches lies the blood money. Light from the fire bounces off the cloth sack, illuminating it.

The doors to the mess hall burst open once more, destroying every sense of self-loathing I was granted. Xavier, Zander, Veronica, April, and a girl I recognize but don't know waltz in.

The way she walks exudes confidence and grace. I hardly notice as everyone sits on the couches near me. I can't tell if it is the firelight bouncing off her face, but the occasional ray exposes features of her face that enchant and completely captivate me. Is it her full, red lips that form a gracious smile? Perhaps her brown hair that symmetrically cascades down her back? Or her eyes that sparkle with alluring depth? My heart is beating so hard, I'm worried it is visible to everyone. There's a faint voice sounding deep within my brain, and I can't seem to focus. My soul will never be mine again.

A pillow slams into my face, causing me to jolt.

"Amis, stop staring, you creep! Haven't you seen a beautiful girl before?" Xavier teases.

My skin crawls, redness blushes my lightly freckled face out of pure embarrassment.

"I'm sorry, my mind has been racing all day, and I must've lost my thoughts looking in your direction," I mumble out the odd excuse.

"It's okay, I get it a lot. I'm different and used to it. I'm Raelynn, by the way." Her sweet voice replies.

"Oh, you're the girl going to the capital. I'm…"

"Amis, Amis Hastings." She takes the words out of my mouth. "I met you earlier while you were drooling in the med bay."

Laughter echoes across the room. Goosebumps emerge on my arms, causing the hair to stand straight up.

"Knock it off, you wankers!" Zander grins.

"What, you can't handle a little chuckle in your direction? Do you suffer from little man syndrome?" Xavier winks, raising his little pinky.

I raised my arm and whipped the pillow swiftly back at Xavier's face, skimming Veronica's nose on the way. Then, I swiftly get up, jumping on Xavier, coming down with my left elbow on his stomach. "How's this for a little wanker?"

"Okay! Amis!" Xavier wails.

"Knock it off, insulant children," Veronica hollers, slapping me across the head.

Xavier kicks me off of him, causing me to stumble flawlessly back into my spot on the couch. I exhale in satisfaction. Breathing steadily for a few minutes while everyone carries on.

"For you to be a duelist in the capital, you must be one hell of a fighter?" I ask Raelynn, trying to redirect the attention.

"Sort of, luckier than anything. You, Hastings, are the ones everyone always describes as invincible."

Her sweet voice fills my ears. This woman is perfect. My eyes began to wander, looking upon her petite frame. Something about her makes me feel whole…

"It's not just me who's heard wild things about your family, Amis!" April chimes in.

"My family isn't the only one that has had multiple duelers. Look at Zander's family. The Jaspers have been popping out fighters left and right for years. They breed like rabbits." I say in protest. Zander just shook his head in disbelief.

"That reminds me! Look at this wound Zander gave me last week!" Xavier lifts his shirt, exposing everything. "Zander hit me with a blunt arrow, and it took my nipple completely off! Carrie said they don't grow back either!"

The whole room breaks out again in a frenzy of laughter. There was pure pride across his face as he disclosed that bit of unwanted information.

"Pull your shirt down before I slice your other pepperoni nipple off!" Veronica hisses.

"Were they like this in your last guild?" I ask Raelynn as even keel as possible.

"Oh no. Havensburg is a bunch of brown-nosing sticklers. I was close to Addison, before…"

Before my brother stabbed him with a trident, I think, but dare not say.

"I'm sorry. Amis' brother killed mine too; he knows no restraint. I'm sure you'll meet him in

Harpstedt." Zander says slyly, making me feel an abundance of guilt.

"It's just the nature of what we do. My instructor saw Amis's last duel. He said that Amis did everything in his power to provide mercy."

"He did and almost died himself for it." Zander acknowledges.

I look away at the fire, as a piece of wood is engulfed in flames. Looking back at Raelynn, I changed the subject, "What's your preferred weapon?"

"Well, I'm extremely accurate with throwing knives. I know them like the back of my hand; I'm accustomed to their weight, and my hand-eye coordination is off the charts. I'm able to flip any object high in the air and catch it with perfection. Wanna see?!"

"Sure..." I say with hesitation coursing through my veins.

Raelynn sits up and casually pulls a knife from behind her back. My eyes widened wildly.

"Did she just pull that out of her-" Xavier stops mid-sentence.

"Yup." I nod nervously.

"Amis, sit right here." She says, pointing to a spot right in front of her.

I don't dare say no. Not when I have a chance of getting closer to this mysteriously sexy girl. I sit on the rug with my legs crossed, gazing up at her toned physique. It still seems like I'm half her height in this position.

Raelynn looks up at the fifteen-foot ceilings. She rotates the knife casually in her hand and then whips it up in the air. It flings end over end, barely brushing the ceiling, and begins to missile back down towards me. My eyes are locked on her. She seems concentrated, and for some reason, I am utterly dumbfounded by her confidence.

For a moment, it seems like the knife is going to penetrate right into my skull. There's no retreat on my part. If I die right now, that's fine by me. With a lightning-quick snap, Raelynn catches the knife, taking it off its imminent, deadly path. I don't flinch but keep my eyes pinned on her.

"That was ballzy!" April spits out. Everyone else was stuck in a state of pure shock. Silence pierces the room.

Sighing heavily, Raelynn gasps with a straight face, "I think I'd better go to bed." She turns about and rushes away.

"What was that about?" Zander mutters.

Everyone shrugs their shoulders. I'm still stunned, sitting on my ass, Xavier seizes me underneath my armpits, and brings me up to my feet.

"Get your legs under you. She really left you weak in your knees?" Xavier sneers.

Grabbing my sack of coins, I hotfoot out of the mess hall and hit the stairs, skipping steps along the way. Walking to my room, I secretly hope to see Raelynn again. Just another glimpse. The hallway is silent and vacant. My countenance changes dramatically; disappointment creases the corners of my face. I enter my room, and it is more of the same. Empty, barren, and lonely.

I slept in late today. I'm expecting Bruce to knock on my door at any moment. My eyes are heavy, my mind swirling, and my heart beating differently than it ever has before.

'Bang, bang, bang.' The noise ripples off the walls of my room. Fully dressed and ready to be equipped with armor, I take long strides towards the door, opening it fully.

"Mr. Hastings, master Kilroy is in the gym waiting." Bruce squeals, urging me to come.

"Heading that way now."

I blow past Bruce with speed. My family's fate is tied to this Dan fellow from the Loyalist guild. He has to be just as nervous as I. With a piece of toast in hand, I bypass everyone, not stopping long enough for any substantial conversation.

Entering the gym, I see an array of metals, chain mail, and cloth. Kilroy is standing with his hand on his hips, looking rather flustered. Dressing in a complete set of armor is never enjoyable, especially for the person doing the dressing.

"Ahh, there you are. You made me worried, son. Are you ready for this?" Kilroy asks, gazing at me.

"Yes, sir. I'm ready as ever."

"Very well. Stand here and follow my orders. We need to get you squared away. This will take some time."

I put on a long-sleeved padded shirt, a padded hood, cloth pants, and cloth form-fitting footwear. Then Kilroy assisted me in putting chain mail on my entire body, including mail around my cloth feet. The padded cloth undergarments provided a slight relief from the mail being uncomfortable. Kilroy then spent time buckling armor to every inch of my body, from the metal greaves covering my shins to the gauntlets on my wrists. My body is lathered in metal, including a breastplate, metal sabatons, and a metal tasset skirt. My body was now encased in a silvery glow.

Kilroy hands me my helmet, insisting I understand, "Good, it fits you well enough. The visor on your helmet doesn't latch. Keep that in mind. I know you are well aware that your face, armpits, knee pits, and palms are your most vulnerable points. You'll be given a long sword as your primary weapon and a dagger as your secondary. Either bludgeon him to death or hit him in one of the accessible points."

I shake my head in agreement. My body clunks and rattles with each step. We walk out of the gym and eventually make our way to the street. Bruce has prepared two horses for us. We rode to the courtyard steadily and proudly. There was a sense of authority in riding a horse to an event like a knight, empowering me as if I were the champion before entering the ring. That feeling soon escalated as we entered the courtyard.

Citizens gathered from all around to witness the duel. Shoulder to shoulder, they are tightly packed like sardines. The two-story buildings surrounding the yard had their windows open, allowing people a bird's-eye view.

My heart sinks seeing more bettors placing wagers. To think, people are gambling money in my name. Do they know the extent of my past injuries? Does that affect the odds? Dueling is becoming less about politics and more about entertainment. I am no entertainer.

Dismounting, I found the Federalists' corner, along with my family and friends. Given my current steel-plated condition, I stand out like a sore thumb. Someone grabs my head and brings me in close, whispering.

"Don't forget yourself." Rupert's deep voice surprises me, and I pull away and examine him.

Why isn't he up on the balcony judging? The thought crosses my mind, and I'm immediately pulled to another place mentally. Mom, Sofia, and even Dad brought me in close for a hug, giving their support. My duel-mates and Raelynn are on my side of the ring with an impeccable view. My heart skips a beat as I see Raelynn. I need to impress her, but I can't get distracted right now if I want a chance at pursuing her.

The armor clangs loudly as I take a big step up into the ring. The metal is annoying and awkward, putting an extra fifty-five pounds on my body. I can manage this easily, though. I may not be as agile as usual, but I'm protected. The sandy terrain could pose some potential issues, I note, as I drive my metal shoe along the slippery terrain.

I put my helmet over my hooded head and draw my long sword. I'm holding it in both hands, at the ready. Looking up on the balcony above, Mr. Flemming was preparing to call out the grounds of our combat engagement. Tarron and the futile Rass-hole stand at his sides. Across from me, Dan emerges into the ring. He was fully armored up just like me. His build is bulkier than mine, but he is much shorter. He put his helmet on; his visor was still up, and his smug face was still visible.

A thundering voice projects through the yard.

In the name of Tyren,
let this be known as,
'The Duel of the Hastings Farm'
Daniel Rowley of Lyon,
representing the Loyalists.
Vs.
Amis Hastings of Lyon,
representing the Federalists.

"Please show each other respect and dignity. If Dan is the Champion, the Hastings family will be forced to leave Lyon for the wrongful killing of the Loyalists, Bryson. If the gods' will be that Amis is victorious, the Loyalists will be required to pay for the damages of the Hastings property." Mr. Flemming expanded his lungs, drawing a deep breath. "Let the duel commence!" A whistle simultaneously shrieks.

With one hand, I held my visor, pulling it down over my face. My eyesight is immensely limited by the slit of light peering through my helmet and visor. Dan advances toward me. My body begins to squeeze frightfully against my armored shell. My claustrophobia has enhanced my anxiety to a new extreme. My lungs can't reach their full capacity; inhalation is almost nonexistent.

Pushing all that stress to the side, I converge on Dan. We approach each other in a wide-measure stance, with the hilts of our swords resting on our belts.

This short guard position, held by each of us, is the ideal technique for fighting in armor, allowing us to keep our swords up and pointed towards each other. We circle one another, adding to the tension of our fight.

From Dan's short guard stance, he aggressively thrusts his sword directly at my neck. In confusion, I step quickly back, dropping my guard. His thrust misses, even with my sword not up in defense. He circles his sword back towards me. The tip passes by my face. Continuing my retreat, Dan winds up and slashes lethally from the other direction. This time, I raise my sword to meet him and force his blade to miss broad. Dan stumbles past me.

We both spin to meet each other again in a wide-measure stance, with our hilts on our belts. I attacked, forcefully beating my sword against Dan's, causing him to lose his guard. Continuing my assault, I thrust my sword in one forceful plunge towards his neck. He smacks my sword away tactfully. Dan proceeds to swing wildly in my direction. His arrogance and lack of control are on full display. I over parry, whipping my sword to block him away. Dan attempts to cut around the opening on my other side, where I'm vulnerable. This causes me to half-sword, where I block the incoming blow by reinforcing my sword's structure with my off hand on my blade. Stinging pain emanates from my hand.

Pushing forcibly against him, we become dead-locked. His hand grips my wrist as he tries to gain control. Using all his momentum, he head butts me, transferring a brutal impact against my steel helmet. The velocity of the blow breaks our deadlock and creates distance between us.

Dan again waves his sword high towards my unlatched visor. At this moment, I duck beneath the swinging blow. Carrying my momentum forward, I grapple him. My sore right shoulder pinned against his waist, driving him backward in an attempt to tackle him to the ground. Dan violently pounds my back with his elbow, attempting to hinder my pursuit. Finally, after a few yards of physicality, I was able to bring him down, slamming him onto his back.

A dust cloud fumes the air around us. Cheers can be heard erupting from the crowd. On top of him, I bludgeon him with brute force. Smacking my fist ferociously, trying to inflict knock-out trauma. To my surprise, Dan unsheathed his dagger and slices my chain mail at my waist. The armor protects against the slice, but I don't think it would survive a direct stab. Moving is crucial. Rolling off of Dan, I get back to my feet with my long sword, back into the wide-measure stance. Dan does the same by throwing his dagger into the dirt and grabbing his long sword.

We clash swords in a synchronized motion. Then, with my free hand, I grab my blade, half-swording, so

I could precisely aim for his vulnerable armpit. He uses both hands on his sword, thwarting my attempt and then smacking my visor with his hilt. I fell backwards. Dan charges me and unleashes a deadly strike that brandishes a gleaming arch. I instantly raise my sword with one unstable hand in an attempt to prevent death. His blow is halted, but in the process, it sends my sword flying.

The tumultuous gathering of citizens began stirring energetically, adding unwelcome energy to the duel.

Immediately, I disengage, reversing course as swiftly as possible. I have to stay away from him. Now, I unsheathe my dagger and wield it as my only weapon. Dan flails his sword belligerently, hoping to hit me with a vital strike. I dodge swing after swing on the heels of my feet. Each of his strokes is more powerful than the next, causing him to step into every motion. He's over pursuing.

The crowd is egging Dan on, only giving him unneeded confidence and momentum.

He launches another wild strike in my direction. Seeing my opportunity, I slid my foot under his, tripping him. Just like Nate taught me. Dan falls to the ground, and I pounce on top of him. His long sword is now obsolete in these close quarters.

In a swift assault, I plunge my dagger into his armpit, breaching his chainmail, causing him to wail uncontrollably. Pushing up his visor, his eyes widen until I see the whites of them. Fear is setting in. Tears streak along his distressed face. A vision replays vividly in my mind of Trisha dying.

I raise my arm and smash his chin with the hilt of my dagger. Knocking him out cold. I chose mercy, that is, if Dan doesn't bleed out.

The crowd erupts with an eerie display of cheers. Their fervent bloodlust was on clear display. This is not how an ordinary society should act when witnessing life-threatening violence. Are we a product of our surroundings or a people who have lost their ideologies as a whole? Relying solely on a corrupt regime that leads us to immorality. I raise my visor and remove my helmet as the chaos of applause unfolds around me. I'm at the root of this broken tradition of bloodshed.

I head directly back to my corner, surprisingly unassisted, without any new gashes. I see my Dad with a wide grin, and then, of course, my perverted eyes find Raelynn. I gravitate towards her unconsciously, and she seems pleased with the outcome. A soft, comforting smile from her breathtaking face emerges, making me extremely uneasy. A swarm of hugs envelops my metal frame. Mom and Sofia bring me close, reminding me that nothing is more potent than love. What people need is love.

"You did it, great execution, son." Mom congratulates me.

"And he did with humility, honestly, that fight could've gone either way, I almost wanted you to lose so we could get out of this shitty town." Sofia sneers.

I'm in too much shock to acknowledge Sofia's silly words; all I do is remove the padded hood from my head, and beads of sweat dribble down from my drenched brown hair. This action causes Sofia to startle backward with a crude expression, as if I had just disgusted her.

Pivoting, I looked at Dan's injured body. A few people gather around him to assist and assess the damage. To my knowledge, I didn't pierce any major blood vessels with my blade; the dirt would be much redder if I did. He is awake but appears to be very incoherent about his surroundings.

A familiar colorless voice speaks. "You did well, brother; Niklas would be proud."

"Thanks, Rupert. Well, what do we do now?" I pose the question to my party in earshot.

"Get the hell out of here and away from these deranged people," Dad says, because he's claustrophobic.

I'm the one stuck in this cramped armor, with chainmail riding up places it shouldn't. We walked away as a family, and my guildmates followed behind.

326 | P a g e

Chapter Twenty-Four:

The Stage

"Aahhh. I can't tell you how good it feels to be free of that metal confinement." I express, as relief washes over my face, as the last metal gauntlet is removed.

"You'd better change your clothes. Every bit of you is dripping wet in perspiration. Raelynn won't find this attractive." Zander cringes, placing the last armor piece down.

"What are you talking about? I don't care what Realynn thinks!" Obviously lying. "Plus, she could totally be into sweaty men."

"Maybe sweat, but not body odor. Clean yourself, mate!"

The door to the practice ring flies open as the most obnoxious individual I know galivants in with pure excitement. Causing unnecessary commotion across the wood floor. His facial expression is more than frightening, with a broad smile raising his cheeks.

"Guess what, guys!"

"What is it now, Xavier?" Zander moans.

"I finally grew balls and asked Veronica out. She said yes!"

"That's it? Wow, so wonderful. You are perfect for each other. Your endless flirting was getting a little much!" Zander hisses sarcastically in pure annoyance.

"Don't be such a negative puss. Anyway, there's more! Tonight, there's going to be a feast in the courtyard hosted by our guild."

I close my eyes, imagining. This is my chance. Raelynn leaves tomorrow for the capital. My eyes pop open, and I kick my sore legs into gear. Bolting out of the gym, not giving any concern to Zander and Xavier's reaction. I'm sure their countenances were unchanged by my abruptness. Going up the spiral staircase, I could hear another shuffle of feet, not my own. Raelynn reached the stairs, scurrying up after me in a hurry. Shit, even when she runs, it's enough to ensnare my mind.

"Amis, slow down! I need to talk to you." Raelynn cries out.

Her order petrifies me into stone. She is so quick that I have no chance to gulp down my nervousness. As collected as I can get, I say lackadaisically, "Oh, Rae, what's up?"

Restraining herself quickly, she takes a loud breath. "I wanted to say excellent job with your duel today. It was refreshing to see another dueler exercise kindness."

"Oh, thanks, I got lucky. I've been taught to give mercy… I don't envy your situation; they don't let you choose mercy in the capital."

A slight frown creases her red lips. "No, they don't, I don't know if I can follow through." Drastically changing the subject, she continues, "I know I don't have much time here, but would you be willing to go to the feast with me?"

I visibly mull over the decision to make myself not look too eager. Rae bites her bottom lip in anticipation. Seeing her luring lips, I lose my willpower.

"Rae, I'm going to change and wash up. I will meet you in the mess hall after." Shit, am I too assertive?

"Okay, only because you're the champion for today." She winks.

"That being the case, you'd better enjoy me while you can."

She closes the gap between us, kisses me on the cheek, spins, and walks away. Eagerness makes my knees buckle.

"Sorry if my cheek is salty from the sweat!" I blurt out awkwardly.

"I don't mind." She disappears down the steps.

I'm in trouble. Rae spikes my nerves but soothes my soul all at once.

This girl can stab my heart, leave me bleeding out, and my heart would still beat for her. Physically, I'm alone again, but mentally, I will never be free. My thoughts will now and forever be focused solely on her.

Clean and polished, I'm fresh and ready to put myself out there again. My clothes now consist of a black leather jacket with the Federalists' red three-headed snake pinned to my shoulder, a white cloth shirt underneath, and black pants. Although Rae's time in Lyon is limited and she could quickly meet her fate in Harpstedt, my heart tells me I need to pursue her. There has to be hope that she'll survive.

As I wait in the mess hall for Rae to show, I see Veronica and Xavier walking hand in hand towards the courtyard. They will have a volatile relationship, but Veronica is capable of handling Xavier. A few minutes later, Zander and April do the same. None of them acknowledge my presence, but I'm sure they all know by now where my mind is.

"Mr. Hastings, I have something to discuss with you." It's the ancient fart Tarron.

I silently nodded in shock. How'd this decrepit man sneak up on me?

"Have you been in correspondence with your brother Nate?" Tarron's raspy voice sounds off.

"No, Sir, I haven't. Not since the duel against Trisha. Is something wrong?"

"Pity. No, nothing is wrong with Nate, just for our duelers. Nate has been brutal, dominating every opponent he has faced. He's killed three of ours in Harpstedt."

Nate's a machine. I avert my eyes from Tarron's rickety frame to the doorway. Rae is standing in the hallway, looking desirable as ever, waiting patiently for me.

"That's unfortunate, sir. Why are you telling me this?"

"News gets around quickly; your skills and abilities are needed to replace those dying in the capital. You will be traveling tomorrow morning with Mykel and Rae."

Thoughts race through my mind; this saggy, aged man is not the one to ask. He hopes to see discomfort and frustration wash over my face. I must remain even keeled and manage my temperament.

Straight face and softly, I ensure no emotions slip out. "Yes, sir, is there anything else I can assist you with?"

"No, enjoy the feast. That little dueler from Havensburg looks more than ready to disappear with you." Tarron sneers.

Tarron wobbly departs the room, whispering something to Rae on his way out. Her eyes widen, and her body language changes. Sadness engulfs her face.

"What did he tell you?" I mumble.

"That you received the same fate as me."

"I'm not going to let you die."

"No, WE aren't going to let each other die." She demands, clearly enunciating each word.

My grip around her tightens; the smell of her hair melts me completely. I don't know her, but I'm a sucker for jumping in with both feet.

A wide smile crosses my face enough so that my teeth are exposed. "Shall we go?" I say, putting my hand out.

"Yes." She takes my hand excitedly, and we intertwine our fingers.

My heart leaps for joy, realizing that I'm the luckiest man in the world. There's no point in complaining about future circumstances. Yes, I must go to Harpstedt; yes, I will leave my family behind; and yes, there's a legitimate possibility that I will have to fight Nate. I have Rae to face those challenges with, I'm not alone.

This is the first time that I've walked to the courtyard without any added stress, uncertainty, or utter concern. I'm actually looking forward to the feast. The stone streets feel different now, and even the nasty aroma of the cesspit gutters isn't ruining my mood.

"So, what were you like before dueling?" I pose the question to Rae in hopes to learn the true her.

"Well, I have two brothers, and I'm right smack in between both of them. They have completely different personalities, but both are extremely book smart. They are two people you wouldn't want to debate, and my older brother is a ruthless scumbag. He's more of a politician, I'd say."

"Why aren't you a politician?" I tease.

She glares at me with her eyes and punches my arm. "Dueling was never my choice. That's why I've never killed and never plan to."

I rub my arm, "Remind me never to piss you off. Are you always this abusive?"

"Oh, just wait and see. Give it a few more days and see if you want to stick around."

"I like that you don't want to slay anyone, but how do you plan to escape that in Harpstedt?"

"I'm not sure, kind of making it up as I go." She sighs.

Changing the troubling subject, I ask, "What are your parents like?"

"My Mom was the sweetest person. She always made me feel safe. I like to think I'm more like her than my father." Rae looks away. Sadness protrudes softly from Rae's lips as she continues. "My Mom was my best friend; she passed when I was young, and I never saw much of my Dad."

"I'm so sorry, I didn't mean to bring that up. Who raised you and your brothers in Havensburg?"

The devil incarnate, my grandmother. If Athren believes in hell, she'd be the devil's Queen." Rae laughs, making light of her past.

"Noted. Let's never cross that witch."

"Someday I will have to, if I want to save my younger brother."

I now know never to pry about her family life. She's been through more trauma than I. A dumb question billows up and spills out of my mouth. "What do you like to do for fun?"

She raises her eyebrows. "Fun? There's not much fun for a peasant girl like me. Cleaning, cooking, and spinning are all routine chores that can burn in hell with Granny."

"Damn, you remind me of my sister Sofia, who is very pessimistic. There has to be a hobby you enjoy aside from the hellish chores. You are the best person I've ever seen with a throwing knife."

"I guess I do love reading, that's something I've really invested in since winning all the blood money. I've purchased a large variety of books, ranging from fairy tales to romance and history. I read to bring peace to my soul, and I throw knives to cut nerve-racking tension."

A smile enriches my naturally mug-stained face. "I have a book I think you'd like to read."

She grabs my hand tighter; sweat is building up between our fingers, but neither of us dares to let go. We reached the courtyard; people were littered everywhere. This is definitely all the elites of Lyon, gathered up in one privileged venue. Below the ring are tables in a singular line. A lavish array of food includes fish, roasted meats, vegetables, pastries, and elaborate desserts.

Seats lined both sides of the table, including plates of all kinds. My Mom, Sofia, and Rupert are in their seats waiting patiently to chow down. Dad isn't here, honestly, I'm not surprised. He doesn't like to socialize, and at the last big dinner event he attended, his parents' heads were disturbingly unveiled before him.

My guildmates find their seats. They've been different, to say the least, since I got back. Tarron sits at the head of the table, looking down upon the large row of people. I sit next to Mom, and Rae sits on my left. Sofia bobs her head around, looking at Mom, and gives me a proud smile. Her hand reaches around Mom's back, and I give her a high five. Clearly, she is impressed with my ability to bring Rae.

I lean up to Mom and whisper in her ear, "There's something I need to tell you and Dad." My tone is urgent.

"Not now. Not the time or place for serious conversation." Mom sternly says.

"My dear friends, associates, and colleagues, thank you for attending this feast of feasts. The Federalists of Lyon are indeed grateful. With our guild now winning the last few duels, I feel that I can express that the Gods' will is aligned with ours."

"The Loyalists have had spurts of success throughout the years that have allowed them to send duelists to the capital. We, as Federalists in Lyon, have not had that same success for many years, until now. Amis, please stand."

Aw crap. I push my chair out; it skids across the stone, making a terrible screeching sound, and I rise, staring at Tarron.

"Amis has been ordered to the capital. There, he will have a chance to represent Lyon on a bigger stage and become the champion not just of Lyon, but of all Athren. Please raise your glasses to Amis!" Tarron's deathly ill voice chimes out.

I dare not make eye contact with anyone in my family. I raise my glass.

"To Amis!" Everyone repeats in unison as they gulp down their drinks.

I sit back down swiftly. Embarrassment flushes my face as all eyes are turned onto me. Rather than sinking into my chair, my Mom puts her arm around my shoulder and pulls me in.

Her soft voice whispers, "Save Nate and come home."

Easier said than done, all I can do in response is nod. The dinner proceeds without any noteworthy events. I made sure to eat, filling myself to the brim. Mr. Brookshard tried to advise on the capital, but it was unwarranted, going in one ear and out the other.

On the dueling ring, a few people began to arrange displays, equipment, and props.

"They are turning the killing area into a stage," Zander says in pure disgust.

"Isn't it a stage already?" Veronica bites back.

They place three barge-like pallets across the now stage, with blue, watery waves of fabric cut out. A person in the corner plays a flute. A trident is on a stand on the center platform. Two performers emerge. This is a reenactment of Nate's first duel. I roll my eyes at Rae as the flute makes goofy satire's music. Are they really trying to make the horrific scenes funny?

Imposter Nate swims in the water with his head rising above the wavy watery cutouts. Addison has the trident, "Exclaiming, where is?" They even depicted Nate rising, sneaking behind Addison, mocking him, and eventually it gets to the point where Nate stabs Addison. The music sounds unrealistic and dramatic in the night air. Then, in another scene of mimicry, the actor emulates Nate by reproducing his words, "Not today, I'm the Champion!"

The crowd applauds with joy, clapping and laughing recklessly. This proves to me that they care more about entertainment than their party affiliation.

Rae turns to me with pain in her shaky voice, "They find comedy in this? First, they make us kill. Then they imitate how we fight and snicker in enjoyment in reflection."

People rush the stage, acting like stagehands setting up the next distasteful scene, removing all the props until the ring lies barren once more. Two more actors emerge, walking to the center of the ring, back-to-back. They are about to perform Nate and Harry's standoff. This isn't entertainment. Zander is in attendance, and now we have to witness them recreate Harry's death. The lighthearted parody of the duel is still too vivid and too sensitive. Zander abruptly stalks away halfway through, clearly emotionally.

The skits continue, recounting Trisha's death and Dan's defeat. I unfortunately stayed firm in my seat, trying my best to black out the scenes. Rae's support being by my side made me stronger and more adaptable to face the resurfaced trauma. The crowd continues to be amused by the satire, their comical giddiness undiminished. These aristocrats and ritzy elitists are not our friends.

Then the stagehands set up for another duel. Not one that has happened, but surely one that will come to fruition. Nate emerges on stage with a sword in hand, and an actor portraying me does the same. They 'brawl' and in the end, Nate dies. The Federalists all around cheer, ecstatically, drunken on their own stupidity.

Mom stands and grabs my shoulders, demanding, "It's time to go."

Getting up with my family, I notice a silence fall over the assembled Federalists. From Tarron to Veronica, their faces look upon us with pure discontent.

"We'd best be going; it's a long journey to the capital. We will need all the rest we can get. Thank you, Tarron, for orchestrating this feast." I announce, looking at each person's facial expressions.

No one utters a single word but continues in their unimportant conversations about duels. It's like they know they'll never see me again. Going to Harpstedt can be considered a death sentence. Pivoting, I put my hand on the small of Rae's firm back, and we walked away.

"So, Rupert, are you not a judge anymore?!" I ask while kicking a rock on the road towards Mykel's.

"Nope, I was sick of being a pawn in corrupt games. I fear that I would become just like one of those arrogant fools. Furthermore, I finished that book. That has been extremely eye-opening, changing my perspective on the entire system. Righteous people must gain power in Athren; dueling has to end." Rupert stammers off.

"Finished already?!" My face is in shock.

"I'll give it back to you, but it'd be risky bringing that to the capital. They'd execute you on the spot if they find it. If you really want it, though, I will give it to you when we reach Mykel's."

Then, Mom changes the subject, probing Rae. "What do you think of Lyon?"

"The people are the same as Havensburg. It also offers some beautiful views; the jagged mountains and expansive meadows are absolutely stunning. I'm always going to be an ocean girl. Something about the salty breeze."

"Havensburg is very beautiful, I've spent time there myself," Mom says agreeably. "How'd your family handle you leave?"

"About the way you'd expect. They are pushed into a corner; this is the only way to free them." Rae says low and sad.

That's an odd way to put it. She looks visibly upset at the thought, which makes sense. She may never see them again in this life.

Breaking the dismal vibes, Sofia teases. "Have you kissed Amis? Does his breath stink like rotten fish?"

A giggle escapes Rae's red lips as she blushes. "No, he hasn't tried, but I'll let you know the fishy level if he ever does."

"We've only known each other for a few days, don't make it weird!" I say, scolding Sofia.

"Amis, honestly, you slept with a blanky till you were twelve; clearly, you're an oddball."

"Rae, speaking of odd, has he told you about his evil ex in the capital?" Rupert asks, adding to the hazing.

"Ooh, ex-girlfriend in the capital. Should I be scared?" Rae questions, encouraging Rupert on.

"Oh no. You could smash Mariam like a stink bug." Sofia chimes.

Mykel's part of the town seems wealthier with much less commerce and congestion. Reaching his fence, a voice rang out towards us. On the porch, Mykel and Dad sit in rocking chairs, clearly awaiting our arrival.

"How was the feast?" Dad bellows towards us.

Unlatching the gate, Rupert responds, "Rather uneventful, except Amis has something to tell you."

Dad changes his view, looking at me. "Thanks, Rupert... Tarron informed me that I'm going to be joining the guild in the capital and am leaving tomorrow with Rae."

"I'm not one bit surprised, son. Mykel received his orders to escort you and Rae earlier in the day. They're trying to expose you."

"Oof, I don't know if I'm ready. Tarron said Nate is killing all the Federalists."

"Indeed. Amis, you're the only person who can stop him." Dad sighs. "On a more important note, who is this girl, Rae?"

"I'm just another poor soul that met the same unwarranted fate as your son." Rae's soft voice quirks up.

"A Dueler's Fate has a way of bringing new people into your life. People don't stick around for long if we don't cherish them. Please watch over my son, sometimes he gets a little irrational, thinking with his heart and not his brain." Dad rants jokingly.

"He's in good hands, trust me!" Rae adds.

"Let's get inside," Mykel interjects.

We were all ushered into Mykel's living space. It's small and cramped, but nothing compared to what our old home was. It's a nice little bachelor pad, though; a girl in his life could help him around the rough edges.

Rae is in a chair, and I'm on the ground on the wood floor in front of her. I like these cramped spaces with her; it gives me an excuse to keep physical contact. Dad stands up in front of all of us like he's about to give a lesson.

"There are important matters I need to discuss with you all. Starting with our farm. Brookshard has approached me with a reasonable offer to purchase our land, and with the payment from the Loyalist guild for the destruction they caused, we will make enough money to travel wherever we'd like. Your mother and I have both agreed that we have outgrown Lyon."

"Dad! That farm is our home, and Niklas is buried there!" Sofia cries out.

"Yes, you are right, Sofi. Brookshard has agreed to maintain the property and keep Niklas' grave protected. He will allow us to visit whenever we'd like. Lyon has been our home for twenty-five years, but we came here to blend in and hide. The time for hiding is over."

"Where are you all going to go?" Confusion laces my face.

"Seems the capital is the most logical place." Mom answers.

"See, Amis, you won't ever get out from under Mom and Dad's thumb!" Sofia laughs.

"Speak for yourself! You're only fourteen!" I say, taunting back at her.

"What about our animals that survived the fire?" Rupert asks in worry.

"We will keep a few chickens and the horses, the rest we will sell," Dad answers.

"Can we eat, Leo?" I blurt out.

"Who's Leo?" Raelynn asks.

"Amis' nemesis, a whittle bitty rooster," Sofia says, grinning. Rae chuckles, placing her hands softly on my shoulders.

Dad continues, "Amis, I can promise you'll never see that rooster again. Now the second item, the road to Harpstedt. Who knows what lies waiting? Plenty of demons want you dead. Be cautious. I'm pleased Mykel will be with you."

"I thought Mykel had to be impartial to train each of the guild duelers?" Rupert questions.

"I do but think of me as a mercenary for higher," Mykel says, rubbing his gray beard.

"Last thing. Amis, you'll get to the capital before us. Try to pull Nate aside and inform him of everything that's happened. Tell him about Rasmussen, the burnt farm, the book, and our real past. Let him decide for himself what route he wants to travel. He has a right to choose for himself and exercise the will God gave him."

"There are things from our past…" Dad motions to Mykel and Mom. "Which has put us in this situation today. Yes, we all used to be duelers, and we did escape the oppressive and corrupt institution of dueling. Yes, I did kill the King, and yes, the Queen and her offspring still live. We don't know who or where he is, but we assume he is trying to reestablish the monarchy."

I can sense Rae tensing as she unconsciously digs her claws into my shoulders. I worry that we're sharing too much about ourselves. I don't want to push her away.

I place a hand on hers and she seems to calm. "I have a genuine question. Would you like us to call you Henry or Gentry?" I pose the prompt.

He ponders for a second and, with a serious face, says, "Dad."

Chapter Twenty-Five:

Journey

I've walked the desolate streets of Lyon at night several times these past few months. None of those times have felt quite like this. Darkness looms around every corner as usual. I never experienced a set of bittersweet emotions like this before. Knowing I'll be without my family, but I will have Rae. I don't fully understand the girl, but I want to. I'm willing to dive all the way in, even if it means I won't make it out in one piece.

"What'd you think of tonight?" I say ruining the quietness. Rae seemed to be deep in thought.

"Which part, the feast, or your family? One of them was misery, and the other was a hoot. Your family is a bunch of rebels!

I smile immensely, "Yes, you could say my family is willful." I laugh, adding, "At least the food at the feast was delightful!"

"I suppose! By the way, champ, your creepy friend Xavier was staring daggers at you the whole time."

"No way. Xavier?" I say incredulously.

"Yup! That little shit has a girl, but apparently, he's jealous of you." She snaps her head at me with a smile.

"I mean, I would be jealous too. Have you looked in a mirror?" I say it as smoothly as possible.

She giggles, "That reminds me of a pickup line my older brother used to use."

"Ya, let's hear it!" I say in explicit encouragement.

"Do you have a mirror in your pants?" I stared blankly, not answering. "Because I can see myself in them!"

The barren street echoes with boisterous laughter.

"My turn."

Rae bites her lip, wearing a flirtatious smile. "Okay."

"You have the key to my heart, and I have the key to your chastity belt."

Rae spits out a cute giggle. "Not yet, Champ."

"Champ?" I squint my eyes at her hard.

"You don't see the back side that I do… Champ."

I laugh, shaking my head. "Rae, do you trust me?" I directed her to the sidewalk next to a store.

"Yeah, I think so."

"Intertwine your hands like you are going to pray," I order.

"Okay, like this?" Her right and left hands clasp together.

"Perfect, now extend your right-hand fingers."

Immediately, I folded my right hand over hers, pinning her hands tight. Walking backwards, I find the wall with my left hand and press Rae's firm body softly against it. I lift our folded hands high above her head, still clasping her hands tight, so she forfeits control. I catch the scent of roses, a sweet, floral aroma with a hint of spice. Rae's eyes meet mine.

"Now what?" She says, biting her bottom lip.

I lose control. Sliding my left hand in her thick brown hair on the back of her neck and pinning her hands against the wall, I plant my lips on hers, kissing. Her lips are soft and gentle against mine. The subtle movement and pressure of her mouth tell me this is precisely what she wants. Our passionate position sends chills down my body; she is willing to trust me while being in such a vulnerable state. I gently pulled away, wanting so much more. Releasing her hands, a radiant grin appears on my face.

"Wow, what if I freaked out?" Rae asks, inhaling a gulp of air.

"To be honest, I'm sure you would've found a physical way to tell me to stop, and I would've listened."

"I've never felt so powerless, but so safe at the same time," Rae admits.

"I felt the same way when you threw that knife above my head. I trusted you completely. How come you left the room after you caught the knife over my head?”

“I’ve routinely flung a knife in the air a thousand times, but that one was the most nerve-racking because you made my heartbeat impeccably fast.”

“Ya let’s not fly weapons at each other anymore.” I tease.

Reaching into my cloth sack, I pull out the book and review it one more time for signs of tampering.

“What’s that?” Rae asks, intrigued.

“Here’s the book I was telling you about.”

“Are you sure you want me to have this? It’s just that you don’t know me well enough to-”

“I trust you.” I cut her off.

She gives a forced smile; I have a tough time reading her face as I hand her the book.

We made it back to the guild, and I walked her to her room. I could spend every moment with her, but alas, she’d grow tired of me eventually.

“I loved your family, by the way! Your parents have their hands full with Sofia. Thank you for tonight, and for the seductive kiss on the street.”

Rae steps into my space once more; my body language was more than inviting. She plants a quick, intoxicating kiss on my lips. Shivers race down my spine. Slowly retracting her hand, she turns and enters her room.

I'm frozen; this girl makes me feel alive. Mariam never made my heart beat out of my chest like this, and I loved her. She was always so much colder and more serious, making me feel uncomfortable in my own skin. Raelynn is different, and I know God placed her here for me. Am I too trusting to loan her the book?

Heading further down the hall to my room, I immediately noticed my door slightly ajar. Reaching down and unsheathing a dagger, I cautiously approach my room. When I reach the open door, I push it hard, so it swings fully open, and I take a hop backward. Surely if this were an ambush, they would've stirred in some capacity by now.

I compose myself by taking a deep breath and keeping my eyes on a swivel. One quick, quiet stride, and I enter my exposed room. Checking every nook and cranny, there are no signs of life. Instead, my room is dismantled. All my clothes were tossed across the ground, drawers open, the closet ransacked, and my mattress flipped.

Shit! Someone is going to die. It's a good thing my book was with me. Well, now with Rae. Taking account of all my personal items, I notice my letters from Niklas are missing. This must be Rasmussen's work. What did the letters say exactly?

- *Loyalist and Federalist are corrupt., egotistical, power-hungry bigots.*

- *Go to the Lyons Library, and someone will recognize you as a Hastings. They will give you a manuscript.*
- *Avoid the guilds.*

I rearrange my bed and secure the door with a cabinet and a chair on top of it. In my paranoia, I even double-checked the window. I won't sleep tonight. Weapons lay at the ready all around me, in case of another intruder. Hours go by, and I close my eyes, only to think about Raelynn; her life is in jeopardy with that book.

Morning comes abruptly, with the streaks of sun rays slicing through my bedroom window. The one pleasant thing about my room being ransacked last night is that it made packing easier.

We will be leaving soon, I'm sure. Whipping my bag over my shoulder, I pursue the front door of the guild. I pat myself down, confirming all my weapons and personal items are properly secured.

The moment I open the front door; I feel the fresh pine air swooping in against me. The sun is brighter today, and its warming rays shine bright, illuminating the day. My eyes adjust to the natural light, and immediately I see the sight of Rae. She is sitting on a stone step, facing away from me, looking out at the bustling street. Her brunette hair falls down her back, braided to perfection, with sunlight radiating off it, making it glisten.

I walk up behind her noisily so she's aware of my presence and sit on the stone steps of the guild next to her.

"Hey, you're ready to get out of here, aren't you?"

"My Dad always told me, 'If you're on time, you're late.' I don't plan on being late, especially not today."

"What's so special about today?" I ask out of pure ignorance.

"I get to leave with you."

Our faces lit up, and our expressions mirrored each other's happiness. We wait together for Mykel to show and for Kilroy to send us off. I told Rae about my trashed room from the night before; her body language showed growing fear.

"Amis, did the letters say anything that could incriminate anyone?" She asks.

"No one, Niklas was very cautious."

"I read the book a little last night. Your parents are bad ass. I hate to say it, but someone knows who they are." She's dead right, somebody does, and it's probably Rass-hole. "Good thing we have a few days on the road to think everything through!" Rae speaks with optimism.

The street matured, holding a larger crowd than usual, with an increased unrest. A cluster of people moves along like blood traveling through arteries. My family is among them, dressed in their best attire, with what they had left over from the fire.

Mykel walked beside them and his horse. Mykel's wearing a leather vest with no sleeves, exposing his toned biceps. He looks like a warrior ready for battle, carrying a large axe strapped to his back and daggers at his waist. His pack on the back of his horse is full. I noticed a bow also strapped there.

I stood up instantly, darting to my Mom and greeting her with a hug. My head towers over her, enabling me to notice people around me on the street. Kilroy and Zander were walking in our direction, steering horses of their own. I look longingly at my parents, with Rae at my side.

"Amis, don't die before we get there." Sofia orders.

"What about after?"

"I give you permission to die once we arrive," Sofia says, shrugging her shoulders with a smirk.

"No one is going to die, don't say stupid things!" Rupert remarks harshly.

"Well, not yet anyway! Keep popping that tone, and I'll kill you right now." Sofia violently gestures with an evil scowl.

"Rae and Amis don't have time to listen to you two goons' banter. Son, remember everything we taught you. Rae, please take care of him!" Dad states straight-faced.

"With my life, Mr. Hastings!" Rae retorts.

"You can call me Gentry."

My head turns back and forth as I view our surroundings. Dad just said that in the wide open. People weave around us in the street as usual. No one seemed to take note of us, and Kilroy was barely out of earshot.

I express my final goodbyes, and we approach our horses. Loading my pack and weapons on the back, I carefully keep my hatchets easily accessible. Zander's eyes are visibly sad and heavy, with bags under them, looking tired.

"Are you okay?" Concern is evident in my voice.

"Don't worry about me, you are the one I'm worried about."

"Thank you for all your help. You are truly another brother to me. Where are the others?" I question, expecting them to walk out of the guild at any given moment.

"They were pulled away, unfortunately. Keep your head on a swivel, trust no one."

His words sting my heart. 'Trust no one.'

Our credulous journey had begun. We head south, leaving the streets of Lyon behind for the countryside as we make our way onward, following the road of Murcia around Ash Reservoir. Shirtless Mykel leads us as our guardian and guide.

The people in Lyon pay no attention to the three of us gallivanting out of town. When we reach the last set of houses in town, I notice an odd detail of a few Athren guards. Their faces seem to be all looking up in a tree with disturbing expressions. When we reach their position by the edge of town, I follow their gazes.

Horror cages me as pain stabs me like a searing knife to the core. The old librarian dangled lifeless from a rope in a tall willow tree.

"What in the name of Harwen..." Mykel says, dragging each word. "Why would they hang this poor old lady?"

Rae looks petrified and sick. "Is this because-"

"Yes."

"Ms. Cunningham knew the risks," Mykel says in comfort.

"It's my fault. Someone broke into my room last night. They found the letter from Niklas."

"Amis, people take risks. This is a risk she took. Now lift your head and mourn when you arrive in Harpstedt. Ride with haste, my young companions, we are surely chum in the water now."

Looking to the west, I see the tall peaks of the Oquirrh Mountains rising close to 11,000 feet. A vast forest full of predators and prey is located in all levels of that unexplored wilderness. The road we traverse is smooth and maintained, but we travel with such swiftness that it's impossible to soak in any of its hidden beauty.

We are traveling at a steady pace, hoping to cover thirty miles today. That will put us only fifty miles or so from the capital. Mykel informed us that this journey can be completed in two to three days easily, but it's significantly slowed when carts and wagons are involved. Good thing we are traveling light.

"How far south have you gone?" Rae asks as she grips her reins tightly for support and leans over to reach into her pack.

"I've been all over the reservoir. We've fished every hole in this area."

"Oh, good, so this is all familiar territory for you." She exhales as I notice her rip a piece of fabric and drop it to the ground.

I squint, intrigued by the oddity, and respond, "Passed the reservoir, I'm in the dark on our journey. So, what did you rip and drop?"

"Oh, 'Hehe,' my Dad gave me a colorful blouse for Harpstedt… I hate bright blouses."

"You and Sofia are similar in that way."

Traveling today took roughly nine hours. We stopped every three hours to give the horses a much-needed rest. Now, farther away from the place I called home, the scenery changed to more open fields and fewer forested trees. Mykel said that as we approach the capital, the landscape will become less and less green, and when we reach the Gulf of Athren, there'll be only thirty miles left in our journey.

We found a campsite off the road to avoid any unwanted visitors.

"Let's erect camp here." Mykel finally dismounts and suggests.

My eyes open wide, and I turn to Rae, holding in a chuckle.

"Is something funny?" Mykel looks at me in seriousness.

"Erect camp? That's an interesting choice of words!" I laugh alone hysterically.

"And you like him?" Mykel sighs in disbelief.

"I'm debating it now." Rae's teeth chatter as she jerks her head in disapproval.

"Right. Like I was saying, we will ERECT a camp here. Let your horse graze; there is a small pond for them to drink from, too. They need the rest."

"Mykel, it's baffling you don't have a woman." I tease.

"What makes you think I don't have a sweetheart?"

"Uhhh. I guess I've just never seen you-"

"Son, you don't eat where you piss!" Mykel admonishes. "Anyways," He glimpses our facial expression, "Janice the politician is who I'm sweet on. She is an extraordinary woman."

"You old birds do fit well together." I laugh.

We were exhausted from our first day of travel. My thighs are sore and on fire, but I dare not say anything. We decided to take shifts to observe our surroundings, the moonlit meadow, for any potential threats. I will start first. With my pack removed from the horse, all my personal items and weapons are accessible.

I prop myself up against a willow tree, much like the one Ms. Cunningham suspends from. Its vines dangle low all around us, making me feel dreadful, but concealed. The air smells sweet, with a floral scent from the wildflowers blossoming all around. An uneasy stillness permeates the air. Crickets create their high-pitched repetitive 'chirping' in their nightly ritual.

I lay there for roughly an hour, watching the dark woods beyond my view and having my ears attuned to unusual noises. My body begins to shut down, drifting off slowly. Fighting to maintain my cognitive function, I rip a piece of tall grass from the ground near me and place it in my mouth between my teeth. The bitterness broadens my eyes. Just two more hours, and I'll be able to switch night watch with Mykel.

Off in the distance, a shadow of a bird abruptly flies into the sky, catching my attention as my star-watching is disrupted. A faint, piercing 'shrill' comes and goes; the noise is unlike the crickets rubbing their legs. I steady my breath in hopes of hearing it again, slightly kicking Mykel awake. Again, the high-pitched noise resonates through the air.

I whisper Mykel's direction, "It's a signal."

Reaching quietly in the direction of the sleeping Rae, I placed my hand on her shoulder, waking her. She abruptly sits up, as if she's been awake the entire time. "Get up, something is coming."

Crouching with my sword in hand, I ready myself for whatever looms in the darkness.

A shadowy figure emerges and swings his sword rapidly at me. I'm able to parry the dark figure and then utilize the torque in my body with a countering blow. Mykel thrusts his sword at the perpetrator at the same time, and in unison, we drive our swords into the attacker's gut. A loud 'shriek' rings out, alerting all the other hunters in the field to our position. There are too many of them.

"Amis, Rae, over here now!" Mykel demands.

"Listen! I don't know how, but they found us. The two of you must go now. Run south on foot and stay off the road. When you hit the bay of Athren, keep going south thirty miles until you reach Lanstring. Take the ferry crossing there. It's a different direction; the normal route is too dangerous. Now fly."

"But Mykel, you'll."

"Go!"

Rae rips my arm, making me stumble backwards. We run into the mist of darkness, our cloth sacks, and weapons in hand. Turning back, I look to see Mykel. I hear only the clashing of swords and screams. He can't die; they can't kill him. Mykel's fierce mastery will uphold him.

"Amis! We need to go; we can't stay here." Rae drags me once more.

Running on the balls of our feet, we sprint through the field into the neighboring trees, entirely out of sight. The natural cover and lack of light on this night have given us prime camouflage. We still hurriedly move southwards, trying to maintain stealthiness along the way within the tree cover. After about an hour of intensity, I threw myself to my knees.

Pain, guilt, and regret swirl through me. I left Mykel to die. He faces a horde of enemies alone. His words from earlier drive me. "Lift your head, mourn when you get to the guild in Harpstedt."

"He sacrificed himself to save us. Amis!"

"How did they find us?" I blurt without thinking, being baffled.

Raelynn's face looks as tortured with pain as she says, "Someone wants you to die. If you don't stop lamenting, that'll transpire. Get up and make Mykel's sacrifice worth it."

I gather my breath. Brushing the dirt off my knees. Reaching out my hand sincerely I say, "Let's move on."

Chapter Twenty-Six:

Sanctuary

Observing our surroundings, there doesn't seem to be a soul in sight. I look up through the tall, towering trees for any sign of night light. There is no source of faint glimmering lights. I don't know if it's the dense canopy of leaves blocking my view or if clouds rolled overhead. The air is cool, and dampened soil lurks beneath our feet.

"I think it's going to rain, and from what I can tell, a substantial amount," Rae mutters.

"Really? Another one of your unique abilities?" I ask flirtatiously.

"Oh no, this one is common sense. The wind changed; see the roughness of the branches above? And listen, what's different? There are no more crickets."

My jaw drops in disbelief. Who is this girl?

Just then, droplets of rain start splattering the plants and trees, causing an enchanting melody. The wind picks up even more rampantly. Water droplets are falling and rolling off the trees in abundance, soaking us and the ground.

"We need to find shelter; this is more than a squall." Desperation sounds in my voice.

I grab Rae's hand and lead her forward. The storm's unfortunate power and ferocity are on full display, as wind gusts batter rain into our faces. We search urgently for some form of shelter in the depths of darkness.

"Look over there in the clearing!" Rae bellows out.

There's a shadowy structure in the middle of a clearing. Our feet carpet the earth, moving nimble and swiftly as they will conceivably take us, finally, within reach of the unknown structure that appears to be abandoned.

I found remnants of what used to be a door, lying off its hinges in shambles. Moving it cautiously to the side, we peer into what looks like an old hunting cabin.

"This will work!" Rae says in pure relief.

"Looks like there's a nasty mattress and even a fireplace! We might make it after all." I say maybe too sarcastically,

"We are soaked; think you could start a fire?"

"Let me try." I enjoy a nice challenge.

I retrieve my hatchet and flint from my pack; the same one I used in the cave. Bless your heart, Mykel.

My hands rummage around the small cabin, looking for anything that could be of use for kindling. Striking my flint, I create sparks, and eventually, I ignite the parchment paper I use for kindling. Luckily, there is some leftover firewood available for fuel.

The room is brightened, and to our joy, we find the cabin to be in better condition than we initially thought. There's only one leaking hole in the ceiling where the rain was dribbling through. Rain continues its onslaught outside, as we cozy up here. I block the window and door to prevent any light from escaping our enclosure.

Rae sits on the bed, "Somehow this might be better than my bed at home."

"Ya? Do you want to test it out?" I say rather nonchalantly.

"What do you mean, test it out, Champ?" Rae's eyebrows raise.

I try to read her face for indicators, so I know how to proceed. I'm left stumped. Rae is a stone-cold fox.

"Sleeping, of course, what else would you do in bed?" A smile etches into the corner of my mouth.

"We are trapped in a small cabin that has a fire going and one bed. It's around midnight. I can imagine a few things happening." Rae sputters with a smirk, enriching her face.

I walk casually toward her and lean down, placing one hand through her hair and the other under her chin.

Her luscious hair is wet and disheveled. To my surprise, her natural perfume still emits a sweet floral aroma. My heart races, and I lean in and kiss her. Soft, full lips match mine perfectly. The pure warmth and emotion our contact evokes eases my soul. The firm sensation felt throughout my whole body puts me on the brink of losing control.

Rae's back falls against the bed; my eyes explore. I seize the distance between us, kissing her passionately. My mouth wanders, and my hands want to do the same. In an instant, I'm lost in Rae.

Jerking back, I stand up abruptly, "As much as I want to continue. I don't have the willpower to stop again. I can't take advantage of you like this. The bed is all yours."

Rae is visibly flustered; I can tell she is feeling the heat of the moment. The red firelight bounces off her wet face, damn, she looks incredible.

"Okay, good night." She says, clearly, with a look of disappointment and confusion.

"Oh, do you want me to hang your clothes in front of the fire to dry?"

"These?!" She placed her hand on her chest in confusion.

"No." A laugh bursts out of my mouth. "The ones you have in your sack."

"Amis, you are going to have to work on something called CLAR-I-FY-ING. You almost saw all of me." She enunciates.

"In that case?" I tease.

"Oh, you're such a jackass!" Rae turns over to sleep.

I turn to set up a clothesline with some rope I found. When I was tying a knot, a wet shirt whipped the back of my head.

"Who's the jackass now?" I poke back.

"Watch it, Champ." Rae giggles.

I turned around. Rae, to my disappointment, has rolled over again; my eyes dare not linger now. I could've kept kissing her, but I can't be with her right now, not after what happened to my Dad's closet friend, Mykel. My parents were always sticklers about waiting until marriage, which is growing harder to do.

I hang the clothes to dry in front of the crackling fire. The slight smoky smell coming from the fireplace comforts me. I yank the wet clothes clinging to my body, hanging them to dry, and expose my toned muscles and soaked body.

I guess I'm foolish enough to do this, good thing Rae's asleep. Turning quickly to see if she's peaking, from what I can tell, I'm in the clear.

I review my tall, athletic build for any new damage. To my relief, I'm still put together. I have scars across my body where I was stabbed, shot, and clawed.

They all look pretty gnarly, making me feel like a ba-dass.

I sit down in a chair next to the fire; my eyes are trained on the pure fire crackling, but my thoughts are stuck on Rae. I'll do everything I can to protect that girl. I trust her with all my soul. Taking the book from her pack, I see it's still carefully wrapped in cloth. It must've been in the center of Rae's sack, because it isn't wet. I review the pages, and no water damage appears to have occurred.

Then Rae's voice startles me in my vulnerable state as she says, "Amis, I'm sorry about Mykel."

"It's not your fault; he could be alive. There is still hope."

"No, I really am sorry. My Dad used to say that when storms like this come, it's God's expression of discontent for our actions. I've lived through many storms."

"Could be, but God could have sent the rain to help us escape. Regardless, you were right earlier when you said we need to utilize Mykel's sacrifice even if he's alive."

"Yeah," Rae says with a bleak tone.

∞

The morning light whisps through the cracks in the door. The storm has passed; we ought to be going. I repacked all of our clothes and am now modestly dressed. Rae's dried clothes remain on the rope. 'Grunts' sound the room, and arms shoot out of the bed as she stretches mightily.

"Amis, can you toss me my clothes?"

"Of course." I stand up, walking to the rope, then I pause in realization.

"Hmm, wait a minute… This is a very precarious situation. You lie immodestly in that bed, of your own accord. You threw your clothes at me. Maybe I just ought to let you get up and retrieve them."

"Amis!"

"Yeah, I think I'll just sit down in this chair."

"Knock it off. Please give me my clothes! If you don't, we will stay here forever."

"That's not a bad idea, growing old with you here would be nice. Put all our problems behind us. But Rae, wouldn't you get sick of that bed?"

"Enough of the games! I'll start screaming!" Rae growls, being visibly frustrated.

"Whoa, okay, here you go." I throw them in her direction.

"You know, Amis, you surprise me. I assumed you'd be a very plain person, but there's more to you than I expected. You gave me a free show last night."

"Your eyes were shut! You didn't avert your eyes?" I come off as accosted, but secretly I don't mind her peeping.

"It's hard not to when there's a Champs full moon in your face!" Rae snarls.

Embarrassment warms me to my core, but I'm content with it.

We share the only food we have left in our packs, soggy bread. The texture of it almost makes me hurl, but alas, I survive. We left the comfort of our cabin behind and began our long walk out into the bright new day.

Rae and I decided our goal was to make it to the ferry at Lanstring. Praying all bodes well for us on this leg of our journey; we can achieve it. I quickly got our bearings by locating the Oquirrh Mountain peaks.

We continued south for hours under the tree cover as much as possible. There was no sign of another human life, but the occasional critter scampering into the brush causes me to jump. Rae started joining in with the little rodents, stepping on leaves and sticks, causing them to crackle under her feet.

"You jump at every little noise!" Rae giggles as she stomps down on a branch, snapping it in half.

"In the last few months, I've dealt with an onslaught of attacks. You would be jumpy too."

"I hate to say this, but you are always on edge. That's your personality."

"What do you do to relax?" I pivoted my head.

"The brain is powerful. If you can convince yourself not to fear death, you can actually live free. I also practice deep breathing exercises to center myself. Have you ever heard of 4-4-4-4?

"No."

"Now inhale for four seconds, hold for four, exhale for four, and hold again for four. I like to think of ocean waves when I do it. My older brother likes to think of a box, because he's a black and white bastard that can't ever read between the lines." Rae takes a deep breath, releasing anxiety of her own. Her hands are up close to her chest, making the shape of a box. "Here, let's try it together."

Rae then grabs my hands and continues, "Ready, inhale."

We both suck air into our lungs, filling our chest. Now we hold; pressure is building, like a cork in a wine bottle, ready to pop.

A loud gasp of air exhales from Rae's mouth as she exclaims, pointing, "Holy Harwen! Look at that sight."

I release pressurized air, and my jaw drops in awe.

The scenic view is heart-stopping. A sheer cliff with at least a 300-foot drop, a few feet away. Past that was an unbelievable viewpoint. We could see the blue Gulf of Athren blanketing the landscape in the distance, along with a vague outline of Harpstedt on the other side of the bay. The multitude of colors of plants and the waviness of the hills made the scene even more unreal.

The Murcian road forks when it reaches the big body of water of the gulf. One fork goes west to Harpstedt and the other south to Lanstring. That's where we need to go, south.

"It's so stunning," Rae says, amazed.

My eyes move from the outlook to her. "You're more captivating."

I pull her in for a hug, letting her know that I'm not just being cliche with my words. My arms wrap around her frame. She fits perfectly under my chin. I inhale for 4 seconds and hold, and she follows my lead. We finish the full cycle of her breathing treatment, and I end with a kiss to her forehead.

Then, turning to the scenic view again, I spout off, "Looks like it's just ten miles downhill to the ferry."

"I think we can do that in three or four hours easily!" She expresses excitement.

The downhill descent made our journey much quicker. The stress on our knees, however, was much greater. We continue despite the pain and discomfort we are experiencing.

Trying our best to follow the last words of Mykel, we stay off the roads. It grew increasingly difficult to do, due to the elevation change. The vegetation at this altitude made the plants even more sparse.

When we reached Lanstring, it was late in the afternoon. The town is a close-knit community nestled against the gulf. There are modest-sized family farms scattered throughout, along central street lines, petite shops.

The population is minimal and reclusive. Not a soul was on the quaint dirt street. The general stores that freckle Lanstring are made from wood and thatch. There are no sturdy stone buildings.

We made our way towards the end of the street, where the docks are located. Rae and I are quiet, feeling peering eyes watching us from the windows. There's no welcome committee for this tiny town.

I motion to Rae, pointing to a small business by the water. Ferry Crossings to Harpstedt and On. "Let's check this place out."

As we slither our way through the door of the establishment, a bell dings above our heads. We are met with a putrid stench of rotting fish. Rae almost visibly gagged.

"Who goes there!" A one-eyed mutant man emerges behind the counter. His ragged clothes and leather skin make him hard to look upon.

"Good afternoon, sir, we would like to ferry to Harpstedt," I say politely, trying my best not to cast judgment with my eyes.

"For the two of you? There'll be no more crossing today, lad. My captains have taken leave and are three pints deep."

"Please, sir, we are desperate." Rae's sweet voice begs.

"Ahh, my sweet girl, I recommend you stay here in town tonight. It's been some time since we had a sweet-looking darlin' like you enter our town. I suggest you make your way to the tavern. Take a load off, laddie, and drink some ale."

Unsheathing my sword, I accelerated the tip of the blade to the ferryman's throat.

Fury flames in my eyes, "She is not one you'd want to trifle with. Give us a boat!"

"Whoa, calm down. No blood need be spilled. All I can muster up is a canoe. Everything else is under contract."

"That'll do." I lower my sword. "Show us that way."

"Don't be so hasty."

The ferryman picks up an apple and locks his jaw on it with his one good tooth, biting into it forcibly.

He points at the door, ushering us out, muttering with his rotten mouth full. "This way." Bits of apple fling from his lips across the countertop.

We follow the crooked man onto the dock. A few sailboats and ships litter the harbor.

"Why can't you lend us one of those sailboats?" Rae asks.

"Like I said, those are under contract. The canoe is all I can muster." The man croaks.

"Barnabee, you can't be serious! You're making these two paddle ten miles against these dire head-winds. One strong gust, they will flip." A husky man with a pipe criticizes from the shadows.

"It's after hours, they are pushy, and that's all I have! Unless you're willin' to pilot them across on your boat!" Barnabee, the ferryman, rudely retorts.

"What in the devil are you two doing here?" The maritime pilot questions.

"We are duelers from Lyon on our way to the capital to join the guild there," I answer straight.

"What guild do you swear allegiance to?" The maritime pilot interrogates.

"We serve the Federalists. When it comes to allegiance, if I'm frank with you, we serve Athren. I am willing to pay you double the price in coin." Trying my best to manipulate.

"Barnabee, I'll sail them over. They are going to their deaths as it is. Why make them suffer more?"

"Noah, whatever you say." Barnabee chuckles.

Rae leans in, "I wonder which boat is his."

"Let's get a move on, you two; we will be lucky to get in just after dusk." Noah, the pilot, demands.

We follow him down the narrow dock. Rae waves at Barnabee and blows him a kiss, taunting him. She's brave and steadfast.

Noah jumps onto a sailboat that has one mast with a square sail, a rudder, and two oars. We jump in behind the pilot.

Rae asks fearlessly, "Why'd you agree to help us?"

"That's irrelevant, want me to change my mind? Each of you needs to pick up an oar and row the whole way."

We'll follow the orders and sit on opposite sides, each grabbing a wooden oar. The toned, veiny arms of Noah push off the dock and unfurl the sails. He then positions them precisely the way he wants and sets his rump on the back of the boat by the rudder. My eyes are drilled on him.

"Now row!" He commands.

We follow his decree. Making it far out into the deep black water. Our speed increases as the wind fills the sails. Howling sounds, and the water sways us. Our paddling remains firm. Surely, we would've died out here in a canoe.

After a few hours, we could see the towering city growing taller as we crept closer. It is just as glorious as Dad had described in his book.

The harbor of Athren is striking. Massive ships are located all around, almost in a blockade-like formation. We sail right by undeterred.

Before we reached the impressive docks and waltzed our way into the city, the jolts up in aggression.

"Before I release you, I expect compensation."

I fling a small sack of coins in his direction, half-expecting it.

"From both of you!" Noah insists.

Rae scrambles into her sack and gives off an apprehensive look. While she digs frantically, I flip another bag of coins at the pilot.

"By the way, you two are nothing but political pawns for our corrupt leaders. They use you for sport to keep the citizens distracted from the truth."

"We are well aware. Thank you, sir." I respond in acknowledgment.

"Don't thank me, I pity you duelers." He mumbles.

We get off the boat, not looking back, and walk swiftly off the dock. Unaware of the true terror that awaits us from within the city walls.

Chapter Twenty-Seven:

Harpstedt

The sun has set completely; the city's lights sparkle in the night. Even in the darkness, the shadow of the magnificent city looms all around us. The architecture of it all is so incomparable to anything I've ever seen. Even the sewage is out of sight and not in the streets, making the air aroma actually bearable. Harpstedt has ingenuity and design that surpass Lyon's by miles.

We traveled up one of the main streets by the harbor. Just like Dad's book, the former king's castle was immaculate, with a stone face rising high above the harbor and the arena. We walked by the steps, climbing towards the arena. My stomach lurched thinking about all the people Nate has killed in there; I could be the next.

"Amis, it's getting dark. Do you have any idea where we need to go?"

"Not a clue."

"Oh, there's a guy over there with a torch, maybe we can ask him?" Rae shrugs, walking away without waiting for a response.

A young man who seems to be talking to everyone passing by. He catches a glimpse of us on our approach.

"Good evening! Do you need an escort in the darkness?"

"Oh, um, yeah, is this a kind gesture or do you charge?" A curious look crosses my face.

"Nothing is ever free, sir. You're not from here, are you? I'm what they call a 'Link Boy;' I guide people to their destinations in the dark. It helps them avoid the nastiest of crimes."

"Oh, I see." Hesitation sounds in my voice.

"Don't worry, I've never had any issues with attackers. If I did, I won't stick around to protect you."

Rae giggles. "Don't worry, we don't need your protection."

"Okay, well, where are you off to? I can escort you."

"We are trying to locate the Federalist guild," I say impatiently.

"I see, are you two duelers?" The boy blurts excitedly.

Pride swells up in my chest, "Yes, we are."

"Quickly, then, follow me. Duelers are almost royalty here. The people practically worship you."

The pilot's words come back to the forefront of my mind. 'They use you for sport to keep the citizens distracted from the truth.' Sickness swells in me.

Dueling has never been about the laws, only manipulation.

"Your guild is actually near, just on the other side of the arena."

He walks a few steps in front of us, illuminating the way. We follow him for a few minutes. Again, eyes seem to be looming in on us from the gloomy alleys. It could be fear or paranoia, but I like to think of it as intuition. My awareness of my surroundings has always been in tune. I wish I could be more like Rae and let loose, living freely.

We arrive at a vast stone building, with steep steps rising to a massive door, lit up by two torches. Above the door, there's a three-headed snake, winding down the sides of the door frame. The chiseled architecture was accomplished to absolute perfection.

My attention is ripped away from the building when the young man asks, "What are your names so I can watch you in the ring?"

"I'm Amis Hastings and this is Raely…"

"You're Amis Hastings?! Your brother is Nate?!" The boy exclaims in realization.

The boy continues, "Ahh shit! I'm a huge fan of your brothers! He has been dominating everyone in the ring. They say he might be the greatest dueler ever. Are you ready to fight him?" He blurts the words out before thinking.

Rolling my eyes hard and shaking my head, I flipped the boy some coins and saunter off. The coins clatter against the ground.

"I'm sorry, young man. I appreciate your kindness." Rae apologizes loud enough for me to hear.

She runs up the steps after me. "There was no reason to be a jerk to that boy."

"You're right, I shouldn't react." I grab Rae's hands tightly. "I don't want either of us to fight Nate in the ring."

"It's inevitable, but like I said earlier. Don't fear and breathe. There's nothing you can't do about it right now."

"I don't know what I'd do without you. Thank you."

"Of course, we are in this together." Rae's sweet lips form a crease.

The doors of the guild are heavier than those in Lyon. Once I'm able to get it to creak open, we slip inside. The initial foyer is bright, illuminated by a host of candles lit throughout the space.

The floor is tiled, and the walls and ceilings feature artwork that appears to depict past duels. Stained glass windows line the open foyer, and a grand staircase is at the opposite end.

A fully decked-out guard in chain mail approaches us with his hand on the hilt of his sheathed sword. A host of other guards approach in support of their comrade.

"Can I help you?" A grisly voice demands.

"Where are the new duelers sent from the Murcia province. This is-"

"Live for a month and then I'll learn your names. Let's see your orders." The guard scoffs. I reached into my sack and hand over our orders from Havensburg and Lyon. "Come with me, I'll show you where the gym, cafeteria, and your rooms are." The guard aggressively says.

We follow the sentry around, trying our best to take in every detail of the massive building.

"How many other duelers are here with us?" Rae asks.

"There's one other girl from Blanding. She got injured and hasn't been able to fight. That Hastings dueler for the Loyalists side has been bleeding us dry."

My stomach twists into a knot of pain. I'm bound to fight him soon.

"Report for training at dawn tomorrow. Your instructor, Jameson, will be waiting." The guard adds.

Rae and I hurried our way down to the cafeteria. We feast on bread, vegetables, and fruit. We devour the food and stuff our faces rapidly.

"We look like wild animals." Rae giggles.

"I've never been so hungry!"

"No sense in having manners when we spent the night together in a cabin, eating soggy bread!" Rae beams.

"I wasn't very polite before that anyway!"

"I believe it, after what you did to me against the wall in Lyon!"

"That was just a kiss!" I banter back.

"Sure, but impolite and indecent all the same. Good thing I'm into that." Rae jokes.

She stands up and walks to my side of the table. Rae kicks a leg over me and sits on my lap. Our eyes meet, and her body warmth sends chills down my spine. She asserts her control by pushing my arms downward and bringing both her hands to the back of my head.

Rae straddles me, with her legs wrapping around my body tightly. She seductively bites her bottom lip.

I lose myself in her deep brown eyes and cute nose. Seeing details that were hidden before. There are gold streaks in her eyes, her symmetrical smile, and the tiny freckles that dot her face. Not being able to resist anymore, I lean in to devour her.

She catapults off of me, standing straight up, saying, "You teased me last night; it's my turn to tantalize you."

She stalks off, leaving the cafeteria. Quietness creeps in around me. I'm left alone in a profound silence. My heart races still, and my blood is pumping.

I take a few deep breaths just like Rae taught me and then get up to clean the table, leaving alone for my room.

∞

The next day, I arrived at the gym around dawn to assess the situation. Their training equipment and weaponry are the best available. Even the workout clothes I found hanging in my room are pristine. They spare no expense.

I sit on the ground, stretching, trying to loosen up my muscles for what will be a tiring day. A new place, a new day, and I need to earn my keep.

Rae enters the gym with dark circles around her eyes. She's definitely not a morning person, but she is still early for training. I notice she's not in their workout clothes, but her own.

"Good morning, Rae. How'd you sleep?"

"Eh, the cabin's bed was better." A smirk forms on her face. "What's with the clothes?" She asks.

"I just saw them hanging and thought I'd try to fit the part. They are cozier than mine. Why aren't you wearing them?"

"Someone who died probably already wore them." She says pessimistically.

"Do you really think it's that bad?"

"Look around you, where is everyone?"

My eyes scan side to side, she's right.

A strong woman's voice echoes across the room. "She's right, you know. In the past year, we've lost ten duelers in our guild alone."

"Hello there, you must be the other dueler." Rae puts out her hand to greet her.

"Yes, I'm Iris. You two are?"

"Amis and Raelynn from the Murcia Province." A tall, dark man with thick hair proclaims. "I'm Jameson, your instructor."

"Nice to meet you, sir." We respond in unison. He looks much more adequate as an instructor, compared to Kilroy.

Jameson's deep voice grabs our attention again. "Amis, your brothers have done a number on our guild. Eliminating six duelers from our guild on their own."

"Wait, he's a Hastings!" Iris's arms fold; her pissed off face tells me she isn't a fan.

"Yes, Iris, but he's on our side. Trust me. You're a day early; we weren't expecting you just yet." Jameson states.

"We had some unexpected events that led to us taking a different route," I express, sighing.

"Ahh, I see, that's a subtle way to say that someone tried to murder you. I'm glad you're both here. We have quite a list of events this week." Jameson reveals.

Rae and I remain silent in anticipation of his subsequent words.

"Today and tomorrow morning, we will train."

"Tomorrow night there's a dinner in the capital castle with all parties from both guilds. Our guild currently looks a little sad, but Amis, your presence will stir things up."

"In two days, we will rest and prepare for the duel on the third day."

My eyes immediately drop to the floor.

Iris blurts out, "Who will fight Nate?"

"Amis will fight his brother."

Rae puts her hand on my back. I purse my lips together.

"Amis, surely you knew that you'd have to duel your brother!" Iris says loud and unfiltered.

"Iris, someone oughta break your other arm!" Rae threatens. "You guys don't do rankings here?"

Iris bravely retorts, "There's no point when we are all destined to die."

"Jameson, sir, Nate still doesn't know I'm here, right?" I question, ignoring Iris's annoying persona.

"No, he doesn't, no one will be alerted to your presence until tomorrow night's dinner."

"Good, let's keep it that way," I say with slight confidence.

"What's your plan? Tell me." Rae requests in a hushed tone.

"I'm going to follow my Dad's instructions and talk to Nate alone," I say in a whisper.

"Now that is all settled, the next two days we are going to be focusing on the seven points of agility. Iris, you'll participate where you are able. The seven fitness skills are riding, swimming, shooting, wrestling, fencing, and long jumping. We will start with the shooting."

We line up at the end of the huge gym. Rae and I took up bows and a quiver of twelve arrows. We shot all twelve arrows at a target fifty feet away. Jameson said we had to shoot and reshoot until we penetrated all twelve arrows into the target. It took me a few tries, but I was successful on my third attempt.

We did the same with throwing knives and hatchets, hurling them at a target fifteen feet away. I was much more proficient in that. Rae held her own, too; she was flawless with throwing knives.

Iris was able to join us. Her injury reminds me a great deal of Veronica's. It could've been intentional.

We continue our skills practice with fencing. Jameson gave helpful techniques on footwork and defensive counters.

Fencing bled into wrestling, which I enjoyed tremendously with Rae. Any excuse to have her rigid, firm body against mine. She's much stronger than she looks and can contort her body in ways I could only dream of.

The rigorous agility drills continued as we performed the long jump repeatedly into a sand pit. Then we climbed a handmade obstacle-style wall on the side of the gym.

The exercises, combined with our treacherous journey to the capital, really depleted our energy. We ate a high-protein meal that night and went to bed without hardly conversing.

The next morning, we gathered around the stables. Jameson informed us that we will ride to the beach and do training there. Iris attempted to get out of going, but Jameson threatened her with execution if she didn't.

As we disembarked, I rode next to Rae. She seems really down, and I'm not exactly sure why.

"Everything alright?" Concern fills my words.

"Ya, everything is fine. Oh, I finished your book. I thought it was... interesting."

That's not the word I would use to describe it. Did I do something to offend Rae? "If there's something wrong, I hope you know I'm here to help."

"I know," Rae says in a meaningful way.

"Okay, good. Can you bring the book tonight? I want to give it to Nate."

"Yup." She says, clearly annoyed, taking off on her horse.

The remainder of the day drags on. We practiced maneuvers on our horses. We also performed several swimming exercises in the Gulf of Athren. I did well but still feel like I was going to drown the whole time. Around midday, we had finished our training.

Jameson gave us the rest of the day to ourselves. When we got back, I planned to take a nice nap and prepare for tonight.

Rae and I walked the hallway to our rooms. She still hasn't talked to me much.

I walked a few paces behind her to give her space. Something definitely is wrong with her, and I know she will talk to me when she is ready.

She opened her bedroom door and swiftly entered. The door closed with wicked speed before I could even debate entering behind her. I lingered patiently in the hall.

The door creaked open to a sliver. The book protruded out of the creaking door. I clutched it, pulling it away from me.

"Amis, I'll meet you at dinner."

"You don't want to arrive together?"

"I want to be alone; I have matters to deal with."

"Okay, I know something is wrong. I respect your wishes."

"Nothing is wrong!" The door slams.

I head back to my room and lie on my bed. My thoughts form and race. I replayed every conversation from the last few days. The only thing odd that comes to mind is that everything between us was swift and almost too easy. I just figured that's what happens when it's meant to be. Maybe that's the hopeless romantic within me.

Confusion races through my mind; the mixture of emotions gives me a headache. There's too much going on at once. The first thing I need to worry about is talking to Nate alone.

Chapter Twenty-Eight:

The Castle

I stand fiercely in front of the castle, absolutely stunned at its majestic beauty. The magnitude of engineering that must've taken place to build such a structure. The detailed artwork carved into the stone, the large towers jutting up into the sky, and the surrounding stone walls blend perfectly into their surroundings.

I'm wearing my nicest surcoat, tunic, tight pants, and leather shoes. It's definitely adequate for an occasion like this. I managed to carefully place the book in my waistband, hoping my surcoat would conceal any unusual bulging.

I enter the courtyard of the castle alone. Servants who work on the grounds greet me and escort me into the castle.

Just like Gentry had described, the glorious interior of the castle catches me off guard. In the front room, Athren flags litter the walls along with a giant chandelier. A grand staircase with beautiful marble flowers is located on the far side.

My body freezes up for a moment at the door, taking it all in. Jameson and Iris are huddling together to my right, along with some politicians. They waved me over.

Groups of people in lavish clothing were gathered; there had to be at least forty people associated with the guilds in the room. I'm sure Nate is among the hordes of people.

"They rarely host dinners like this; the last time was when there was a very impactful law presented forth. I think it had to do with the Barbaric Wars in the northwest. Given our grand company here, this must be an important matter." Jameson speculates.

"Don't the politicians meet often?" Iris asks, rolling her green eyes.

"Oh yes, we do, but that is mainly to go over the laws the Federalists want brought forth." A round politician answers.

"The latest spout of defeat has not helped us any," Jameson adds.

"No, we've been on the defensive as of late. Our guild appears to be weakening. Now that we have Amis and Raelynn with us, we may stand a chance. Amis, where is your counterpart?" Another politician asks, looking at the whole room with concern.

My eyes glanced, surveying the room. I don't see Raelynn anywhere. That's odd.

"I don't know her current whereabouts, but I know she will be here," I say in doubt, shifting my weight uncomfortably.

My eyes continue to survey the room. I see a large number of Loyalist duelers on the opposite side of the room. Finally, I pinpoint the blonde-haired, thick-framed Nate.

"Excuse me." My party's concern turns into shock as they watch me cross the center of the luxurious room in the direction of the numerous Loyalist duelers.

My strides were not aggressive or loud, but I managed to garner everyone's attention. Am I not supposed to interact with the opposing guild? All the commotion of socialization ceases, and reticence fills the void.

Nate's acknowledgment of my presence is gut-wrenching; he seems upset to see me. Murmuring begins amongst the crowd.

I walked confidently toward my brother, less than five feet from him and his guild. Everyone's body language is defensive and closed.

I uncork my mouth to say something embarrassing, but courageous. A hand grabs my bicep, taking me off my collision course. The hand slides down to mine and holds tight as they steer me away.

Mariam turns towards me, with no one else in earshot. The gossiping grows louder.

"What are you doing?" I groaned in frustration.

"Trying to save you from yourself."

"I can't talk to my own brother?"

"Not like this, he's not the same person. Amis, this isn't Lyon. Now that everyone knows you're here, they are going to hunt you."

"Hunt me? I'm going to die by Nate's blade in a few days as it is."

"You threaten everything the Loyalists are working for. We can't talk here. Later." Mariam's hushed voice evokes a sense of uneasiness in me.

"Well, well, is this the ex you were telling me about?" Rae's voice sneered.

"Who are you?" Mariam questions in confusion.

"I'm a dueler for the Federalist, oh, and Amis' girlfriend." Jealousy sounds through Rae's voice.

I take a few steps back from them. Rae brings me back to her, gripping my arm like I'm her property. Mariam shakes her head in disbelief, walking backwards, fleeing up the grand staircase from the dramatic scene.

"Where have you been?" I say, berating Rae.

"I'm here now, that's all that matters. I'll tell you everything after dinner. I promise. Let's get back to our people. Everyone keeps staring at us while we stand here in the middle of this godforsaken room." Rae insists.

Back in our smaller group, everyone is hesitant to mention the recent dramatic scene. But of course, there's always one who isn't afraid to speak their mind.

"Amis, what the hell were you thinking?" Iris scolds me.

"It's none of your business, you worthless mouth breather!" Rae hisses.

"Calm down. We are glad everyone is present and accounted for." Jameson lectures.

Trumpets bellow a loud, brassy sound throughout the room. At the top of the stairs stands a tall, lanky fellow and a beautiful, mature woman.

"He's the leader of the Federalist, and that's his wife," Jameson whispers the words into mine and Rae's ear.

"They're a gorgeous couple," Rae says in awe.

They began their descent down the long staircase, and another couple emerged. Rae visibly trembles with fear. My heart stops: the slithery man stands holding the hand of a girl I no longer love. Mariam.

"That's Rasmussen and Mariam. He's the leader of the Loyalists, and she is a politician." Jameson ignorantly says.

"We are well acquainted with them!" Rae snarls.

Watching them graciously walk down the steps makes me more mortified. Every part of me wishes Rass-hole would slip down the stairs and break his neck. That would be too easy a death for that evil prick.

"Good evening, we are grateful to have you all gathered in the castle of the former kings. Rasmussen and I are proud to unite both guilds here on this special occasion." The Federalist leader rattles off.

"In two days, by the will of Tyren, Nathaniel Hastings of the Loyalist guild and Amis Hastings of the Federalist guild will have a brotherly duel for the most important law that Athren has witnessed in years." Rass-hole's words roar out with a cold tone.

"First, let us eat!" The Federalist leader says, pointing to the dining room.

Everyone shuffles into the next room.

"Whatever game that asshole is playing, we cannot file in and join," Rae whispers in her sweet voice. "Amis, please, let's leave while we can."

I'm stuck in a daze, unsure of what to do, ignoring Rae's plea. We were the last to enter the dining room. It is white and glorious, like the rest of the castle. The same round table that my Dad had depicted in his book circulates the room. In the middle of the round table was an open space, the same space where my Dad saw his parents' heads on platters. This place's history is sickening.

We slowly move into the room, giving us a chance to survey everything as it unfolds. Rae's face still looks visibly flustered and worried.

"You better not attempt anything on our champion!" A voice cries out. It's a Loyalist in a bright orange tunic that I don't recognize.

"Who are you to talk to me about my own brother?" I scowl.

"I'm one of his closest acquaintances. I'll stab you right here if I must." He snarls.

"Let's see how far that gets you, bud. Go ahead." I taunt, raising my arms, giving him a clear shot at my chest.

The Loyalist, in his creamsicle tunic, takes out a knife. I know Rae has a knife of her own at the ready.

"I'm ready to receive," I mock him.

He grunts and tenses his arm, poised to strike. No fear is present in me.

"There'll be no bloodshed here! Sheath your knife." Rasmussen declares from across the room.

The duelist does as ordered and shuffles off to his seat.

"He was all bark, no bite," Rae utters.

"He's lucky I'm facing Nate and not him. We'd see how loud he barks then."

Everyone takes their seats. Rasmussen, Mariam, and the Federalist leader and his wife sit first. Assigned seating was dispersed throughout the circular dining table. The Federalist politicians, down to the Federalist duelers. My name was the last among my guilds.

The Loyalists were situated similarly. The Loyalists outnumbered us by more than ten bodies, so they wrapped a little farther around the table. Starting with Rasmussen all the way down to Nate at the end.

They arranged for Nate and me to sit next to each other. Bizarre and harsh.

I pull Rae's chair out and allow her to sit down first; she hesitantly takes a seat. Then, I grab my own skidding, noisily across the floor to obnoxiously signal my presence. Sitting down, I immediately notice Nate unfurl his napkin, gripping his steak knife.

"What's with the knife?" I ask him as if we are still normal brothers.

"You know why. I don't trust you."

"You think I'm going to kill you? Here?" My eyebrows raise as if he is absurd.

"I don't know what to believe after you killed my Fiancé and joined that oppressive guild." Nate scolds.

"Look, there is obvious animosity between us. Let's be brothers for tonight, like we were before Niklas' death. Then you can kill me in two days."

"We aren't brothers anymore." He shoves the words like a dagger in my heart.

"Dad wanted me to tell you something. Please hear me out, after dinner." I invite.

"Fine, shut up until then."

This dinner is delicious, consisting of exquisite dishes to which I wasn't accustomed to, such as fowl of exotic kinds, pomegranate, and sugar plums.

Conversations scatter throughout the table. Talking of past duels and rumors throughout the land. Such as a dueler in the south who is seven feet tall and is supposedly on his way to the capital, or the disturbing reports of Barbarian raids in the territory near Eagle Valley. Iris and Rae talk for a bit and are at least amiable towards each other.

I remain silent, and so is Nate. When people attempt to involve us in any conversation, we are quick and to the point in our response. The round table gave me an adequate opportunity to look at everyone.

Rasmussen is carried away in discussions with many different people. Due to his impeccable dress and sociable personality, he was able to garner much respect and attention.

"I know you don't like him, but you shouldn't stare. You'll create more enemies." Nate says while looking straight down.

I moved my gaze to a beautiful mural of Harpstedt on the wall. It displays the incredible structures of the city, streets filled with happy people, and even depicts the arena. "Rass-hole is the devil," I say with firm lips, trying to keep my mouth still.

"Ya, well, he's been kind to me, and he did just save you from my friend."

I pick up my steak knife and balance it in my hand, gauging its weight. "I suppose I could claim revenge against Rass-hole now."

"Revenge? You wouldn't, you would die where you sit." Nate's voice rises in concern as he glances at my knife.

"Watch me."

I grip the point of the knife and flick my wrist. It's forcefully propelled. A loud 'thunk' sounds as the knife is planted into what sounds like a skull. Alas, I nailed my target, the depicted mural of the arena.

"Very bold of you, Mr. Hastings." Rasmussen stands up and projects his voice as he walks to the mural.

"I never liked that painting much; I don't believe it illustrates what the capital truly is."

His hand reaches up and rips the knife out of the painting, dropping it to the ground. 'Clattering' is heard against the tile.

"You remind me of your brother."

I glance toward Nate. "Oh no, not that brother. Niklas. You are untamed and stubborn, unable to control your own emotions."

Rae is not impressed with my careless actions. The audience drops lower into their seats as tension fills the air. Nate squirms wildly, stuck in a precarious situation.

"If my father were still here, he would have had you executed for that act of childish behavior. All your good fortune will come to a screeching halt in two days. You'll meet your-"

The tall Federalist leader interrupts, hollering, "Enough! Is the precision he just displayed making you nervous?"

"Nervous, no amused perhaps." Rasmussen side eyes the Federalist. "We gathered you all together to announce the historic ramifications that will take place if Nathan Hastings triumphs over his little brother. Boys, please stand."

Nate gets up first, looking tall and strong. Any normal man would quake at his pure size.

I rise slowly, making sure everyone has been given adequate time to view us. I straighten my shoulders and stand up to my proper height.

My build is big, but not as big as Nate's. I do have two inches on him. Not a lot, but enough to notice the difference.

"He's not much of a little brother if you ask me. Seems like the duel could go either way. They are cut from the same cloth." The tall Federalist interjects.

Rass-hole ignores him, continuing with his course, "When Nate defeats Amis, Athren will become a monarchy once more. I will assume the role of my father before he was assassinated. Becoming the King."

Every fiber of my being wants to yell, 'You are no King.' I bit my tongue, showing restraint I didn't know I had. Rae grips the back of my leg hard, trying to calm me, but it only fuels my emotions more.

My body sways with adrenaline. I sat down and sinking into my chair. Rae moves her hand in the process to my shoulder.

Nate rests back into his chair, and Rasmussen's voice continues in the background. I take deep breaths calmly, trying not to draw more attention, as I soothe my unpredictable state. Rae is here; she is my peace.

"You said you wanted to talk?" Nate asks.

"Yes."

"When everyone disperses, immediately leave this room through the door on your left. Follow the hall, and there'll be a small staircase at the end of it. Go up one flight, into the first room on your right, and out onto the balcony."

I nodded in understanding. He is too vague; I can easily get lost.

Rasmussen belts out a loud, "Thank you for your time, our dinner has concluded."

A ruckus erupts in the room as chairs all move at once, and chatter commences.

I follow suit, quickly getting to my seat and grabbing Rae's shoulders from behind. I put my mouth to her ear and whisper, "I need to take care of something. Meet me in the front room."

My hands release her shoulders, and I walk swiftly out of the room before anyone can pull me aside. My strides continue down the long hallway; I pass servants along the way.

A young fellow in complete white steps in my way. "Sir, where are you off to?"

I stutter for a moment and formulate my thoughts. "I need a toilet, now."

"Oh, I see, there is a toilet just behind you. In that room, there." The servant points with a slight smile.

"No, you don't understand, I need space to relieve myself."

"Oh, my apologies. Go down the hall and upstairs. The first room on your right should have a washroom."

I clasped his hands, gesturing thank you, and speed down the hall and up the stairs in pursuit of the balcony Nate described.

Once I reached the balcony, I immediately noticed that no one else was there. It's secluded enough; the view is blocked by tall green trees rocking back and forth near the ledge. The door behind me is the only entry point.

I sit on a stone bench and listen as the trees rustle together relentlessly. What an odd place for a balcony; there's absolutely no view. Smart of Nate to arrange our meeting here, but it is strange that a location like this exists within the castle.

Suddenly, I hear a faint voice call my name, "Amis, Amis. Psssh over here."

My head whips back and forth, trying to pinpoint exactly where the noise came from.

"The trees!" The voice squeals again.

I stand up and lean against the stone railing of the balcony. "Nate, is that you?"

Nate steps on a branch closer to me. I can barely make out his shadowy figure.

"Who the hell are you, swinging from branch to branch?"

"Climbing the trees is the only way I can talk to you alone. If they spot us together, we'd both be executed."

"They wouldn't execute their champion," I laugh, teasing.

"We don't have time for joking. What is it you wanted to tell me?" Nate seems eager.

I take a deep breath, knowing this is my only opportunity to divulge the truth.

"Dad requested that I be candid with you. Rasmussen is a despicable man. He killed Heather, framed Niklas for murder, scorched our farm to rubble, ambushed Mykel, and blackmailed Trisha."

"You killed Trisha! Not Rasmussen. Don't try to place blame. You drove your dagger into her." Nate gasps, releasing built-up anger.

"I will never forgive you. My own damn brother slayed the love of my life." Nate chokes in emotion.

"Did you hear a thing I just said! Rasmussen framed Niklas and is trying to ruin our family! Wake up." My aggression escalates the situation.

"I am awake! You joined the wrong guild. This is your fault, Amis!"

"It's not my fault; it's your damn kings! We are pawns in his bloodthirsty game."

"You're lucky I'm dueling you and not your new lover. Honestly, you don't know the immense pain I live with now. My sweet Trisha is dead, the only person who made me whole."

"I'm sorry! If you won't listen to me, read Dad's book." My two hands willingly offer the book to Nate.

"I can't! Our fate is already predetermined. One of our graves has been unearthed. Be a man, greet death, and stop your fruitless begging."

"Wake up! Stop sleepwalking, you zombie." I plead with Nate.

The door crashes open vigorously behind me. The servant from the hallway exclaims, "Who are you talking to?"

"Oh, hello there, no one. I came out here for fresh air." I improvise.

"This is a restricted area. I must ask you to leave." The servant urges.

"Of course." I turn to the trees to see if Nate is still there. His shadowy figure disappeared.

I walk back to the front room of the castle. My pace quickens as I try to find Rae.

Chapter Twenty-Nine:

Rasmussen

Rae and I left the castle property hand in hand. It was extremely dark, making it extremely difficult to find our way in a city still very unfamiliar to us. Where's our 'link boy' to guide us home?

Shadows crept and stretched down every street. It is impossible to see what lies ahead, making our eyes obsolete. The best thing we can do is stay close together and rush back to our guild as quickly as possible.

"I'm not scared of the dark, you know." Rae shutters.

"You're not scared of anything." I grin back at her.

"I am afraid of one thing. Losing you." Her eyes drop low.

"You won't lose me, I promise."

"How'd your talk with Nate go?"

"Bad, he's still holding a grudge for Trisha's death. I don't blame him, but he's not listening to me."

"He's blinded by despair." Rae's voice falls as we come into view of our silhouetted guild. "We just might make it." She whispers, raising the hair on my arms.

"What the hell does that mean?" I shout.

"Amis, there's a reason I was terrible to you this morning. There's something I've been holding from you-"

Footsteps approach us increasingly fast. Figures materialize from the shroud of darkness. There have to be a dozen men, all carrying what looks like clubs.

Rae and I stand back-to-back, ready to face them. We're surrounded; there's no way out. All escape routes are shut.

"Follow me." I drew a deep breath.

There's no way we are fighting through this. I observe all the attackers and identify the smallest one.

Two assailants lunge at me violently at the exact moment. One swings his bludgeon down, aiming for my upper body.

I dodge the blow to my head by rushing the smaller attacker. He was taken aback, completely shocked. I grip his shoulders and shove him to the ground. A path opens. I kick my legs into gear and sprint the hole, praying Rae is on my tail.

I lay my eyes on the guild and know that if we can make it there, we'll be safe.

A yell sounds. "Stop him!"

My strides became longer as I reach a speed I know they can't match. I hear Rae's footsteps close behind.

I'm almost to the steps of the guild. Then a 'thud' sounds, followed by grunting. Rae's wrestling with one of the assailants. She finds her hidden blade and stabs him in the chest.

Screams sound ferocious and high-pitched. The attackers encircle Rae, grab her, and hold her up vertically.

"All we want is you, Hastings. Give yourself up, and we will let her go."

Rae cries out. "No!"

A big, bearded freak punches her in the face. A streak of blood trickles down. She goes limp.

"Don't hurt her or you'll die, you imbecile!" One attacker clamors.

My heart sends my body berserk before my mind has had a chance to process how to proceed. I rush the now eleven attackers, striking the bearded freak across the back of his head, knocking him to the ground.

One attempts a tackle, grabbing me at my waist. I raise my knee into his gut and slam my elbow into his back. Causing him to release me, while wincing in pain.

Rae is knocked out cold, still being held up while her head dangles unconsciously. I should've protected her better.

A flurry of close fists launches in my direction. I dodge the first, but the second and third smack on my jaw and chest. A dull, achy pain fills my nerves.

Instinct kicks in. My drive to protect Rae from further harm propels me forward. Blacking out, I remember snapshots of the brawl.

Utilizing an uppercut, causing one of the perpetrator's teeth to mash together and clatter. Evading blow after blow of the uncontrolled barrages. Flipping one small bastard over my shoulders and beating another prick's face in until I see red.

This lasted for a few long minutes until I was no longer able to fend them off. They corral me to the ground, grabbing my arms and pinning them behind my back, driving my face into the coarse stone street.

My swollen eyes witness the prominent, bearded brute place Raelynn's limp body in front of the guild. A moment later, cognizance fades, and darkness falls upon me.

A torment of pain radiates from my face. My eyes open swollen and groggily, from a time forgotten sleep. To my dismay, I'm chained to the ceiling in the middle of a dark and damp room, wearing ragged clothes. Dripping water echoes consistently, and a ray of light shines through a tiny window. Stone encases me in this dreary tomb that has a single steel-plated door.

The isolated, unsanitary conditions, full of rot and mildew, are bleak, to say the least. My chains rattle every time I move, and rats occasionally scurry across the floor. This dungeon is a vile and terrible place.

A deep groan from the metallic door alerts me to an incoming visitor. The clanking handle turns, and a man springs from behind.

The malevolent, degenerate Rass-hole smiles horrifyingly. His black soulless outfit tells me he isn't king yet. The duel with Nate still hasn't happened.

"Oh, good, you're awake," Rasmussen scowls, exposing his wretched yellow teeth.

"Where am I?" My raspy voice laments.

"You're in the dark depths of my home." His lips snarl.

"I know what you did, you corrupt piece of shit."

"Good. When you dig as many graves as I have, you start to forget the egregious choices made. I'm glad someone knows my secrets. Just like my story, I told you a month ago."

"You killed Heather, you bitch, framed and executed my brother, blackmailed Trisha, and burnt my family's farm!"

"Yes, I had Niklas executed, but you credit me too much, my dear boy. I didn't arrange the fire at your parents' farm. Brookshard did. He paid off your own duel-mates and one of ours. I must say his plan was impeccable, and no one suspected it."

Rasmussen takes a raspy breath, continuing. "Brookshard managed to force our guild into paying the damages and then swindled your parents out of their land afterwards."

"Xavier, Veronica, and Zander betrayed me?" My heart pounds.

That explains the awkwardness during the night of the fire and why they've been so distant!

"I did break into your room while you, Federalists, had your feast. I did kill Ms. Cunnigham, or should I say your dumb brother Niklas did with his letter."

"You Bastard!"

"Amis, people are inherently selfish, seeking their own gain. You place too much trust in others. Mariam, Brookshard, your duel-mates, and even Raelynn." A grin crosses his face.

"Rae?"

"Do you really think she loves you? My boy, I thought you were smarter, pity. I'm the reason she went to Lyon. She's my Federalist mole, sent to build a hoax relationship with you. I didn't expect her to infiltrate your heart. Are you that naive?"

"You're lying!" I hiss in denial.

"Am I? Use your brain. How did we know about your hidden contraband in your room? How did we locate your camp while journeying here so effortlessly, in that meadow? Poor Mykel, he picked the wrong side long ago when he assisted in killing my father."

My head drops in realization.

"Yes, now you believe. Rae left torn fabric for us to follow right to your camp. Don't worry, Mykel is barely alive, we are doing our best to keep him on the verge of death."

"Where is he?!" I cry hopelessly.

"Just down the hall. If you listen intently, you can faintly hear his cries."

"I haven't told you the best part. Rae is my daughter." An evil laugh escapes Rasmussen.

A heartbroken moan materializes within me. Tears began to stream down my broken face. I convulse in rage, rattling the chains that string me up.

"Don't worry, Amis. I'll show you mercy and let your brother kill you in the ring tomorrow. Too bad you'll never witness me become your king and you'll never get to call me your father-in-law." Rasmussen shrugged.

"I have some matters to address; I'll be back in a few. Don't wait up!" His fist smacks my jaw, knocking me back into an unconscious nightmare.

Chills electrify my body, and I jolt outrageously. My chains send a wave of vibrations to the floor and ceiling. Another forceful wave of chaotic wetness gushes over my body, followed by a shivering sensation going up my spine, leaving my thin, clothed body drenched.

Water drips excessively off my body. I wake with attentiveness as another wave of water blasts me. A guard wearing leather has three empty buckets on the ground next to him.

His unrecognizable voice sounds, "My Lord, he has awoken."

Rasmussen appears out of thin air from behind the door. "Very good, now leave us!" He orders.

There is still a ray of light left in the day. The guards' footsteps recede. My chest fills with the musty air when I remember my predicament. A dull ache twists like a knife in the pit of my stomach as I recollect all the emotional torment I had just suffered.

The thought of Rae betraying me, that our relationship isn't real, and I was used, overwhelms my mind. The one good thing in my life is a fraudulent lie. I loved her, but she is of Rass-holes' blood.

"Let's see, this shirt is worthless now. Let me assist you. "

Rasmussen tears the cloth off my neck, leaving my chest bare. My arms and chest spasm.

"You are jacked, but I have to say Nate seems bigger." A smile enriches his lips.

"You don't stand a chance against Nate, but why don't we lessen your odds even more?"

Pulling out a small razor-sharp knife, he placed the point of it into my chest. Driving it forcefully into my skin until blood forms. He cut across the entirety of my chest in one horizontal direction.

Searing pain spurts across the filleted area. Carving me in a new location on my face, he penetrates the tip of the knife into a bruise above my eye. The black and blue area pops as blood cascades into my socket.

The blade is driven down vertically, splitting my eyebrow. His face seems unamused by my reaction, yet he remains persistent.

"Appears I can't hurt you as much physically as I'd like to. I do want your guild to view you as acceptable to duel tomorrow. Instead, let me tell you a little story."

Rasmussen reaches behind his back, retrieving a book. My Dad's book.

"Before dinner yesterday, my lovely daughter Rae came to me. She told me about an unbelievable story she read about your father killing my own, the King."

The blood streaks down my body. My one good eye looks upon his hideous, snake-like face.

Understanding why Rae was so standoffish to me. Did she feel guilty? Was she going to tell me the truth?

"Rae was valuable in informing me that you were delivering it to dinner, in hopes that Nate would accept it. My guess is, he didn't believe you. Is he still heart-broken over Trisha?"

I spit my blood and saliva, dotting his face. Anger explodes in his countenance. He winds up and punches my ribs. The air in my lungs escapes me, wincing from the pain.

A coughing fit erupts. It persists long enough that a fit of laughing occurs. Rambunctiously, I continue the chuckles, exposing my bloody teeth. A monstrosity of gore is painted on me, and I notice Rasmussen gives me a disapproving frown.

"You couldn't break Niklas, and you won't break me," I say, laughing.

Rasmussen grabs the book, opens it, and tears out pages. My Dad's history was now in shambles.

"Destroy the book all you want, it's alive and well in here." My lips sneer as my eyes dart down to my bloodied chest.

"Niklas was cunning. Nate is a physical prodigy. Rupert is smart and sociable. Your little sister Sofia is vicious. What are you, Amis! Nothing."

"You have no power over me. God is my king." I stated articulately.

"I know your family is journeying to the capital as we speak. Rae and a few soldiers will intercept them. Killing them will be enjoyable, don't you think?"

"I will butcher you, Rass-hole!"

"Oooh, I love the nickname. Do yourself a favor, have a brisk death tomorrow! If you end up killing your brother, I promise you won't live to see nightfall." He turns on one foot and leaves.

"You want my father, Gentry. I'm not him, Niklas wasn't him. Kill me all you want; Gentry will destroy you just like he did your father." Rasmussen doesn't hesitate to hear my words, stalking off.

Chapter Thirty:

Excrement

My body dangles painfully for what feels like hours. The lacerations stop bleeding, and the glossy reddish-brown color flakes and crusted against my skin.

My thoughts are bobbled from the anguish of all the revelations. Rae isn't who I thought she was; even my friends in Lyon are willing to throw my relationship into the cesspit. My lungs convulse as my vocal cords release a deafening outcry.

I didn't have any food or water, making my lips parched and my stomach uneasy. All sunlight has receded; darkness looms around me. I can't wallow in my misfortune. Yes, I did some foolish shit to get here, being way too trusting. It's time to think critically.

Gentry (Dad) was thrown into a pit infested with vipers. When a snake bit him, he remained calm and patient. I'm in the same pit, but with the venomous Rass-hole. I need to stay calm and take a deep breath. 4-4-4-4, I create a box and think of my solitude under the apple tree next to Niklas' grave.

My heart rate steadies, and breathing becomes more manageable. The mind is a powerful thing, and if I can change my perspective, I can change my reality.

A loud 'bang' comes from the metal door, as its joints begin to move and swing its heavy frame open. My eyes were up and ready to face another onslaught against that vile viper.

A small girl emerges from the door; I can tell by her shadowy figure in the now dim room. She scampers to me quickly, breathing hard.

"What the hell happened. Your cuts and blood… I'm so sorry, Amis! You tried to tell me back in Lyon. I… I should have listened to you about Rasmussen." Mariam's voice is remorseful.

"How did you find me?"

"Rae came to the Loyalists guild frantically searching for you, and she ran into me."

"Rae did?"

"Yes, she broke down begging me to help. That's when I came looking for you."

"But-"

"Amis, no more questions, we don't have time." She cuts me off with an urgent voice.

To my surprise, she has a key and unlocks my chains from my wrists and ankles. The weight of my body collapses on her. With her support, I hobble to the door, reaching the dismal corridor.

"This way, we need to be quick." Mariam points madly.

"Mariam, Mykel is here somewhere. We need to save him."

"There's no time! I'm risking everything by stealing the keys and saving you."

"He sacrificed himself for me. I can't just leave him."

"And I'm sacrificing myself for you; we have to leave."

Mariam lifts me higher and purposefully walks down the hall. My limp body could only follow behind. She is in control of what direction we take.

"I hope you have a plan to get us out of here."

"I have a plan to get just you out."

Lanterns are scattered intermittently to light the hallway. Down the hallway, twenty feet, we pass incomprehensible, bleak prison cells. I can only imagine the atrocities that have occurred in this dungeon.

Mariam stops hesitantly and lingers in front of a cell door. She's contemplating something, then she whips her keys out while I lean on her and opens another cell door.

A giant man with a grey beard, whom I recognize, is chained similarly to how I was. Pools of blood drip to the ground, puddling. His face is unrecognizable, and his body battered. Sweat and blood line down the man I viewed as indestructible. Mykel's hands are gone, left to stumps with bandages on them. Tourniquets squeeze both his arms, keeping him from bleeding out profusely.

Mariam unchains him. He splatters to the ground like a meteor. A 'bang' echoes loudly in the cell.

Leaning next to him, I whisper, "Bloody damn, Mykel. Janice wouldn't want you to die like this. Time to go."

He rises to his full brute height, like a jolt of lightning has struck him, and walks out. His club hands and misfortune are now irrelevant.

Back in the corridor, Mariam abruptly squats to the ground. Below us is a tiny metal grate. She slides her hand under a bar and rips up the grate.

"Here's a torch and the keys. Drop down and follow the tunnel. I know it ends at some point."

I slid my legs into the hole with my butt on the edge.

Mariam hugs me, "I made some poor decisions that really hurt you. Please forgive me."

"Forgive me, I was an insufferable jerk. Mariam, I'll see you again someday, if not this life, in the next with God."

I squished through the hole where the grate once was, raising my arms above my head. Gravity does the work. I plummeted fifteen feet and landed in shallow water, causing a minor splash.

"Ahh shit!" I shriek.

Rushing out of the way of the hole, Mykel makes the same putrid splash.

"Good luck, Amis, enjoy the fecal matter!" Mariam giggles and closes the grate..

The river of wastewater and feces is shallow as it runs slowly and oozes down the nasty tunnel. This was worse than any waste gutter in Lyon, and there's no escaping the putrid smell. I take small breaths while pinching my nose.

I feel a slight ocean breeze from the night air and trek towards it. I'm not sure why Mariam gave me a torch. Maybe she wanted me to see the disgusting biome vividly? Was this another sick joke by Rasmussen, or was she actually trying to help?

We whoosh our bare feet for about twenty feet when the red torch light brings into view a barred gate. There's a lock on the right side of the gate. The nightman uses the sewer gate when they sweep the wretched tunnel. Jingling the ring of keys, I try one after another on the lock with no luck.

A splash sounds from behind us. I hear what sounds like footsteps approaching. Fumbling the keys anxiously, I drop them in the mildew water.

"Ah, come on!"

Mumbling the word, I search in desperation for the keys in the nastiness.

"We're so screwed!"

The stomping increased loudly. Finally, my hand finds the metallic keys swirling around in the once stagnant waste.

A voice rings out, "They're down here!"

Looking back, I haven't seen the attackers yet in my torchlight. I try another key in the lock, and when I twist it, there's no resistance, as the lock clicks.

A force suddenly propels me into the gate with such speed that the gate flies open, and we barrel through it. A man stands over me and snickers while Mykel is immersed in the water, helpless.

"You really think you can escape?" My torchlight reveals a smirk lining the prison guard's mouth.

"Taste fire!" I shout back and simultaneously jab my torch into his eyes with such intensity that it lodges in place.

A shrill scream emits from the man. My arms grip him around his neck and careen him forward, so he somersaults, landing hard on the ground.

I kick him hard, and he rolls once more, right off the edge of the castle. Standing on the edge, there's a sheer drop from the castle into the gulf below.

The very steep and vertical descent alarms me. It has to be at least a sixty-foot plummet into the water below, and lord only knows if there are rocks at the bottom. I scanned the walls of the castle for another path. The walls are completely flush in all directions; there's no other way.

I hear more movement from behind me. I knew everyone was now alerted to our position. I motion Mykel to jump, and to my surprise, he does with no hesitation. I close the gate with haste, relocking it into position.

Grabbing the keys, I turn towards the opening. Fear begins to grip my inner organs. I press my back against the gate, getting as much room as possible, and preparing to make the impossible leap Mykel just made.

Hands lurch through the bars, holding me firmly in place, as their fingernails rip into my skin. I hear the clanging of keys on the gate; another guard is trying to open it.

"Amis, you can't run!" A guard snarls into my ear.

The gate clicks, and I know they have found the right key. One of the guards' arms is around my mouth. My teeth clenched into him until I broke skin.

Naturally, he retracts his arms, and I jolt forward, rushing for the castle's edge. My feet plant against the last bit of stone as I spring off the side, jumping towards the dark abyss below.

Immediately, a sensation of weightlessness overcomes me, and the feeling of a rush of air brushes past my body. My legs broke through the surface of the water, creating a ripple. An invigorating chill runs through me as I descend deeper into the vast watery depths.

The saltwater affects every part of my body. A nerve-burning jolt sends pain through me. The contact with the salt made my wounds shrivel like a snail.

My body buoyantly bounces to the surface of the dark water. I cautiously swim to the shore until I reach the docks in the harbor. There's no sight of Mykel anywhere. Did the fall kill him?

Back on land, I could not wait for him. Rasmussen would've alerted the city's soldiers by now. I rushed down the same streets Rae, and I traveled on the day we sailed in. Everything is barren due to the nighttime atmosphere, but I still hurry as fast as possible to the guild.

Rasmussen's henchman will surely be after me. My bare feet slap the ground as I follow the same track by the arena that the linkboy had taken us before.

Finally, back on the steps of the guild where Rae's limp body had lain unconscious the day before. My fist clanged on the door with great urgency. The Federalists guard opens in shock.

"Master Hastings, what happened?!"

"I thought you didn't want to learn my name?" A smile washes across my face, and my feet enter the building. I immediately feel safer. If those Loyalists came in here, it'd be an act of war.

"I normally don't, but you and Raelynn left an impact on us with your sudden disappearance. You look terrible, what happened!?"

"Not now, please inform Jameson I'm here and will be ready to fight tomorrow."

I walked away to the nurse. In the wee hours of the night, I managed to wake her. I was thoroughly cleaned, sterilized, and stitched up. My body is now whole, pieced together by strings and bandages.

This may be my last night, and I decided to make the most of it. I ate and drank a tremendous amount and retreated to the comfort of my bed.

434 | P a g e

Chapter Thirty-One:

The Duel

I find myself in the pit of the arena, by the dark gates leading into the giant ring. This morning was less than eventful. I had a light breakfast and saw the nurse once more to double-check all my trauma areas.

I haven't seen Rae. I'm assuming she followed Rasmussen's orders in killing my family. If I saw her this morning, I wouldn't know how I would respond, considering I'm confused about why she would tell Mariam. Regardless, her deceitfulness is a knife to my heart. She's too much of a distraction.

When Jameson and I walked to the arena, there wasn't much to say, but he did try to offer some encouragement and told me that this duel would be strictly swords and light armor. That's probably for the best; any metallic weight on my chest would be cause for concern.

I hope that Nate is ready and able to follow through. We are sparring off just like we have our whole lives, except this time, one of us will meet our end.

The commotion of the crowd grows as citizens all file in. Wagers are being made, goods are being purchased, and seats are being claimed. They all come eager for bloodshed and violence, but always seem to miss the actual ramifications. Our Federalist tunnels are completely barren, with only Jameson and me.

"Amis, there's no advice I can give you for what you're about to face. The gates are about to open. Make sure to bow to the politicians above, and when the judge announces, please pay attention." Jameson admonished.

"Bow and pay attention. Got it." I acknowledge.

The gate doors open, revealing the empty grounds before me. The expansive size of the arena is an awe-inspiring sight to behold. White sand is scattered across the surface. The circular walls are matte black with sharp spikes protruding out everywhere. The Loyalist gate entrance is on opposite sides. Towers rise high above, and the stands all around provide ample opportunity to witness brutality. The far side of the ring is the politician's platform, where Jameson told me to bow and pay attention. The castle's height is intimidating; following the wall up is a balcony platform just like Dad described.

I step out onto the firm, white sand, and immediately notice the weather conditions are clear, with not even a breeze. This is optimal dueling weather.

The arena atmosphere is crazier than I could ever fathom. Citizens pack together tightly, again, these wild people are butt to gut wanting violence.

I try to avoid the scene by keeping my eyes forward at the Loyalist's gate. The crowd's cheers erupt as I make my way to the middle; deafening roars fill the void in my head.

Then suddenly, Nate emerges from the Loyalist's gate. Their champion has appeared, and the sea of boisterous people let it be known. The citizens' individual voices blend, forming a powerful chant: "Kill, Kill, Kill…"

Coming into view, his walk and attitude exude pure confidence. His skill, experience, and posture make him look undoubtedly fit to be the Champion of Athren. He wears a leather vest, girdle, and shoes, making him appear light and agile. His bulky thighs and arms are exposed, and on his wrists, he wears bracers. He grips his sword tightly, as if the duel had already commenced.

My focus is solely on him; there is no way the roars all around are going to distract me. Nate and I are now ten feet apart, in talking distance. His eyes grow broad as he sees my stitches lining my head down to my cheek. I know he's intrigued to hear the story behind it, but he doesn't dare say a word.

Our attention shifts as we look up towards the platform. The political leaders come into view, and the judge. Rasmussen deserves to die just as his dad did.

Nate drops his shoulders low in a bow, while I, in defiance, do not. Instead, I stab my sword into the earth and rip my cloth shift off my torso. Leaving only my girdle and shoes on.

An audible gasp rolls through the crowd. Nate looks baffled, seeing my battered body, scars, and another stitched wound cutting horizontally across my chest.

My arms raise, and I circle Nate, proclaiming to the people, "Is this what you want? For the Loyalists to impair their competition! Wake up, Athren!"

I repeat it several times, which in turn causes the crowd to go into a frenzy, littering the grounds with rotten fruit. Nate remains focused, keeping his attention on the lawmakers above.

The judge steps forward onto the platform, readying himself for a loud speech.

"Silence, citizens of Athren! Silence!"

A hush sweeps over the crowd.

In the name of Tyren,
the God of Justice and Order,
We welcome you all to a duel of death.
Before the fight commences,
I have an extra announcement to make.
A citizen has been found committing interference.
Mariam from Lyon within the Murcia Province.

The judge motions her forward. Her hands are bound, and her mouth is gagged with a cloth. My heart stops with guilt racing through my veins. She is guilty of saving me.

"See what your side does to our friends!" I shout in Nate's direction.

"They are your friends, not mine."

"What demon have you become?!"

"This is what comes when you break the laws set in stone by blood."

The judge makes a motion to two guards to put a rope around her neck.

"Nate, we need to stop this!"

"There's no reason for your outbursts; you will die along with her," Nate states plainly.

The judge flicks his finger. A guard kicks Mariam off the platform.

"God no!" My knees hit the ground next to my sword.

Her body drops with speed until the tension in the rope causes gravity to take effect. Her neck snaps, and she dies in that instant.

Mariam saved me; I failed to save her.

Rage boils up within me, hate and revenge grip every part of my soul. I don't care who sees, I'm sick of this barbaric style of life.

I breathe heavily. Once that whistle blows, I will be unleashed.

The noise of the arena is rowdy again, with the sight of my mangled friend swaying back and forth below the politicians. Mariam's eyes are closed, her arms drift down at her sides. She is with God now.

What a sadistic style of entertainment, have we really descended this low?

Tears well up in my eyes as I remember her sacrifice for me. A quote penetrates my mind: "The worth of every soul is great in God's eyes." While still on my knees, I say the words plainly for Nate to hear.

"I've taken too many lives for God to forgive me. Now I must take yours." He glares, holding his sword firm.

"As long as your heart beats, there's a chance to change."

"Now, my dear citizens of Athren, today there will be a historical duel. Athren abolished a monarchy after King Harper was assassinated thirty years ago.

Today, his son, Rasmussen, will have a chance to inherit the throne and become King."

Nathaniel Hastings of Lyon
Representing the Loyalists
in favor of the reinstatement of a monarchy
Vs.
Amis Hastings of Lyon
Representing the Federalists
against the reinstatement of a monarchy

"Now I will turn the time to Rasmussen Harper, heir to the throne of Athren, to commence the duel."

I cannot bear the sight of my hanging friend and that diabolical swine. Nate bows deeply, showing respect. I turn away completely, exposing my back to the platform.

"Citizens of Athren! It is the Gods' will that I am allowed to speak. I was born to be King, just like my father before!"

"Our society has been wayward and lost, much like the original Athrenians that settled this land, while they fended off hordes of barbaric tribes. My people, you are no longer in darkness. I am here to show you the light!"

"With that, let us witness this monumental moment together as these two brothers clash, deciding my fate, more importantly, the fate of Athren!" Rasmussen's loud bark ends.

I hear Nate's shoes crackle on the firm sand beneath them. We study one another, just a few yards apart. Our swords are now upright, firmly held within our hands.

Nate forms a frown and vents, "I'm sorry, little brother, for what I'm about to do."

"Where is your humility, you cocky prick?" I counter.

Nate draws a substantial breath and digs his feet into the ground. He seems ready.

On the other hand, I'm still in shock at the situation. My ex-girlfriend is slumping in my peripheral view, Rasmussen will be made King upon my demise, and Nate is eager to kill me.

My body tenses, and my senses are now heightened on high alert. My veins tingle with a hit of adrenaline, making my airway open excessively and my legs restless.

A distinct, high-pitched sound squeals through the air. Nate and I stare at each other for what feels like eternity. Until he strikes. Immediately, I parry, stopping the blow.

The clanking of the swords is like an orchestra to my ears. Each swing is a symphony of strokes with perfect placement and purpose. We match each other accordingly in the long guard stance to maintain our distance and protect our vital organs.

My older brother Nate and I now battle to the death. He always starts high above his head with his sword, attempting to strike down in a single mighty swing. I have practiced with him enough to know the exact counters needed to stand a chance at least. My base is sturdy enough to withstand his onslaught of slashes. Dad always said a firm foundation will help you weather any storm.

Nate wears his intent on his face. As he bites his lip in pure concentration, he plans to make this quick. The aggressive swings and movements show that he wants to be freed of this. It may hurt him as much as it does me.

I lean into a conservative approach, focusing on defending every hack of his sword. Patience is key, considering I'm the injured underdog.

Nate swiftly strikes from side to side with such force that I stagger backwards in an attempt to gain my proper footing. He rushes me, placing his leg behind mine, as he tries sweeping my legs out from under me.

I hold my ground and riposte. Our swords are stuck in a deadlock.

"You've gotten smarter, baby brother." Nate sneers at me.

I rush him, eliminating all the space between us, and headbutt him. Nate stumbles in retreat, dragging his sword through the sand.

Cheers from the public mob are energetically animated in approval. I'm sure Rasmussen is panicking from above.

My assault is halted as blood begins rushing down my eyebrow. The stitched incision broke open. Headbutting was a foolish thing to do.

Blood dribbles in my right eye and down my cheek. I rush to grab my shirt, which I had thrown like a bimbo. Nate cuts me off in my pursuit.

His sword slashes through the air at my back. I somersaulted forward, barely escaping harm. Coming from the other direction now, Nate torques his core muscles and swings forcefully in a left-to-right diagonal motion. Out of pure instinct, I parry his aggression and deflect his saber into the ground.

"AAHHH, just die already!" Nate wails out.

Screw the shirt, it's a death wish. Nate is frustrated, good. We start circling each other, all the other noise and surroundings have faded away, it's just us.

"Nate, you should have listened to me!" I say, wiping my bloody eye.

"Listen to you?! How can I when you killed the only person who understood me?"

"She was going to kill me! She should have gone for a knockout!" I wipe blood from my eye, keeping my gaze upon Nate.

"From my viewpoint, she was trying to put you in an unconscious state! You just refused to go cold!"

I shake my head in disbelief. We will continue to go in circles, both physically and socially. Nate will never change his perception. I need to change my perspective to his.

"You're right, Nate. I did kill her. Nothing will ever change that."

My sword rises above my head, and I charge. He's caught off guard; his little brother had never taken a page out of his book before.

Nate's sword is still as I charge from an overhead position and slice downward. His sword meets mine as he upper parries, a loud 'cling' of metal sounds. Persistently, I continue a barrage of strikes, but each swing is deflected and evaded.

Our footwork is flawlessly executed. When our blades meet midair, our footwork is not far behind in a mirroring dance. We both duel relentlessly in the long guard stances, keeping a great distance between us.

Amid the sequence, I change my fighting rhythm by thrusting the point of my sword at Nate's chest. His heavy-handed defense knocks my blade down, causing me to miss my target. In a fluid response, Nate veers his own sword in an upward motion.

With an agile step, I jolted away unprotected. Nate's blade nicks my chest in the process. The sharp tip of his blade slices my naked stitched wound.

More blood begins to gush forth in abundance. I continue my retreat; the crowd now sees sure signs of defeat as blood reddens the earth beneath me. The Athrenians love it when the white sand turns blood red.

Nate forms a victorious half smile. He struts confidently toward me, closing the distance between us. Sweat builds profusely on his golden skin, and he runs his hand through his blonde hair, spiking it.

He thinks this is his moment! He is bracing himself to be crowned champion once more. In suddenness, Nate thrusts at my face. Instantly, I over parry, blocking Nate's stab. This allows Nate to cut around to my open side and brandish his weapon.

The awareness I now possess anticipates the incoming slash. I drop my head and shoulders low, dodging the blade that now travels overhead.

Nate's botched attack leaves him vulnerable. Allowing me to close the gap and pin his sword-wielding arm across his body. I drive him backwards with such ferociousness that he shuffles his feet toe to heel, trying to free himself.

My free hand locks around the hilt of his. I extend my foot, attempting to trip his massive frame. His heel slams down against mine, causing him to topple over. His muscular frame crashes to the ground with a 'thud.'

With the help of gravity and my grip strength, I rip Nate's sword from his hand, disarming him. He lies on the ground, with disbelief painted on his face. He suddenly looks pale, as his diaphragm noticeably moves, and his respiratory rate increases rapidly.

A sudden hush permeates the crowd like a crashing wave. Emotions run high, and time stands still. Rass-hole must be shitting bricks now.

I throw Nate's sword far behind me and wield my own.

"Amis! I'm your brother, please don't!" Nate whimpers. He shoots out his hands with his fingers apart, begging me to stop.

I brandish my sword, swinging it down towards his right hand, chopping off his pinky finger. My adrenaline is peaking, and a black void fills my mind. My instincts kick in as I struggle to comprehend what I have just done.

The severed finger falls into the sand, and Nate squeals in shock. He rises to his knees, with tears in his eyes, preparing to die.

"You understand, don't you?" I inquire earnestly.

"No. You chose the wrong path, and I will die cursing your name. Trisha and I will be together again, and our blood will stain your hands."

"Am I supposed to let you kill me! This is not about us; Rasmussen cannot be made King!"

A mixer of blood and perspiration dribbles from my dark, bearded frame. I move, positioning myself behind my kneeling brother, so I don't see his face.

Nate leaned his head forward, exposing the back of his neck. With two hands, I raise my sword above him, readying myself to thrust down into the back of Nate's neck, in hopes of generating enough force to end his life swiftly.

"Do it," Nate pleads.

I breathe steadily, pinpointing a place on Nate's neck to aim. Then my arms began plunging the sword down. Mariam's suspended corpse quickly averts my eyes.

Mercy. That's the last thing Niklas told Nate on the farm.

Addison, Harry, Trisha, and Mariam all deserved mercy.

A flash of Niklas' beheading, Harry's braving death, Trisha's dying breaths replay in snapshots in my mind.

My compassion materialized as I shifted the blade's course away from Nate, skinning his neck and smashing the earth next to him. The sword vibrates as it sways back and forth.

"I will not kill you." I declare.

I slowly trudge past Nate towards my deceased friend. The posture of the politicians on the platform above becomes so clear as confusion and anticipation lace their faces.

"Kill me!" Nate demands.

I remain silent, but Nate's voice rings out again. "Amis! You have to! One of us has to die!"

Footsteps increase from behind me, and an audible grunt sounds. I turn to witness Nate's arm in full motion, slashing my own sword at me.

A metallic 'clang' explodes as swords clash. A savior has intervened.

Loud booing and hissing ensue from all in attendance. Soldiers storm the giant ring that encircles us.

My eyes widen in disbelief as Dad blocks Nate in his tracks. Nate instantly withdraws, dropping his sword and embracing Dad. Rupert, Zander, and Raelynn rush to my sides. Her face seems worried as she surveys my blood-splattered body.

"What are you doing? They'll execute you with us!" I frantically cry.

Rae smiles and attempts to press her soft lips against mine. Subconsciously, I jolted away, knowing who and what she was. Heir to Rass-holes' throne. Her expression is telling as a frown creases her mouth.

"There's no time." Rupert motions to the wall of soldiers homing in on us.

Each of us wields our swords, standing shoulder to shoulder. Nate and I remain separated by Dad.

"What do we do about the archers?" Rupert asks desperately.

"They don't dare to shoot, not with me here," Rae expresses confidently.

"Prepare to fight." Dad's deep voice orders.

The six of us now face what seems to be fifty ground soldiers and archers that have emerged on the walls. There's no escape.

The judge's voice radiates over us. "Silence, please! Due to the interference, Loyalist dueler Nathaniel Hastings has been named champion, and Rasmussen Harper will be crowned King!"

A mixture of boos and applause sounds out from all around.

"According to the laws of Athren, Amis Hastings, and all who stand in the way must be put to death. Soldiers, please." The judge gestures with an open hand.

Rasmussen's arm extends overhead. A line of identical, grey-clothed shirts over chain mail advances toward us in perfect unison. Their marching boots 'thud' on the ground, creating a feeling of intimidation.

"This is a much better way to die," I say, receiving a nervous laugh from Rupert.

The judge raises his arm once more, and all the archers on the wall notch their arrows, waiting for the command to fire.

"Welp, we're dead," Rupert says literally with a groan.

The sea of people grows restless, chanting vulgarity, fighting, and booing in disapproval. Surely if they kill us, riots will break out!

"When they converge on us, follow me. We will fight our way to the Federalists' gates and escape the way we came," Dad insists.

"And the arrows?" Rupert asks.

Dad exposes a grin towards Rae. "I think we will be just fine."

Rass-hole's voice roars, "My people! Be still... They will either be sentenced to death, or I will-"

The crowd rampages before he can finish. Cries of citizens ring out, declaring, "Not my King."

Off in the stands, violence spreads, and a soldier uses the deadly force of his bow to subdue a citizen. It propels into an uncontrollable scene of chaos. Violent riots and fights erupt hectically, causing mayhem amongst all the people.

The soldiers in the ring are now staggered and unorganized. Gawking at the pandemonium.

"We may yet escape. Quick after me!"

Following my father's lead, we rush across the now red sand to the gates. I lead from the rear, making sure Rae is within my sight this time around as we take flight.

A few soldiers attempt to impede our credulous attempt. Dad and Rupert launch a wild array of attacks with their swords, eliminating four of the captors in the blink of an eye.

Many of the soldiers retreat to the walls, attempting to quell the uprising within the stands. The resistance we encounter is minimal, and to my surprise, Jameson and the other Federalists hold the gates open and unbarred, creating a clear path for us to run through.

I greet Jameson by grabbing his shoulder, expressing my thanks.

"You fought well; everyone knows who the true champion is." Jameson gestures proudly, grasping my shoulders.

"Till we meet again," I say with gratitude, swiftly dashing on.

We fly through the veiny, dark underground tunnels, going a way I'm not accustomed to. There are no souls in sight, not that we are stopping to find out. The darkness of the halls is reminiscent of the nasty castle sewage I had to wade through.

Dad's powerful strides and quick, light feet scamper in front of us, leading the way.

"Where are you taking us?!" I question.

"This underground tunnel leads towards the outer walls of Harpstedt. Soldiers mainly use these corridors!" Dad says, turning back to me. "Rupert, I see the torch, time to ignite."

"Aye, Aye!" Rupert and Zander stop at a torch on the wall, where two baskets of hay sit below.

We hurry by. My head turns to see Zander, emptying the baskets of hay abundantly across the ground. Rupert drains a vile of oil onto the kindling in hopes it will accelerate the flames.

Rupert hands the torch to Zander, "You wanna do the honors?"

Zander's eyes flicker in awe at the torch. "Please."

He takes the torch and drops it on the hay and oil kindling.

"There's some satisfaction, uh, we better be going now," Rupert says, tapping the mesmerized Zander's shoulder.

"Run, the fire is going to spread, and the tunnel will collapse when the wooden supports burn!" Dad yells.

"I'd hate to die from smoke inhalation, too," Rae adds, catching a smile from Rupert.

We move again with haste farther down the tunnel. I grow weary and exhausted. The bloodied parts of me dry. I'm sure Nate feels the same way, considering I cut his pinky finger off.

Dad halts suddenly at a ladder leading upwards to a hatch.

"Mom and Sofia have our wagon and horses outside. Rae, Zander, and Rupert, you will walk beside the wagon as we leave the city. Nate, Amis, you will need to try your best to be concealed within the wagon, and don't kill each other!"

One by one, we climb the rungs of the ladder. I was visually able to see Nate's missing pinky as he ascended. It's a clean cut, I think to myself proudly.

We rise out of the floor of a vacant house where hood cloaks await us and travel into the streets, locating the wagon. Mom and Sofia hardly glance in our direction, not even sputtering a word. To not draw attention.

Nate and I crawl into the covered wagon in such proximity that the hostile tension between us is malleable. Nate's furrowed eyebrows, clenched jaw, and narrow eyes are fixed on me. He looks uncomfortable and perturbed, sealing his lips tight together.

My own gaze grows longing as I press my head into the palms of my hands. Our family is together again, but at what cost?

Chapter Thirty-Two:

Tyren River

Right when the wagon begins moving, a loud crash echoes in the city. Commotion builds outside as we hear people shouting, "Fire, fire! A building has toppled." Shit, Zander's and Rupert's arson ability is making Harpstedt grow even wilder on this day of anarchy.

The wagons' rickety frame rolls through the streets, unconcerned with the problems within the city. Soldiers and citizens in this part of the town don't even know what's happened in the arena. It will be an easy escape.

Time passes, and I hear less outside noise. We made it out of the city walls. We dare not look, fearing we might compromise our whole family.

Hours roll by, and we sit in silence the entire time. Relief washes over me as I am finally able to reflect and unwind the terrible events of the last few days.

"Do you think it's safe yet?" I mumble to Nate.

"My guess is as good as yours. They'll let us know when it's safe." Nate scowls, taking a deep breath. "Amis, I almost slashed you across the back."

"I know, I'm guilty of the same." My eyes meet his.

Redness rushes to his face, and tears form, giving him watery eyes. Nate put his head down deep into his dirt-ridden and bloodied hands. Gasping for air as if he were suffocating. His body shakes as if all the built-up trauma from the past few months had just been uncorked.

"I, I, killed so many people... There's nothing I can do to atone for my actions." Nate laments deeply, wheezing between each word.

My face softens, and a frown creases my mouth. "Maybe not, but I think the first step is forgiving yourself." I placed my hand on his shoulder. "I forgive you, and I hope you will do the same for me."

The cloth of the wagon opens abruptly. Sofia whips her freckled face into view, "Dad said you can come out now." A perplexed look travels her face after seeing Nate.

I nodded and raise my index finger, symbolizing one second. Sofia departs quietly as I notice her holding Leo the rooster.

The wagon screeches to a standstill. In the distance, I hear a consistent sound of rushing water.

"Nate, we should probably go out there and see everyone," I whisper.

"You're right." He rubs his face and takes a deep breath to reset.

Leaving the cramp wagon is freeing. My limbs can stretch to their proper lengths as the fresh breeze rushes through my hair. We are parked in a clearing next to a giant river. This must be the great river that stretches through the heart of Athren.

"Sofia!" I roar in anger.

"Calm down, Amis. Untwist your panties. Leo is part of our family, too!" Sofia beams widely.

"That demonic rooster is supposed to be dead! Bring it here, I'm snapping its neck!" In a sprint, I catch up to Sofia and hug her. She drops the dumb rooster and hugs me back.

"Are we heading west?" Curiosity shoots out of me.

"Amis! Nate, my turn!" Mom cries, giving each of us individual loving hugs. "Sit, sit, we need to clean your wounds."

The rest of the family gathers around tightly. Rae and Zander are with us. Zander fits in great, but Rae is a traitor. I missed her beautiful brown hair braided to perfection, her cute dimples, and her perfect frame. Can I trust her? Does my family know what she is?

Again, she holds out her hand to me, like nothing is wrong. I have every natural inclination to take her hand. Still, I refuse to take her bid, even though a weird, twisted part of me desires her.

"Yes, we are heading west away from the capital. If it weren't for Rae finding us on the road to

Harpstedt, the results of today would've been much different." Dad's deep voice reveals.

"What about the soldiers sent with her to kill you?" I ask incredulously.

"They tried to ambush us. Rae gave away their position. Once she betrayed the twenty soldiers, we disbanded them rather seamlessly. It was quite a sight to behold; your girl is rather skilled." Rupert says.

"There's so much that happened. Mykel is missing and helpless, Mariam executed trying to save me, Rasmussen is now King, and Mr. Brookshard, along with my guildmates in Lyon, burnt down our farm!" I mutter and proceed to tell them everything about my being tortured, including Rae's deception.

"Let me get this straight. You were tortured, sliced up, saved by Mariam, and you trudged through shit?!" Sofia recaps, giggling.

"Yes, Sofia, I swam through a bunch of shit."

"Amis, we will need to clean these cuts even more rigorously!" Mom adds.

"And Mykel is out on his own with no hands?" Dad can't hold back a smile.

"For all I know, he drowned in the Gulf of Athren. He wasn't exactly himself and was treading water with no hands..." I shrug, trying to picture Mykel.

"Mykel doesn't die easily.. It's terrible to hear that about Mr. Brookshard; he was an old friend of mine.

He must've seen the opportunity. Greed is a terrible thing." Dad sighs.

"Rae, Zander, he called you out. Do you have anything you want to say?" Rupert's bushy brows rise, noticing their apparent uneasiness.

Zander speaks up, swaying his weight back and forth on each foot, looking nervous as hell. "Amis, I should've told you sooner. Guilt festered in my soul, and I couldn't bear to be without you. You have filled the void of Harry in my life."

Nate's posture plummets to the ground with the memory of killing Harry. Mom rubs his back to comfort him.

Zander continues, "Xavier and Veronica threatened me. They wanted to put you down; they are jealous of you. Their new lackey, April, is the devil. The truth is, they didn't expect you to ascend. I'm sorry, your Dad saved me and invited me to join."

"They will kill you for abandoning the guild," I exclaim in fear.

"Amis, they will kill all of us." Zander shakes his head in confusion.

Silence falls on us as the gravity of the situation grows. They will kill all of us if they find us, but not Rae.

"Dad, Rasmussen destroyed your book, I-I'm-"

"It's just words on paper; our true stories exist in here." He placed a hand on my bandaged chest.

"Amis, Nikas would be proud of the courage you have demonstrated these last few months. Now it's time for us to take some of the burden off your shoulders."

Nathan stands up and looks me in the eye with a deep stare, then hugs me. Tears stream down our faces. "Amis, I forgive you."

My eyes peer over his shoulders, looking at Rae.

"Enough of the mushiness," Rupert demands.

Nate and I separate, creating a hole in our circle once more.

"Rae and Aims need their privacy. Remember, Amis, we can't help what family we are born to." Dad states.

"Come on, Dad! I need all the drama." Sofia whines.

Rae and I walk down by the Tyren River that flows to the Gulf of Athren. My stomach knots as emotions swirl. She opens her mouth, preparing to speak.

"Amis, I'm the daughter of a tyrant. He is an evil man who has been manipulating me all my life. You don't have to forgive me, but you do have to trust me." Rae says, her eyes fixed on the flowing river. "My father killed my Mom when I was young and sent me and my brothers to Havensburg, where my devilish Granny raised us. I hate my Dad. Gentry has given me a chance at redemption."

"Is that where your brothers are now?" I responded, looking into the same river.

"What?" Rae gulps, being caught off guard.

"Are they in Havensburg?"

"Yes. Amis, my younger brother, needs me."

"And your older brother?" I ask with a raised brow.

"He's a deadly problem."

This river is like us.
Some parts are rough with rapids,
Others are smooth and placid.
There are falls and big bends,
but we continuously flow on until we end.
Now jump in, tread, and transcend.

The End of Book One.